THE TRIDENT SERIES

FROST

Book 3

Jaime Lewis

The Trident Series - FROST
Copyright © 2020 by Jaime Lewis

ISBN: 978-1-952734-08-3

Printed in USA

TABLE OF CONTENTS

Prologue 1

Chapter 1 9

Chapter 2 22

Chapter 3 31

Chapter 4 45

Chapter 5 49

Chapter 6 64

Chapter 7 78

Chapter 8 99

Chapter 9 104

Chapter 10 107

Chapter 11 115

Chapter 12 125

Chapter 13.. 136

Chapter 14 143

Chapter 15 157

Chapter 16 166

Chapter 17 175

Chapter 18 185

Chapter 19 193

Chapter 20 200

Chapter 21 206

Chapter 22 215

Chapter 23 216

Chapter 24 225

Chapter 25 232

Chapter 26 237

Chapter 27 239

Chapter 28 254

Epilogue 259

PROLOGUE

Autumn Kauffman stood beside her car staring at her good friend Nathan Coates.

"Autumn, I really wish you would reconsider this move."

Autumn wanted to roll her eyes at him but thought better of it. "Nathan, I've thought long and hard about this decision, and moving is what I feel is best for Cody and I. It's a fresh start we both need. Plus, I'm already committed to the Naval Hospital in Norfolk. I can't renege on my contract."

Nathan, her late husband's best friend, wasn't thrilled with her decision to leave town, but it was something she had to do. Saying goodbye to the life that she'd known for the last eleven years was going to be tough.

Having to bury her husband ten months ago had been the hardest thing she'd ever had to endure. The toll it had taken on her emotionally was enough to warrant a clean break from her past, even if it upset her friend.

Knowing Kevin would never walk through their front door again had pushed her into a deep depression for several months after the funeral. She'd been stuck in a fog while she let everyone around her dictate her life. She wasn't usually a needy person, or one who relied on others to take care of her, but that was exactly what had been happening. Her son, Cody, had suffered as a result of her manic meltdown. In her opinion, her parenting had sucked, and that was not how she wanted her son to remember her. She had always been strong, and she believed that she would regain that strength by starting a new chapter.

Out of everyone who had graciously offered to help after the funeral, Nathan had been the most supportive, helping her cope with the loss while also encouraging her to move on.

Nathan had been assigned to the same unit as her husband and had been with Kevin that fateful day. What had started as a normal routine patrol quickly escalated into an ambush. As Kevin lay dying in his best friend's arms, he made Nathan promise that she and Cody were taken care of. Nathan had honored that promise and then some. For the past ten months, Nathan had unselfishly put his life on hold for her and Cody. She'd never be able to repay him for everything he'd provided, whether it was as simple as helping her fill out paperwork, helping Cody with homework, or just being a shoulder for her to cry on. He had also opened his home to her and Cody while she contemplated what her next move would be.

Then one day, she'd been searching the internet, and a job board website popped up. Something inside her told her to click on it. The second job listed was an ad for a position in her field at the Naval Hospital in Norfolk, Virginia. Not expecting to hear anything back, she took the chance and applied for it. To her surprise, she received a call back the following week, and the rest was history. Even with everyone saying she was making a mistake by moving, she put her foot down and decided the new start was the best thing for her and her son. The two of them would begin the next chapter of their lives in Virginia Beach.

She walked over to Nathan, standing by the driver's side door with his arms crossed in front of his chest as if he would block her from getting in. He was tall, just over six-feet, dark crew-cut hair and dark brown eyes. She hugged him and tried to hold back the tears welling up in her eyes. This was a difficult decision, and one she did not take lightly, but it had to be done; she was suffocating here.

"Nathan, please don't be angry with me. You have to understand; Cody and I need this. I promise to keep in touch. You can even come out and visit. Actually, I'd be upset with you if you didn't." She grinned, hoping to get him to smile. She didn't want to leave with him angry.

Hugging her shoulders, he gave her a good squeeze, then kissed the top of her head. "I'm not upset with you, Autumn. I'm just worried. I mean, what happens if you need something?"

"Nathan, I'm thirty years old. I'll be okay." Dammit. This was why she had decided to leave. She hated being treated with kid gloves.

"I didn't mean it like that. I meant being in a new town and all, driving across the country in your deathtrap of a car, not having anybody to call if you need something."

Knowing Nathan meant well brought a smile to her face. Ever since he had accompanied Kevin's body home from Iraq, he'd been her rock, but it was time for her to move on and time for Nathan to have his life back. "I know, Nathan. I appreciate your caring and being worried about us, but we'll be fine. We'll make new friends. Besides, I don't want to cramp your bachelor status by being here longer than we have to." She gave him a wink.

He gave her a stern look. "Hey, I've been on dates since you and Cody moved in, so don't go trying to find excuses."

She looked down at her watch. Dang, it was already after seven. She had wanted to be on the road by now. Giving Nathan one last hug, she assured him they would be okay and promised she would call him every couple of hours to check in. She had their entire route planned out, making sure the journey would be an adventure for Cody by stopping in specific cities for a little sightseeing.

She got into her 2005 Nissan Altima; truth be told, it had seen better days, and with a sigh, she buckled her seatbelt. As the car's engine sputtered then roared to life, she took one last look at Nathan and waved. He waved back. As she started to drive down the main road and off the base for the last time, she kept telling herself that this was what Kevin would've wanted. He would want her and Cody to move on and live their lives instead of grieving over him.

She glanced in the rearview mirror and saw Cody staring right back at her from his seat. His shaggy brown hair, just like his dad, was sticking up in all directions. She winked and smiled at him, and her heart melted as responded with the sweetest little grin. "Are you ready for this, buddy?" She asked, trying to put on a brave face, even though she was a nervous wreck.

He smiled wide. "I'm ready if you are, Mom."

CHAPTER ONE

"Oh, good! You're still here."

Autumn turned from her locker, where she was gathering her purse and gym bag to leave for the day, to see her manager Nancy rush into the employee lounge.

Nancy was a very eclectic woman. In her late fifties, she stood probably just shy of six feet. Her blonde hair with pink streaks throughout was cut into a bob. She was fun and easy to work for as long as you did your job.

"I'm still here."

Nancy smiled. "Sorry, I know you're trying to get out of here for the day, but I need to speak with you about a patient."

Autumn wondered if there was an issue with one of her patients. She loved her job and took it seriously. As a physical therapist, she got to meet many people of all ages, although the majority of her patients were current and former military personnel. When she first started, she had taken on some of the more elderly patients. But lately, they'd been assigning more active-duty personnel to her. According to Nancy, she had apparently made a name for herself, and now patients were requesting her.

Her thoughts must have shown in her expression because Nancy touched her arm and started to explain.

"I'm sorry, Autumn. I didn't mean to make it sound like something is wrong. I received a new patient file from Dr. Ingram. I know you already have a full plate, but is there any possible way you could add this patient to your workload? You would be doing me a huge favor. This one is kind of special, and you're the best therapist I've got. He'll be here for a few days, then transferred to an outpatient facility closer to his home once he's discharged. Since he was only going to be here for a few days, I had suggested that they wait and start his physical therapy at the facility, but Dr. Ingram insisted he wanted him to start working his leg as soon as possible."

Autumn thought about it, and Nancy was right; she was already loaded down with more patients than most could handle. But from the desperate look that she was getting from Nancy, if this particular patient was indeed important, then she'd make some adjustments in her schedule. Plus, staying later would mean overtime, which meant more money in her bank account—money that she desperately needed. Whoever this person was must really be special to have the doctors pushing his recovery. If the doctor said to do it, then she would. She gave Nancy one of her bright smiles. "Sure. What's his story?"

Nancy thanked her and handed her a folder containing all of the patient's information. She scanned the information. Even though she had been getting ready to leave, she wanted to go and introduce herself to the patient before she left and see about setting up an appointment first thing tomorrow morning.

She grimaced when she read he was recovering from a gunshot wound. Even though it was clean through and through, Autumn knew it still had to hurt like hell.

She scanned further down the page, and her eyes widened at the doctor's sense of urgency. The patient was no other than one of American's finest warriors. A Navy SEAL. The government invested a lot of money in these guys, so, of course, she understood why they would want him back to active duty as quickly as possible. She'd heard all about the SEAL teams who were based out of Little Creek, which wasn't that far from where she lived. In fact, she always saw men from the base at the local Stop-n-Shop down the street from her house. She had treated a couple of them here at the hospital in the last few months. Those guys were a handful. Most were hard men, full of muscles and intimidation, who could snap her in half in a blink of an eye. Just the thought sent a slight shiver through her body. The sound of Nancy's voice shook her from her thoughts.

"If it helps any, I hear this one is pretty easy on the eyes," Nancy said, waggling her eyebrows up and down, and Autumn couldn't help but roll her eyes, making Nancy laugh. Nancy had a habit of checking out the prospects and trying to set Autumn up on dates. She had enough offers from men working at the hospital alone. Thankfully, her schedule between work and taking care of Cody didn't give her any time to even think about dating. She wasn't even sure if she was ready to venture down that road yet.

Autumn snorted. "Good looking or not, these types of guys are difficult to work with. They never listen, then try to act all macho and tell you they're fine when they're not so that they can get back to active duty. Just because they are full of muscles and carry the title of SEAL, they think their shit don't stink." She set the folder down while she put her purse and bag back into her locker.

"I hear ya, honey. I've been around here for a long time. But in their defense, those men are trained to be that way. It's ingrained into them. But I know you can handle it, or I wouldn't have asked." She tossed Autumn a smile and winked as she gave her shoulder a friendly squeeze.

Autumn shook her head as she prepared to go meet the SEAL. Chief Petty Officer Rhoades was his name. Brushing her red hair from her face, she started down the hall toward his room. Nancy was right; she could handle this. It was just another day at the office. But then why was she so nervous?

"So, Frost, how long are they keeping you here?" Dino, Frost's teammate, asked as he leaned against the wall with his arms crossed.

Frost looked up at him and the rest of the team. They had come by to visit before they headed home. He was pissed that his ass was stuck in a fucking hospital bed and not with them. He'd had injuries before; knife wounds, pulled muscles, bruises, and sprains, but he'd never been shot before. However, there were plenty of near misses in his career as a SEAL. Either his enemies were just bad shots, or he was just lucky.

He didn't understand why he couldn't sit at home in his own damn bed and take the damn antibiotics they were giving him intravenously. Stitch, his best friend, teammate, and roommate, was a combat medic. He surely could handle playing doctor for a few days.

11

Since the day he had been admitted to the hospital, he'd been a cranky son of a bitch. Most of the nurses were understanding in dealing with his ornery behavior, while some nurses stepped over the line of professionalism and were just trying to vie for his attention in hopes of him asking them out. Hell, some even left their phone numbers on a piece of paper. At least, he'd have some peace and quiet at his apartment.

He was tired of how women were always throwing themselves at him when they found out he was a SEAL. When he was younger and new to the teams, he loved the attention, especially when he was looking for an easy lay. Now that he was older and wiser, he was tired of that scene. In fact, he hadn't been with a woman in over a year. Hell, maybe that was his problem. Maybe he just needed to get laid.

He looked at Dino and gave a half shrug. "A few more days. The doctor wants me to start physical therapy tomorrow."

"So soon?" Ace asked, giving Frost a once over. Frost knew his team leader was probably making sure he wasn't pushing it too fast. He was surprised as well when the doc told him he wanted him to start tomorrow, stressing that it would be very light exercises to begin with. Again, probably shit he could do from the comfort of his own home.

"That's what the doc said. They are going to start with some light exercises. Once they release me, I'll continue PT three days a week at the outpatient facility by the apartment."

"Just don't over-do it. We want you back as soon as possible, but we want you healthy with no setbacks," Ace told him in a stern tone, which meant he'd better listen, or there would be hell to pay.

"Yes, sir." He gave Ace a salute. He wanted to be back on active duty as soon as possible. He just hoped he got a decent physical therapist who knew what they were doing. He'd heard stories from friends who had to endure some sort of therapy, and most of them sounded like nightmares. From his experience and the rumor mill, most hospital personnel and employees at VA facilities didn't really give a flying shit about a soldier's recovery. All they were interested in was collecting a paycheck.

This was a big proponent of why one of his best friends, Alex, started her 501c3 organization. The Jacob Hardesty Foundation was created in memory of her father, Jacob Hardesty, a SEAL who was killed in action. The Foundation served veterans and their families and included a medical clinic that catered to patients in a timely manner. They don't make them wait for months to see a doctor like they would have to if they went to the VA. It always upset Frost when he'd hear the horror stories of how veterans were being denied medical treatment because of backlogs, or because the VA said their treatment wasn't covered and the patient couldn't afford it. Hopefully, the newly elected President could untangle the web of destruction left by the former administration.

Alex's Foundation was run strictly off donations and grants. The only overhead costs were the utilities. The doctors and other staff were volunteers donating their time and service. The Foundation was so well received amongst the medical community that Alex had a waiting list for doctors, nurses, and other specialists wanting to volunteer. The grand opening was scheduled for October, and Frost couldn't wait to see it open and succeed. The community was anxiously awaiting as well.

Frost looked at Ace. "How's Tenley doing? Since I'm stuck here, I haven't been able to talk with her. She called last night, but we only had about a minute because the doc was here."

"She seems to be taking things in stride. Alex knows an attorney that agreed to help Tenley sort through all the paperwork her dad left her. Potter is with her right now at their first official baby appointment."

Frost grinned, something he hadn't done since he'd been shot. "I can't believe they're pregnant." He was happy for Potter, his teammate and friend. Potter and Tenley had a rough go around for a couple of months, but in the end, they got their happily ever after. They were married, had adopted a seven-year-old girl from Ecuador, and now had a baby on the way.

Tenley had her life upended over the last few months. She was one of his three best friends. The other two were Alex, who was engaged to Ace, his team leader, and Stitch, who was also a team member. All four of them grew up together in Virginia Beach.

Tenley's recent situation was why he was laid up in a hospital bed with a bullet wound to his thigh. Not that it was her fault. That blame belonged to a drug and arms dealer named Esteban Sanchez.

Long story short, Tenley's ex-boyfriend and the arms dealer were using Tenley to blackmail her biological father to get their hands on his heroin business. Tenley had never met her father until she went to Ecuador the day after Christmas on a humanitarian aid trip. When she met her father, he wasn't exactly forthcoming with his identity. He knew that Sanchez, along with her ex-boyfriend, would stop at nothing to get what they wanted, including putting Tenley in danger. When Tenley finally found out who her father was, it had been too late. Her ex was apprehended by the FBI and currently serving time behind bars, but Sanchez had escaped and gone after Tenley. Tenley had been kidnapped on Frost's watch, which bothered him, although he couldn't do much with a bullet hole in his leg.

After Tenley was rescued, she got checked out at the hospital, and that was when they found out they had a baby on the way. He couldn't be happier for Potter and Tenley. With everything they'd both been through in the past year, they deserved a happy ending. It didn't hurt that Tenley was loaded since her father's entire estate had been left solely to her.

Ace nodded his head and smiled. "I know. Potter's ecstatic, but it's only been two days since they found out, and he's already treating Tenley like she's made of glass. Alex said Tenley's already giving him shit about it." He chuckled.

A light knock on the door, followed by a woman's soft but husky voice had Frost glancing at the doorway.

"Excuse me. Sorry to interrupt, but I'm looking for Chief Petty Officer Rhoades?"

Frost rolled his eyes. Great, another nurse coming to "check up on him," though he didn't recognize the voice of this one. She probably worked on another floor and heard from her co-workers that he was there.

He took a deep breath and got ready to say something sarcastic, but then the woman emerged from behind Ace and Irish. Not only was he left speechless, but he about tumbled out of the bed as he found himself leaning towards her to get a better look. He shook his head to refocus as the most beautiful woman he'd laid eyes on walked towards him. And that was saying something because he'd seen his fair share of women in his thirty-one years.

Frost closed his mouth when he realized it was gaping open as he looked her over. She was petite, with a shapely figure—plump pink lips, little pixie nose, and large, almond-shaped eyes the color of shamrocks. He was speechless by her beauty. He took note of her tits and ass; they were perfect. He liked a woman with a shape to her. But what had his heart racing was her long, wavy red hair that fell below her shoulders, framing her face beautifully. Even in what he assumed was her hospital attire—a purple polo shirt, and black khaki pants, she was a fucking knock-out.

As she walked closer to the bed, her bold green eyes twinkled under the fluorescent lighting. "Since you are the one sitting in the bed, I'm assuming you're CPO Rhoades?" She asked again, grinning at him as if she knew her looks alone were tormenting him. He noticed the guys checking her out, and he couldn't blame them a damn bit.

He cleared his throat. Jesus, he was staring at her like a teenage boy. It was like he'd become brain-fried as all the blood left his brain and flowed straight to his cock. Thankfully, the blanket was pulled up to his waist and covered any evidence of his arousal. Just to be sure, he placed his hands in his lap and adjusted himself slightly to make sure his manhood wasn't creating a pop tent. That would surely send her running, unless she were anything like the nurses before her.

"I'm CPO Rhoades," he said in a gruff voice, which made some of the guys snicker. *Assholes.* They knew how she had affected him, and he was so going to beat their asses for it too. Once he recovered from his injury, of course.

Flashing him a bright smile, she held out her hand, "I'm Autumn. I'm one of the physical therapists here at the hospital and the one responsible for getting you back on your feet as quickly as possible. Well, at least while you're here, that is."

When their hands touched, an electrifying feeling coursed through his veins. He felt alive. Her hand felt tiny and delicate compared to his much larger one, and her skin felt so soft against his calloused fingers that he couldn't help but hold on to it a little longer than a normal handshake. When she gasped and pulled her hand away quickly, looking away from him, he realized she felt something too.

Well, hell...so it wasn't just me. The Irish beauty felt the connection too.

She started fiddling with his IV pole, trying to avoid eye contact with him when she started talking. He couldn't hide his smile at her cuteness as she wrinkled her nose and looked down at her watch.

"I apologize for stopping by so late in the day, but I just received your chart. Since your doctor wants to start your therapy tomorrow, I wanted to come by to introduce myself and see if you had any questions, but since you have company, we can wait until tomorrow. I'll adjust my morning schedule so we have some extra time to go over any questions or concerns you may have before we get started."

He didn't have any questions about his rehabilitation process, but he definitely had some personal questions he wanted to ask her. For starters, was she single?

He needed to keep it together so he didn't scare her off, so he flashed her a flirtatious smile—the one he knew that women ate up. "That sounds good, sugar. Tomorrow morning would be perfect, but can I ask a favor?"

Her lips parted, and her breath hitched slightly when he called her "sugar," which aroused him even more. She quickly recovered and narrowed her eyes slightly, placing her hands on her hips as she gave him a staredown. He wanted to laugh at the sight, but he knew better. If she were anything like Alex and Tenley, there was a lioness under her beautiful exterior.

"And what would that be, sailor?"

He smiled, already liking her sass. "Promise me you'll go easy on me?"

She let out a husky laugh and damn if his cock didn't harden even more at the sound. And, the way her red silky stresses swayed at the shake of her head had his fingers itching to run through them.

"Not gonna happen. Listen, I'm going to be upfront with you before we get started. I'm a 'tell it like it is gal.' I don't take shit from my patients, especially hard-headed ones like yourself. My job is to get you back on your feet as quickly as possible so that you can return to active duty. I take my job seriously. I'll push you so hard you'll probably want to kill me, but I'm hoping it won't come to that because then you'll be assigned another therapist who most likely doesn't know their ass from their head and won't give you the effort and care that I guarantee you will get from me. I will respect you, and I ask the same in return. I don't work with quitters. If you're not ready to give me a hundred percent, tell me right now, and I'll make other arrangements for you." She stood at the foot of his bed with her arms crossed in front of her chest, giving him a serious look and waiting for an answer.

Frost didn't know if he should laugh or be a little scared. Not only was this woman a total knock-out, but she was a total bad-ass. She was one of those women who kicked ass and took names later—a woman with attitude and a sense of humor. In a matter of minutes, she had made his body come alive.

"Damn, sweetness. Are you single? Because if so, I'd love to take you out."

Leave it to Irish to open his mouth. Everyone laughed but not Frost. He gave Irish an annoyed look, and Irish just shrugged his shoulders and winked at him. He'd be lying if he didn't want to know the answer. She didn't answer; instead, she smiled and shook her head. But if the blush that painted her cheeks was any indication, he believed he had his answer. *Thanks, Irish, now fuck off.*

He smiled. "Please excuse my ignorant friend over there. He's just jealous he doesn't get a beautiful therapist to spend time with."

She lowered her head, and he swore her cheeks turned a deeper shade of red. She was gorgeous, and he found himself wanting to know more about her.

After meeting with the CPO, Autumn left the room feeling flushed; that room had enough testosterone for ten men, and damn were they gorgeous. Christ on a crutch, Nancy wasn't lying to her when she said the patient was good looking. She hadn't wanted to stare, but it was hard not to. The man was gorgeous, especially when he grinned, and a slight dimple on his right cheek appeared, adding to his appeal. But he was also very intimidating, not to mention a total flirt. His friends were just as easy on the eyes. Her male patients over the last couple of months had mainly been older, married men. If the chart was correct, this guy was a year older than her.

After dropping the chart off at the nurse's station, she walked to the employee lounge. She needed to pick up Cody at his friend's house, then drop him off at his Naval Sea Cadets meeting. The Sea Cadets organization had been great for Cody. The organization was a leadership program and lets kids, both boys and girls, get a look and feel of what the military could offer them should they choose to go that route after graduating high school. It taught discipline, keeping them out of trouble, and making them maintain good grades in school. Cody didn't need those things, but he really enjoyed being in the program. They usually only met once or twice a month on a Saturday for a couple of hours, but they were planning a trip to Washington, D.C. next month right after school got out for the summer, and Cody was going. She was nervous because she wasn't accompanying him. It was only for two days, but he'd never been that far away from her before; however, the Commanding Officer in charge of their unit assured her he would be in good hands. The best part was the unit covered all of the travel costs. All she had to provide was some spending money.

Money was tight for them. The money she got from her husband's death benefit only amounted to $1,200 a month, which went toward Cody's school tuition. Her salary from the hospital barely covered all their living expenses. The rent for the duplex she rented was outrageous for the size of the place, and the area was sketchy. Plus, she had the utilities to pay, along with groceries and gas for the car. She also wanted to make sure Cody got to do fun things, so she needed money for that as well, though she was really good at finding great deals and discounts for places and activities for them to go and do on the weekends. Nancy knew she had been looking for a part-time job to earn some extra money, and when she mentioned to Autumn about the hospital needing someone to do some transcribing work, Autumn had been quick to jump on it. The extra income helped tremendously, and the plus side was that she could do all the work from home after Cody went to bed.

As she approached her car, she noticed a piece of paper stuck under one of her windshield wipers. When she got closer, she realized it was some sort of a flyer. She felt relieved. Last week, she had walked out to her car, and there had been a note taped to the driver's side window. In big red letters, it said, STAY AWAY FROM HIM. That had freaked her out because she had no interest in any man, and no man had been interested in her. Well, except for a few of her patients that flirted with her, but again, they were old enough to be her father and weren't serious. She assumed that whoever left the note got her vehicle mixed up with someone else's.

She pulled the flyer out and looked at it. It was for the new café that just opened down the street. She and one of the other nurses had made plans to go there for lunch tomorrow. She stuck it in her bag and hit the button on her key fob to pop the trunk to her car. She threw her gym bag in and shut it. As she walked to the driver's side of the car, she felt the hairs on her neck stand up. She looked around, but nothing seemed out of sorts. Just some other employees were walking to their cars.

CHAPTER TWO

"Jack Rhoades, you are one stubborn son of a bitch!"

Frost laid in the hospital bed and glared at Alex.

Day three since he had taken a bullet in his thigh, and he was so over all bullshit hospital stuff and ready to climb the walls. He was tired, sore, and just full of piss and vinegar.

While his injury was only considered a flesh wound, it had hurt like fucking hell. The doctors wanted to keep him in the hospital for a few days longer because some redness had started to appear around the wound, indicating a possible infection.

But, the truth of it all was that he was starting to get depressed. He hated being laid up, and he missed his team, although they'd come to see him every day. A couple of them would come by in the morning and the others after work, but it wasn't the same. Ace told him yesterday that there was some chatter about the team getting sent out. He hoped like hell they wouldn't deploy until after he was back on active duty, which was still weeks away. He looked down at the white bandage wrapped around his thigh. He was glad that the piece of shit responsible for that whole fiasco with Tenley was rotting in hell.

He watched as Alex reached into her large black designer purse. He always wondered how in the hell she ever found anything in that suitcase she called a purse.

She pulled out a black case similar to a square necklace case. "Here," she said, shoving the case into his hands.

He knew immediately what it was when he saw the SEAL logo and motto 'The Only Easy Day Was Yesterday' embossed on the top. He scrunched his eyebrows together and looked at her.

"Where and when did you get this?" He asked, sounding annoyed. He was a hard person to begin with. It was why his call-sign was Frost. As in Jack Frost. He could be one cold son of a bitch when he wanted to be. Plus, he didn't like people snooping through his shit but considering it was Alex, he'd forgive her, as she was like a sister to him. At least this time.

"I had Stitch get it for me last night. I stopped by the base this morning and picked it up from him."

Frost opened the hinged case revealing his gold Trident Pin. He'd endured a lot of sweat and tears to earn that piece of metal.

Alex rested her hand over Frost's, and she looked him in the eye. "Frost, let this serve as a reminder of everything you worked for to earn that pin. Just because you are down and out of commission right now doesn't mean you won't be back out on the battlefield. Hell, think about all the men and women who have sustained career-ending injuries. Yours is just a minor setback. Consider these next couple of weeks as somewhat of a vacation.

"Every time you start feeling down and crabby, I want you to look at that pin and think about everything you endured to earn that priceless piece of metal. You are one of the few who have conquered the grueling training. You are a goddamn Navy SEAL. So, start acting like one. Use that as your motivation to get your ass back in fighting shape instead of moping around and feeling sorry for yourself."

He lowered his head and stared at the pin again. Mentally, he berated himself. She was absolutely right. He was being an asshole and had been moping for the last two days. The only thing keeping him somewhat grounded was his friends and family. Plus, he had a little motivation now—the feisty Irish beauty. He glanced down at his watch and smiled, seeing she was due here shortly for his appointment. At least her presence would perk him up a bit. She was a firecracker. Her personality matched her fiery red hair.

"Well, I'm glad something got your hard-ass to smile." He glanced up to see Alex grinning like the Cheshire cat. "Care to share what just went through that big head of yours?" She asked with a twinkle in her eye.

Before he could answer, the sound of a shoe squeaking on the tile floor had Frost looking toward the door. There she stood dressed in a pair of tan khaki pants and a short sleeve, black-collared golf shirt. Today, her red hair was pulled back in a ponytail, making the little diamond stud earrings she wore in her ears stand out.

She wore a look of surprise as she glanced at Alex, then to him.

"Oh, I'm sorry. I didn't realize you had company. Just ring the nurse's station when you're ready, and I'll come back," she said in a hurry and turned to head back out the door.

"No!" Frost shouted as he struggled to sit up quickly. He cringed as he felt the ache in his leg, but he noticed his hard, abrupt tone had stopped her in her tracks. She stared at him, probably waiting for him to say something else. Fuck! She got him all twisted up inside. Never, not once in his life had a woman gotten him all tongue-tied. Something about her had piqued his interest; he found himself wanting to get to know her more than wanting to fuck her.

He dismissed the thought as Alex smiled and leaned down to hug him. She kissed him on the cheek, then whispered in his ear, "Now, I understand what that smile was all about. She's gorgeous." She righted herself and straightened her shirt. She pointed at him and then directed her finger to the case in his hand. "Remember what I said. Oh, and your mom and dad called. They were getting back on the cruise ship. I filled them in. They were worried, but I assured them you were fine and already back to your ornery self."

"Geez…thanks."

She smiled. "Anyways, they'll be home in four days. You should be discharged by then. I'll make plans to get you home."

He grinned and then gave her a mock salute. "Thanks. I'll see you tomorrow."

She laughed and turned to walk out. As she walked toward the door, Frost heard her say hello to Autumn.

Autumn watched the beautiful brunette interact with the CPO. She wondered if that was his girlfriend. Why that made her stomach churn, she wasn't sure. It wasn't like he belonged to her. He was just a patient.

Yep, keep reminding yourself that.

22

She walked towards him and set her papers down on the chair next to the bed. Today, she would be going over his physical therapy schedule and then start with some light exercises.

When she read his medical chart yesterday, she'd admit that the injury had brought back memories of her husband and how he died. Kevin was dedicated to the Corps. With him deployed for most of their marriage, they didn't have the most romantic relationship, but even so, she still loved him. After losing him, she vowed she would never put herself in that position again. She didn't want to have to worry every day.

So why then was she experiencing these small flutters in her belly being near this SEAL? She couldn't be attracted to him. Could she? Their line of work was even more dangerous than her husband's had been. She didn't know what her husband's job had entailed as he never spoke about his work, but she preferred not to know either. She could only imagine what type of situations SEALs were put in. Not that she knew exactly what they did since everyone knew that their missions were classified. Well, at least those missions where the details weren't leaked to the media. There was a reason why their identities and missions were kept under wraps. Leaking the teams' whereabouts and what they did just painted a bigger bull's-eye on all the troops who were out there trying to make the world a better place for all human beings.

Just thinking of that made her sick. *Yeah, no, thank you. When I decide to date again, it will be someone with a less dangerous job.*

She looked at the CPO. He was watching her closely, but he had this little smirk on his face as if he knew what crazy thoughts were running rampant through her head. Well, that was going to change. He was her patient, and that was all their relationship was going to amount to. She'd be professional, do her job, and once he was discharged from the hospital, that would be the last she'd see of him.

She walked closer to the bed. She thought it might help if she could put an imaginary wall up. Plus, it seemed that the CPO had a girlfriend. Knowing that now angered her a tad, as he'd flirted with her yesterday. That in itself should be a warning to stay clear of this guy. "Your girlfriend is cute," she said as she pretended to read over his chart, not wanting to look at him. She already had his chart memorized, as she did with all of her patients, but she needed a distraction right now.

Christ, Autumn. Keep your mouth shut! What happened to keeping this professional? Don't ask him any personal questions. Do your job and get the hell out of there.

He grinned, and that damn dimple became visible, and holy god, was it sexy. Add in the fact that he hadn't shaved and had some gruff growing on his cheeks and chin. He looked sinful.

"Are you jealous?" He shocked her with the question and gave her a hard stare. One that she swore she could feel the depth of.

Yep! Her libido needed to stop controlling the part of her brain that operated her mouth before she really embarrassed herself. She rolled her eyes, trying to give the impression that his looks alone didn't get her insides all fired up.

She waved her hand in the air, waving off his comment, although he was spot on. "Hardly, just making small talk."

Frost chuckled, and his deep laugh made her belly do flips. The next few days were going to be torture. At least her interaction with him was limited to only an hour each day. She could survive it. Couldn't she? Shit, maybe this wasn't a good idea. *Damn, Nancy.*

"Alex, the woman that was here, is one of my best friends and practically a sister to me. And for your knowledge, I don't think my team leader would appreciate you assuming his fiancé was a cheater."

"I sure as hell wouldn't." A deep raspy voice from behind startled her, causing her to jump. As she turned, she swallowed the lump in her throat, and her eyes widened as the large man stalked toward her. He was bulkier in comparison to Frost's build, though not by much. Jesus, what was the military feeding these men?

She glanced at Frost, who was trying to hide his amusement at her blunder, but it wasn't working. She turned back toward the other guy. This must be the leader of their team, as Frost mentioned. She felt herself squirm under his glare. The unreadable expression on his face unnerved her. *Fuck me…* She thought to herself and wished for a hole to appear and swallow her up magically. So much for acting professionally.

"I am so sorry. I didn't mean it that way." The guy raised a questioning eyebrow at her, and all the while, Frost couldn't hold back his snort of laughter.

Oh god, of course, she meant it, or she wouldn't have said it. She was so flustered she lost her grip on the papers she was holding, and they fell to the floor in a big heaping mess. *Still waiting for that hole to open.*

As she crawled around on the floor, she was planning in her head on how to ask Nancy to assign someone else to this guy. But the green monster inside of her was telling her no. If she withdrew as his therapist, then Nancy would assign one of the others, and they were all women. She didn't want any of them sinking their claws into him. Several of them had already told her that they would take him if she didn't have the time. A couple of others had snuck into his room just to get a look at him.

She needed a quick reprieve to calm herself down, so she could think rationally.

After gathering up the papers on the floor, she stood and turned to Frost. "Well, since your friend is here, I'll come back. When you're ready to start, just ring the nurses' station."

She didn't even give Frost time to respond. She turned to Ace and apologized again, then quickly extricated herself from the room.

Frost watched Autumn retreat from the room like her ass was on fire. He felt bad, knowing how embarrassed she was, but, on the other hand, he liked knowing she was jealous. However, Ace's timing was unfortunate.

"Well, it looks like you're the next one to fall," Ace said, smirking at Frost.

"What do you mean, the next one?"

"You like her."

"Like who?"

"Don't give me that shit. I'm talking about that feisty redhead who just ran out of here. She would fit right in with Alex and Tenley. On second thought, I don't think those two need another 'buddy' to get into trouble with."

Frost laughed. Ace was right. Just from his two encounters with her, he could see her getting along well with Alex and Tenley.

"I don't know anything about her, though."

Ace chuckled. "Damn man, when was the last time you actually dated someone? That's the purpose of dating. You get to know each other. Once you get discharged, ask her out. Keep it to something simple, like meeting for coffee."

Frost thought about it. He couldn't remember the last time he dated someone, meaning he went out on more than one date with the same woman. High school, maybe?

"Your silence tells me it's been a while. I'm telling you, I was the same way until I met Alex. That woman knocked me square on my ass the day we met. You saw what it did to me. Take the chance. You won't know if you don't try. Who knows, maybe in a few months or so, you'll be putting a ring on her finger and joining the club with me and Potter."

Frost quirked his eyebrow. He hadn't even asked her out, and Ace was already talking about rings. What the hell? "Yeah, what club is that? Washed up married men's club." Frost grinned. He loved ribbing any of the guys when he got the chance. Plus, it took the attention away from him. At least for the moment.

"Watch it, wise-ass. I'll have you inventorying all our gear when you're cleared for duty." He grinned at Frost.

Frost wondered if he and Alex had a set new date for their wedding since their original date was postponed because of a mission.

"Does that mean you and Alex set a new date for the wedding?" Frost asked, repositioning his leg when it was started to ache a little.

Ace ran his hand through his black hair. "No. I thank god every day for bringing her into my life, and I'll love her for the rest of my life with or without a piece of paper saying we're married." He looked at Frost, and Frost knew there was more. "This might seem silly and make me sound like a pussy, but just having that piece of paper, stating she's officially mine will make me feel a lot better."

Frost wondered if there was trouble in paradise. "Things good between the two of you?"

"Yeah, things are great. It's just that we can't seem to get a weekend where both of us don't already have something planned. As I said, it's silly. Probably just my insecurities are getting the best of me. Especially when I see other men checking her out, but at night when she's in my arms, I can't help but wonder why she chose me." He gave Frost a look. "Anyway, how in the hell did we end up talking about my love life instead of yours?"

Frost chuckled. Yeah, he was good at redirecting the conversation. "I don't have a love life," Frost scowled and crossed his arms over his chest.

"Not yet, but I'm betting you will real soon."

"Whatever. Don't you have a team you need to go order around?"

Ace laughed and looked at his watch. "Actually, I do need to get back. I told the commander I was heading out here to see you and that I wouldn't be too long."

Frost reached out and shook Ace's hand. "Thanks, man. I appreciate it."

"No thanks needed. You've been around the block enough times to know this is what teammates do for one another. Stitch and a couple of the others are coming by tomorrow. I have a meeting, or I'd come with them."

"Sounds good. Tell everyone, hello."

"Will do, man. And don't forget to ask her out." Frost rolled his eyes as Ace walked out of the room, laughing.

Frost laid his head back on the pillow and thought about what Ace said. Maybe asking her out for a cup of coffee wouldn't be bad. First, he needed to apologize for embarrassing her. He'd do that when she returned for his therapy session. He reached over and pushed the call button for the nurses' station. He was looking forward to spending some time with the Irish goddess.

CHAPTER THREE

Later that afternoon, Frost awoke with that eerie feeling that he wasn't alone. His SEAL training brought on a sixth sense. He'd been feeling restless all afternoon ever since Autumn finished working his leg over in therapy this morning. It was probably one of the nurses coming by again. Thank God, he got good news from the doctor saying they were going to release him in two or three days. He was getting annoyed with some of the nurses and their overzealous care for him. It had gotten to the point that he was ready to ask for a male nurse for the remainder of his stay.

Shifting his leg, he felt the muscle ache and silently swore to himself. Autumn hadn't lied when she told him she would give a hundred percent. His session with her was grueling, and she had pushed him hard. He had to bite his tongue a few times when he thought she exceeded his limitations, but then he remembered that this was her job. She knew when he was about to spout something off because she would raise one of her shapely eyebrows at him, daring him to say something, but he knew better and kept his mouth shut. She was probably getting her revenge from this morning when he had embarrassed her. That still made him laugh.

Even though she was a ball-buster and didn't cut him any slack during therapy, he had to admit he enjoyed their hour together. After apologizing to her, he had gotten her to open up a little. He was shocked to find out she had been married to a Marine. His heart hurt when she told him he had been killed while serving. Frost wanted to ask more questions, but could tell she started to get uncomfortable with the conversation, so he steered it in another direction. If things went well over the next two days, he decided he was going to follow through with what Ace had suggested and ask her out for coffee.

Slowly, he opened his eyes, expecting to ward off another handsy nurse, but instead, he was surprised to see a young boy sitting in the chair beside his bed, holding his Trident Pin.

He eyed the boy who hadn't realized Frost was awake watching him. The kid had short brownish hair, with what looked like some auburn color throughout. The outfit he wore reminded Frost of a school uniform. Glancing down, he saw the backpack next to the kid's feet.

He watched the kid as he ran his fingers over the pin. His eyes held a sparkle to them. Then to his surprise, the kid snapped the lid closed and placed the box exactly where Frost had left it on the table. When he looked up at Frost, his eyes went wide as saucers, and Frost had to hold back his laughter. Obviously, he had surprised the kid, and now the kid looked frightened.

Frost nodded toward the pin lying on the table. "You ever seen one of those?"

The boy shook his head side-to-side but then found his voice. "No, sir. At least not a real one. It's real, isn't it?"

The kid's well-mannered reply surprised the shit out of Frost. Nowadays, parents rarely taught their kids good manners, and whoever his parents were deserved a pat on the back.

Frost nodded, then reached over and picked up the case. He looked at the boy again. "Not many people can say they got to hold a 'real' trident pin." Frost knew there were stores out there that sold replicas.

"I'm sorry for touching it without asking. It's just I've never seen one up close before. I swear I wasn't going to steal it if that's what you were thinking."

Frost raised his eyebrows, and though he'd known this kid for just a few minutes, he was impressed with the boy.

"What's your name, kid?"

"Cody, sir. Cody Kauffman," he stated as he sat up a little straighter in the chair.

Frost held his hand out and leaned toward Cody. "I'm Frost. It's nice to meet you, Cody." Cody shook his hand but still looked a little intimidated. Then again, Frost was an intimidating man. Hell, all of the guys on his team were intimidating. It was their nature.

"So, Cody, do you make it a habit of coming into patients' rooms?"

29

Cody swallowed hard. "No, sir. My mom works here, and after school, I come here and wait for her shift to end. After I do my homework, I try to visit the patients who don't seem to have friends or family. I walked by your room, and you were sleeping, but I noticed nobody here, so I came in and just took a seat. Nobody should be alone when they're in the hospital. I like to talk to them and listen to their stories."

Frost wasn't sure if this kid was for real. Was he going for some sort of sainthood, or maybe he was trying to earn a Boy Scout badge?

"So, you're interested in the military?" Frost decided to ask.

"Yeah. My dad was a Marine," Cody answered but looked down at the floor, and a sad expression crossed his face; Frost wondered what was up with that.

"Was a Marine? Is your dad retired now?"

Cody looked up, and Frost swore he saw the kid start to tear up. "No," Cody said softly, then cleared his throat. "My dad died while serving."

Well, shit… Frost was at a loss for words. Damn, he knew plenty of good men and women who lost their lives protecting their country. Some were even good friends. Losing friends was awful, but he couldn't imagine losing a family member to war—especially a parent. He needed to quickly think of something to say, so Cody wouldn't be uncomfortable but also acknowledge what Cody shared with him.

"I'm sorry to hear that, Cody. I've lost a lot of good friends over the years, myself. I'm sure it wasn't easy, but always remember, your dad was an honorable soldier."

Cody smiled, "My mom tells me the same thing. I try to stay positive, but sometimes it's hard." He shrugged his shoulders. "Sometimes I wish he was here to talk to, you know, even though he wasn't home all that much. I mean, I love my mom, but she doesn't get stuff sometimes."

"What type of stuff?"

Cody shrugged his shoulders. "Guy stuff."

"Don't you have any other family members you can talk to? Uncles, Grandfathers?"

Cody shook his head. "It's just me and my mom."

Damn. That sucked. He felt for this kid. Having only his mom to raise him for the past two years, that had to be hard. But whoever his mother was, she was doing an excellent job at raising this kid. She must be one hell of a woman because Cody seemed like a terrific kid with a good head on his shoulders, and he respected his mother.

He went to respond when a familiar voice interrupted him. Frost looked up toward the door and focused his attention on that husky voice he had come to love in a matter of a day.

"Cody…there you are!"

Cody turned toward the door and smiled wide. "Hey, Mom. I was just talking to Frost. Have you met him?"

Frost's head snapped to Cody and then back to Autumn. *Mom? Is Cody Autumn's son?* Holy shit, what were the odds? Now it all made sense. When she told him today about losing her husband, she kept referring to 'we.' He never picked up on it until now.

Autumn walked closer to the bed and smiled at both Frost and Cody. She ruffled Cody's hair. Seeing the two of them next to each other, Frost could now see the resemblance. He had bright green eyes, just like his mom's, which should've been a telltale sign. *Damn, Frost, you're getting rusty sitting around in this hospital bed.*

"Are you about ready, kiddo? I'm sure that Chief Petty Officer Rhoades needs his rest. I heard he had a brutal PT appointment today with a drill sergeant." She looked over at Frost and winked.

"Is that so?" Frost said, raising an eyebrow and grinning back at her.

She held her hands up in surrender and laughed. "Hey, it's just what I heard."

Frost chuckled. The two of them had been going back and forth, teasing each other during his therapy session this morning. When she bent over to grab Cody's backpack from the floor, he couldn't help but check out her ass. She had a perfect round ass. His cock started to harden. *Fuck!* Just what he needed, to be caught with a boner while her kid was in the room. He placed his hands on the blanket covering his lap, hoping to conceal the bulge that was forming underneath.

When she stood back up, she glanced over at Frost, and he knew he was busted as his eyes ran up her body and met hers. She lifted one of her eyebrows, but what could he say. He was a man, and she had some nice features. He just smiled and shrugged his shoulders.

Cody was looking between them both. Then he focused his attention on Frost. "Umm...Frost?"

Pulling his gaze from Autumn, he turned his attention to Cody. "Yeah, buddy?" He really liked this kid.

"Would you mind if I stopped by after school tomorrow to say hi?"

Frost smiled. Maybe it was his good manners that had him wanting to get to know the kid. However, having a mom that was attractive with a great personality didn't hurt either. "Sure, kid. Some of my teammates are stopping by tomorrow around this time. Come by, and I'll introduce you to them."

Cody's eyes widened. "Really?!" He asked excitedly, making Frost smile.

"Really, Cody. You're a cool kid, and just so you know, I don't introduce just anybody to my team."

Cody was smiling from ear-to-ear. "I get it, Frost. I've read about SEALs and how you guys like to lay low. I won't say a word. Not even to my friends."

"I appreciate that, Cody. So, I'll expect to see you tomorrow then?"

"You bet." He turned to his mom, who was silently watching the interaction between them. "Mom, isn't that awesome?"

Autumn chuckled and kissed the top of Cody's head. "It sure is kiddo."

"This is so cool! Can I go grab a juice out of the vending machine before we go?"

"Sure, honey. I'll meet you in just a minute." She adjusted her bags on her shoulder.

"Later, Frost!" Cody said, waving over his shoulder as he hurried out of the door.

Frost chuckled and waved back. "Later, Cody."

Autumn turned to Frost and stepped toward the bed, bringing with her the scent of her perfume. Frost tried not to be obvious as he inhaled, but she smelled really good.

"I hope he wasn't a bother. He normally has his regulars he visits."

Frost waved her off. "Not at all. He seems like a good kid."

"I like to think so. Then again, he is my kid," she said, smiling. "But it's nice to hear it from someone else once in a while." He laughed, and she stepped even closer and looked him over, giving him a sincere look. "How are you feeling after the exercises this morning? And don't lie to me," she said, grinning. "I've worked with a few SEALs, and I know you guys tend to hide the truth. But, believe me, when you do that, it'll only cause setbacks and delay your return to active duty."

Frost was taken aback by the sincerity in her voice. She really did care about her patients. He'd been through several medical professionals during his career, and none of them had the bedside manner that Autumn brought. Most doctors and therapists treated you like you were just a number in the system, and would rely on what the patient told them. But Autumn wasn't like that. She watched closely for any signs, whether it was verbal or physical. And the others sure as hell didn't look like her either. Hearing her talk about working with other SEALs made him jealous. He wondered if any of those guys ever hit on her.

What the fuck am I thinking? She isn't mine. But I want her as mine. Goddammit!

Frost was startled when he felt her soft, warm hand on his forearm.

Shit! I completely zoned out. What the fuck is wrong with me?

Autumn pulled her hand back quickly. "I'm sorry." She swallowed hard.

Frost looked directly into her eyes. Her green eyes shimmered.

"I'll always be honest with you, especially when it comes to my health and wellbeing. If I'm not, I'm not only endangering myself, but I'd be putting my teammates' lives on the line as well, and that is something I'd never do.

33

"So, to answer your question, yes, my leg is sore, but that's expected from the workout my beautiful drill sergeant put me through." He winked and knew immediately he had embarrassed her as he watched her lower her head submissively at his comment. And dammit if his cock didn't start to harden, again. *Shit!* He was losing control. Earlier today, when she was leaning over him during PT, he had to use every fiber of his being to keep from getting an erection. What the fuck was happening to him?

When she raised her head, her gaze held his, and they both stared at each other for a few long seconds until she cleared her throat and tucked a loose strand of hair behind her ear. "I'd better get going before Cody engages in another conversation with someone."

Frost smiled, but deep down, he wasn't ready for her to go. He wanted her to sit and talk, so he could learn more about Autumn Kauffman.

"I'll see you tomorrow, bright and early, Rhoades."

"It's Frost."

She gave him a weird look. "What?"

"Frost. My friends call me Frost."

She smiled. "Okay, Frost. I'll see you tomorrow."

He grinned. "I'm looking forward to it, Autumn. Drive safe."

She nodded her head, and before she turned to leave, Frost noticed her cheeks were a little pink. He watched her walk out the door and couldn't resist taking another look at her ass again. His mom always said love could come out of nowhere and hit you in the head when you least expect it. He began to wonder if Autumn could be that woman.

He laid his head back on the pillow and started to think. He was turning thirty-one in a couple of months. Seeing his best friend Alex happily engaged to Ace, and his other best friend Tenley, now married to Potter, another one of his teammates, made him contemplate what he wanted with his future. He wouldn't always be in the Navy, and he wouldn't mind a family.

His thoughts drifted to Cody. He couldn't be any older than ten or eleven years old, though he acted a lot older. But considering his father was a Marine and then having to deal with his death probably forced him to grow up faster.

He wanted to know more about Autumn and Cody. Something about the duo touched him deep inside. He wanted to do something for Cody, and he got an idea.

Reaching over to the table next to the bed, he picked up his cell phone and dialed Stitch.

"What's going on? You calling to have me come rescue your sorry ass from that place?"

"Shit, I wish." He rubbed a hand down his face.

"Oh, come on, it can't be that bad. I've seen how those cute nurses cater to your every whim and need."

"Yeah, well, that's part of the problem. Anyways, I need a favor."

Stitch got serious. "Sure, man. What's up?"

"Tomorrow, before you guys stop by, can you swing by the commander's office and ask him for a Team 2 t-shirt and hat and bring them with you. Men's size small if they have it."

Stitch snorted a laugh. "Please tell me you're not resorting to offering SEAL novelties to get a date."

Frost laughed. "Fuck you! No, it's for Autumn's son."

"Autumn? Oh! Your physical therapist. The hot redhead? Wait, she has a kid?" Stitch asked.

Frost rolled his eyes. "Yeah, that Autumn. And yes, she has a son. Look, I'll explain later, just bring the shirt and hat with you."

"You got it."

"Thanks, I'll see ya tomorrow."

"Later."

Autumn flicked her blinker on as she turned into her housing complex. It was a few minutes after seven, and the sun was starting to set. She was still smiling inside from spending time with Frost today. Though their day didn't start great, at least it ended on a good note. Gosh, she was so embarrassed and couldn't believe she had insulted Frost's team leader. She never meant for that to happen. Thankfully, they managed to make up during his therapy session. Frost didn't really talk too much about himself, which didn't surprise her. However, she was surprised how easy it was for her to talk to him, especially about her late husband. She was grateful Frost didn't ask questions, which made her respect for him grow.

She pulled into her assigned parking spot in front of the duplex she rented. She hated arriving home when it was dark out. The complex they lived in wasn't the greatest or the safest, but for now, it was all she could afford. Just as she did typically before getting out of the car, she glanced around, making sure nobody was nearby. As her eyes scanned the house, she noticed her bedroom window was pushed up, and the screen was missing. Her stomach clenched. She didn't remember opening the window this morning, and even if she had, she never would have left it open when she wasn't home. Not in this crime-ridden area. She looked around again and saw all of the hoodlums loitering in front of another duplex a few homes down, and she got a creepy feeling.

She noticed that Mrs. Higdon, her seventy-three-year-old neighbor, who lived in the duplex connected to hers, was out walking her poodle. Maybe she saw something. She instructed Cody to wait in the car and lock the doors while she went to speak with her. She didn't tell him why because she didn't want to alarm him.

When she stepped out of the car, her foot landed in a pile of cigarette butts, and she silently cursed. Someone had been emptying their ashtray right next to her parking spot. It was the fourth time in the last two weeks she would have to clean it up. Letting out an audible sigh, she continued toward Mrs. Higdon.

"Hi, Mrs. Higdon," Autumn spoke as she approached the older woman. Barney, the little white poodle, jumped up on his hind legs at the sight of her. Barney knew Autumn usually carried around little treats just for him, but she didn't have any today. She bent down to pet him. "Sorry, buddy. I don't have any treats. I'll bring you one when I get a chance." He gave her cheek a little lick and barked, making her laugh.

"You're getting home late tonight, Autumn." Leave it to Mrs. Higdon to know everyone's business around here. But being nosey in a good kind of way might be why nobody ever bothered her.

"Yeah, I left work a little late, and then I needed to run to the store." Her mind drifted to Frost. For some reason, the man got her insides all twisted up when she was around him.

She saw Mrs. Higdon look toward her car, where Cody sat watching them. "Why is he still in the car?" She asked.

"Well, I wanted to ask you if you noticed anybody hanging around the house today. When I pulled in, I noticed my bedroom window was open, and I don't remember opening it this morning."

Mrs. Higdon gasped and covered her mouth. "Oh, dear. No, I haven't seen anyone, but I was at my quilting class at the Senior Center for a few hours this morning. Do you think someone broke in?"

"I don't know. I'm afraid to go in and check. If someone did, I don't want to contaminate any evidence left behind. But then again, I don't want to look like a fool if I did open it and just don't remember doing it." Damn, this sucked.

"Why don't you call the non-emergency number to the police department and explain the situation to them. They'd still send someone to check it out just to be sure. Go ahead, call them, then you and Cody can come to my place while you wait. If someone did break-in, you need to contact Mr. Voight, the landlord, so he is aware. Now that I think about it, wasn't that the window that the lock broke about a month ago?"

"Yes. I spoke with Mr. Voight about it, and he said he would get it fixed."

"Let me guess, he never 'got around' to fix it," she said using air quotes, and Autumn just nodded.

Mrs. Higdon let out a sigh. "I swear that man is a cheap ass son-of-a-bitch. He pulled that crap with me when I first moved into my place when the handle to the faucet in my bathroom broke. It took the bastard almost two months to replace it. And he only did that because I threatened to sue."

Autumn loved Mrs. Higdon. The woman was a spitfire for her age. She wasn't afraid of anybody, and that included the three-hundred-pound landlord of theirs. In a way, Autumn considered Mrs. Higdon a mother figure to her. She was someone she could talk to about anything.

"No matter the outcome from tonight, you and I are both going to call Mr. Voight tomorrow and demand he gets his ass out here and fix that lock. Next time something breaks or needs to be repaired, you stay on his ass until he gets the job done."

Autumn just nodded her head in agreement. She would certainly do whatever Mrs. Higdon wanted her to do. There was no use in arguing with the woman because, in the end, she'd get her way whether you agreed or not.

"Now, go get that wonderful son of yours and come in while you make that phone call to the police department."

Autumn smiled, not even trying to argue with the tiny but powerful woman. "Yes, ma'am."

"Let me know if you see anything missing or out of place." The friendly officer told her as he escorted her through the house. Autumn thought escorting seemed like a funny word to use because the house was so small, the guy could stand in the living room and see every nook and cranny.

He was good looking, she guessed, probably in his forties. Tall with dark brown hair with a little grey starting to show and light brown eyes. The color reminded her of caramel. She referred to him as the nice officer because the other officer who was on the scene earlier was young and cocky. He looked annoyed at having to be there. God forbid the man actually had to work to earn a paycheck. After he pretty much accused her of forgetting that she'd opened the window, the officer in charge who was escorting her now, had stepped in and dismissed him from the scene. At least he apologized for the young officer's behavior.

They walked through the living room, then Cody's room. Nothing looked to have been tampered with or missing. They got to her room, and again, nothing seemed out of the ordinary, just the window was wide open. They did have their evidence team dust for fingerprints around the window. They were able to get a couple of partial prints, but they could be hers or Cody's. The officer lectured her about needing to get the lock fixed on the window as soon as possible. She explained for the second time today how it had broken a few weeks ago, and she called the landlord, but nothing had been done about it. She however assured the officer she would try calling again, just like she assured Mrs. Higdon.

As they were exiting the room, something caught her eye; her husband's dog tags. They were sitting on top of the small jewelry box she kept on her dresser. She let out a low gasp and covered her mouth, catching the officer's attention.

"What is it?" He asked her.

She pointed with a shaky hand to the dog tags. "My husband's dog tags. I know for sure they were not left there."

He looked at her as if he was trying to scrutinize her. "Are you positive?"

She nodded her head as her eyes started to water. Seeing those brought back memories. Both the good and the bad. She sniffled. "They haven't been out of that jewelry box since the day I buried him two years ago."

He gave her a sympathetic look and put his hand on her shoulder in a friendly and caring way. "Let me call back in the crime scene technicians and get them to process this area. Go ahead and wait out in the living room for me, okay?" She nodded her head and went to the living room to wait.

Forty-five minutes later, the officer came back out. Knowing the dog tags had been removed from her jewelry box confirmed her fear. Someone had definitely been inside her home. But why had the person targeted the dog tags? She didn't understand.

"Mrs. Kauffman, we are just about done here. Just another five minutes, and you'll have the place to yourself. I've arranged to have extra patrols in the area through the night and for the next few days. If we get any information or if we have any further questions, I'll give you a call."

She gave him a faint smile. "Thank you, officer. I appreciate your help."

He smiled, then handed her a card. "This is my card. My office line is on there, along with the general number. I've written your case number on the back. If you notice anything else or if you have any questions, just call one of the two numbers, and either I or someone else can help you."

She nodded her head.

"Now, before I go, is there someone I can call to come over and stay with you?"

As much as she would love to have someone come over, she didn't have anyone she could call. She had Nathan, but what could he do 3,000 miles away? She had a few friends at the hospital and Mrs. Higdon next door. But that was really the extent of her 'friends'. Why, at that moment, did Frost's name pop into her head?

"Ms.?"

"Oh, sorry. I was just thinking. No, there isn't anyone. We'll be okay. I'll make sure I call the landlord first thing tomorrow about the lock."

She escorted the officer out and promised again she would get the lock fixed and notify his department right away if anything else occurred.

After picking up Cody from next door, she got him into the shower and tucked in bed. Thank goodness, Mrs. Higdon was kind enough to fix him a ham and cheese sandwich with some chips for dinner.

She changed into a pair of loose cotton shorts and a tank top, then gathered her bucket of cleaning supplies from the linen closet before getting to work cleaning the filth that the crime scene technicians had left behind. The powder they used to dust for fingerprints covered her bedroom. Although, she planned on disinfecting the entire house anyway, knowing a stranger had been in her house. Only then would she try and get some sleep, but it didn't seem likely. She was on guard and didn't plan on letting it down anytime soon.

CHAPTER FOUR

Skinny stood just down the street and watched the police leave the hot redhead's house. A woman he wouldn't mind sinking his dick into. But that wasn't what he was getting paid to do. Although it was tempting, it would be easy to break into that crappy-ass house. He and his buddy 8-Ball, who'd been helping him mess with the woman, could tag team her. Man, the thoughts that went through his mind, imagining her tied up and gagged while he fucked her rough and hard. The fear in her eyes alone would drive him wild.

He reached down and adjusted his throbbing dick. Just thinking about her sweet body made him hard. He needed to head to the club he belonged to and find an easy piece of ass. His boss, who financed the club, always made sure there were women at all times of the day and night available to satisfy the club members. It didn't matter that the women were drugged. He only cared about the pussy. Maybe he'd mention the redhead to his boss. His boss had a particular taste for women. And this one seemed to be right up his alley. Yeah, he'd give Cecil a call.

First, he needed to call the woman he was doing the job for. He couldn't fuck this up. It was easy money.

He pulled the burner phone from his pocket and hit the pre-programmed number. It rang twice.

"Is tonight's job done?" The voice on the other end, asked.

"Yes, ma'am. The police just left."

"Was the item where I told you it would be? And, were you sure not to touch or take anything else?"

He rolled his eyes. *Did this woman think he was an amateur?*

"Everything went according to your plan."

"Good." He could hear the smile in her voice. "I'll be in touch in a few days with your next assignment. In the meantime, if you see or hear anything, let me know."

"Will do." He heard the click ending the call and slid the phone back into his pocket. He wondered what the redhead did to piss this woman off. But, then again, he didn't give a shit. As long as the contact kept giving him assignments and paying him on time, he could care less about their beef.

He turned and walked toward his motorcycle. Unlike the redhead, he'd be getting a good night's sleep. Tomorrow morning, he'd stop by the Western Union to collect his pay.

As he mounted his bike, he thought about his boss.

Cecil was working on a huge deal, and if everything panned out, it would be a huge payday for all involved. But the problem was, Cecil needed to find a wife. Not that it would be hard for him to find a woman because Cecil was a good-looking man and never had a problem taking a woman to bed. Most were high priced escorts and wouldn't work for this deal. The man that Cecil was in talks with was a traditional family man with a wife and kids. Cecil was trying to impress the guy, and he led the man to believe he was married. Since then, Cecil had been searching for the "perfect" housewife. He was running out of time because he was due to sign all the handover contracts in a couple of months, and he promised the guy that he would bring his wife.

Skinny took out his phone and pulled up the picture of the redhead. He took her picture the other day while she was in front of her house, talking to that nosey neighbor of hers. She was laughing at something, but she looked smoking hot. Plus, she had a kid. She could be just what Cecil was looking for. He dialed Cecil's number.

"Are you still in the market for a wife?"

"Maybe. Why you asking?"

"Well, I might have a prospect for you to check out."

"Tell me about her."

"Shit, let me just send you a picture of her, so you can see for yourself and make a decision."

"Send it over."

Skinny heard the click and knew Cecil had disconnected. But that was Cecil, abrupt to the core.

He put his helmet on and started up his bike. Yeah, he was going to stop by the club and get himself some pussy before heading home.

Cecil Hughes studied the picture of the woman. Skinny hadn't been exaggerating. She was stunning; however, she looked to be much younger than his fifty-six years of age. Not that age made a difference for what he was looking for.

That red hair of hers was a showstopper and went along with her gorgeous and infectious smile. When he enlarged the picture, he almost swallowed his tongue. Her green eyes were mesmerizing. She would be perfect for what he needed. He thought for a moment and remembered Skinny had mentioned she had a young son. Perfect—instant family. An evil grin spread across his face.

Time was running out to seal the deal for the new business venture he had been working on for the last few months. If he didn't find a wife, it could ruin the deal with the Russian.

Vadim believed in family values, especially when it came to his shipping business. His dad started the export company back in the day with just two hundred dollars in his pocket. Now it had grown to a multi-million dollar operation. Numerous shipments were loaded onto cargo ships every day, their destinations worldwide. It was a brilliant way to operate his side business of exporting stolen luxury vehicles. Having full control of manifests and what went into the shipping containers and ships alleviated a lot of headaches, and it allowed him to broaden his client base. He used a local gang to scope out and lift certain vehicles. When the prior leader of the gang went rogue, it had been a perfect opportunity for Cecil to fill the role. Those guys would do any job as long as Cecil kept their clubhouse running, including providing all the alcohol and women.

Money wasn't the issue in getting Vadim to sell the company to him. Vadim stipulated that whoever he sold to must share the same values he believed in, meaning Cecil needed a family. During the last meeting Cecil had with Vadim, Cecil lied and told him he was married. Cecil didn't want his lack of marital status to be a reason Vadim pulled out of the deal. They were due to close the deal in a couple of months, and he promised Vadim he would bring his wife to the closing. There were other possibilities that Cecil could use, such as hiring an escort to play the part, but that was risky. This deal was too important to be foolish. He could lose everything if this deal went south, and time was running out.

He wanted to know more about her. He hit a button on his desk phone, and a voice came over the line.

"Yes, sir."

"I need you to look into someone."

"Trouble?"

"No, nothing like that." He actually smiled as he looked at the beautiful woman's picture again. "I think I may have just found my wife. Get with Skinny, and he can give you the details."

"Yes, sir."

He hit the button again and turned in his chair to look out the window. He enjoyed living on his 161-foot Trinity yacht and sailing to new places; however, there were times he wished he could settle in one place. Maybe after this deal closed, he could. With the money he was going to make, he'd be set for eternity. And what better way than to settle down with a beautiful wife on a private island away from society.

CHAPTER FIVE

Autumn stood back and leaned against the wall as she watched Cody interact with Frost and some of his buddies from his team. Cody was in total hero-worship mode being around these guys.

Stitch was hilarious to watch as he kept fiddling with Frost's IV and checking everything out, although she could sense that Frost was getting irritated with his best friend. Then there was Irish, Dino, and Potter. Irish was a hoot. He was a touchy-feely kind of guy. She was shocked when Frost introduced him to her, and he pulled her into a hug. Irish had blonde hair, blue eyes, and a slight scar that ran just under his bottom lip to his chin. Autumn had a feeling he could get any woman to drop her panties with his charm. Dino was gorgeous; black hair, brown eyes, an olive complexion, and a smile that most women would eat right up. Besides their good looks, they all had exceptional manners and were surprisingly easy to talk to, considering what they did for a living. Well, except for the Potter guy. He was freakishly tall and quiet.

Her main focus, though, was the man in the bed, currently smiling and laughing at something Cody said. She hadn't a clue what they were even talking about. Frost was sitting there, looking comfortable in a pair of gray gym shorts and a black t-shirt that read in big white block letters, "Don't Touch Me." She hid her laugh at the meaning behind the shirt. During their PT session this morning, Frost had mentioned how he was tired of the female nurses' unprofessionalism. He didn't know it yet, but she had spoken to Gianna, the nurse in charge, and explained what was happening and how Frost was very uncomfortable and upset about how he was being treated. Gianna was a hard ass, and most of the nurses hated to work this floor because of her, but in Gianna's defense, she had to be, as the patients on her floor were her responsibility. To say Gianna was unhappy about Frost being handled like a prime piece of meat was saying the least. She had assured Autumn that for the remainder of Frost's stay, he would be treated just like any patient should be. With dignity and respect.

She yawned and tried to stifle it, using her hand and turning her head, hoping nobody noticed. She was tired, considering it had been almost 11:00 pm when the police left her house. Then she spent another couple of hours cleaning and disinfecting everything. She finally crawled into bed around four o'clock in the morning but was then too wired to sleep. She drank two cups of coffee later in the morning, but as it was now almost four in the afternoon, her butt was dragging big time. She was lucky she functioned enough to get matching clothes on.

"Is our company boring you?" She heard Frost ask. She looked toward him, and he was grinning. Well, shit, so much for being subtle. She was busted and felt her cheeks warm, and she shyly dipped her head. "Sorry, it's definitely not the company. I just didn't get much sleep last night." He grinned, and that damn dimple she loved so much appeared.

"Aww…were you thinking about spending the morning with me? I know I'm your favorite patient." He teased her, but before she could answer, Cody decided to inject himself into the conversation. "No, she's tired because the police didn't leave our house until late last night." Cody's voice was filled with excitement. Well, so much for keeping the lid on last night's events. She guessed a ten-year-old would think it was exciting to have the police at their house. Thankfully, he didn't truly understand the harm.

She put her hand on Cody's shoulder. "Cody, I don't think these gentlemen care to know about our little hiccup at home last night." She loved her son dearly, but she swore there was no filter on his mouth sometimes. These men didn't need to know what was happening in her personal life. Nor would they care to know. So, she tried to minimize it as much as possible, though it had really freaked her out. Hell, she was still freaked out knowing someone, a stranger at that, was inside her home and went through her belongings.

She realized the room was now silent, and all the friendly joking in the room had ceased. Frost sat up straighter, and all the other men in the room seemed to stand at attention and were now staring at her with some very fierce expressions. She looked at them. "What? Why are you all looking at me like that?"

"The police were at your house?" Frost asked her in a low but deep serious tone that made her insides quiver.

"It was nothing, really," she said, trying to appease them

Apparently, he didn't like her answer because he turned to Cody. And, of course, Cody being the kid he is, he told them everything.

"Someone broke into our house yesterday. Mom saw the window to her bedroom open when we got home." He looked at Autumn as if asking her if he was telling the story correctly.

Was it illegal to place duct tape over your child's mouth? She took a glance at Frost, and holy shit, the glare he was giving her made her shiver. Now she got why his call sign was Frost. As in Jack "Frost." The sexy man looked lethal and ready to kill.

"Don't you keep your windows locked?" Dino interjected into the conversation, looking concerned despite his accusatory tone. She turned her gaze to the man and caught a fierce look from him as well. Talk about intense!

From their expressions, these guys probably thought she was some dumb, irresponsible parent. God, if they only knew where she lived, then they would likely believe her, but she wasn't even going to go there. They would probably try and convince her she needed to move. However, they wouldn't have to try to convince her. She had already decided she was gone as soon as she could afford another place in a nicer neighborhood. Deciding she wasn't going to let these men push her around, she channeled the tough, independent woman she knew she had in her.

She looked Dino in the eye. "Of course. I keep our doors and windows locked, but the lock on that particular window broke about a month ago."

"Locks are relatively cheap, why didn't you just get a new one and replace it?" Stitch now asked, joining the party of 'let's gang up on Autumn.'

She huffed out an annoyed breath. "Because I don't own the home. I'm just a tenant, and my lease agreement states that the landlord has to do any type of repairs."

"Have you talked to your landlord?" Stitch countered, looking at her like she was guilty of a crime. Now she was getting pissed off. How dare these men to question her like this whole situation was her fault. Damn Cody for opening his mouth. Actually, she couldn't be upset at him. If she was upset at anyone, it was herself. She was the one who set off this chain of events. She crossed her arms in front of her chest and shot daggers at Stitch. She didn't care that he could probably kill her a hundred different ways.

Autumn cringed, as the conversation with Mrs. Higdon came back into mind. She feared she was getting ready to get the same lecture from these guys.

"Do I look like a complete moron? Not that it's any of your business, but yes, I informed my landlord the day after I noticed the lock was broken, and he said he'd get it fixed. He just hasn't gotten around to it."

Stitch glanced over at Frost, and the two men seemed to exchange an understanding before Stitch turned back toward Autumn and grinned. "I like you, Autumn."

"And…What is that supposed to mean?" She asked, raising an eyebrow, clearly not understanding where this conversation was heading.

Stitch just grinned. "Oh, you'll see. But let's get back to your situation. I don't think you're a moron. I may be wrong, but I think your landlord was just blowing you off."

"Why do you think that?" She already knew Stitch was right about her landlord. Her talk with Mrs. Higdon last night confirmed that.

"You mentioned 'he' when you were referring to your landlord. Am I correct?" Autumn nodded. "I know first-hand how a lot of landlords operate. I've dealt with plenty in my lifetime. Most of them are shady and only looking out for their investment. They will try and push repairs off, especially when dealing with someone who won't keep on top of them when something goes wrong. Not to mention, you are a beautiful woman.

The guy is probably taking advantage of you." She went to speak, but he held up his hand, and from the stern expression she got from him, she snapped her mouth shut. "I don't personally know you, but I'm a pretty good judge of character, and I'm going to be a hundred percent honest with you. You will come to learn that us guys here are honest and good men." Autumn was really starting to wonder where this talk was heading. "I can already tell you are smart, strong, and independent. Not to mention a kick ass-mom." He grinned at Cody before glancing back at her. "For our sake, please call your landlord again tomorrow and tell him that if your lock is not fixed in the next couple of days, you are going to file a complaint with the Housing Authority. And, if that doesn't work, you call one of us, and we'll handle it."

Autumn gulped. She looked around at all of the men in the room, including Frost, who hadn't taken his eyes off her. He held her gaze, and holy shit, was it intense. They were all nodding their heads in agreement and looking at her with such serious and powerful expressions that she started to feel a little nervous. She was quite sure those men could get anything they wanted; they were so intimidating.

She knew her mouth was gaping open as she stared at Stitch. She was at a total loss for words. She didn't know any of them, nor did they know her, yet they all were acting protective of her, and she wondered why. Was it a shared trait amongst SEALs? They were all about protecting people and interests, so maybe that extended into their everyday lives as well. But if she were being honest, they were kind of freaking her out right now. This was too much.

"Cody mentioned something out of place. What was it?" Frost asked.

Were these guys for real? Did they actually care, or were they just pretending to be interested to impress her? Would Frost really do that? They barely knew each other, but she had felt a connection to him over the past two days. She knew it was a bad idea to feel an attraction to this guy. She was only going to get hurt. She needed to put an end to this madness. She wasn't going to be their next little plaything or project that they could just set aside when they were done.

She stood taller and pushed her shoulders back, trying to look like the confident and independent woman Stitch had just described her as being. "Look, I really appreciate that you all seem to care."

"Honey, you don't get it. If we didn't care, we certainly wouldn't be standing here, asking you questions and giving you advice. Now, answer Frost's question. What was out of place? And, don't you dare try to lie because I'll know if you do." Now it was the big guy Potter's turn to speak up as he interrupted her and stepped toward her, causing her to take a step back only for her to back against the wall. She swallowed hard. Jesus, he was huge and mean looking! She looked at Frost, and by his expression, it seemed he was a little insulted and pissed.

Was she trying to find something wrong so she could push them away?

From their looks alone, she could tell she wasn't going to win this battle. But if she answered Frost's question, she knew it would lead to other questions and conversations she didn't feel comfortable answering or talking about. These guys didn't know her background. Frost knew some. But how could she ignore the big man towering over her?

One thing she'd never been was a liar, and she wasn't about to start now. She took a deep breath and hoped her voice wouldn't give her emotions away, but that was a long shot. She could already feel the sadness starting to bubble its way up from her heart.

"My husband's dog tags weren't where they should have been."

She saw a few of the guys shoot a quick glance in Frost's direction, but Frost never took his eyes off her. She saw how his eyes softened a bit, and she knew now that he understood and knew how difficult this conversation would be for her.

Stitch scrunched his eyebrows together. "Husband? Are you married? And he's a soldier?" Stitch looked back at Frost. "I thought...." Frost held up his hand to stop Stitch from saying any more.

She gave Frost a pleading look. She felt drawn to him to help her. And it seemed so natural to do so. She had shared a little about her past with him, and she hoped he would help put an end to the interrogation tactics of his friends. If not for her sake but for Cody, who was still in the room listening. He must have gotten the message because he interrupted Stitch.

He turned his attention to Cody. "Hey, Cody. Would you mind running down to the nurses' station and ask them to get me a pineapple juice?"

Thankfully, Cody didn't appear to understand what was happening around him, and he smiled, wanting nothing more than to help out Frost. "Sure. I'll be right back."

Once Cody was out of the room and out of earshot, Autumn took a few deep breaths and turned toward the men. They all were looking none too happy, and although their looks should have scared her, she really didn't give a shit.

"Look, I appreciate the mementos you've given Cody and how nice you've all been, but I ask that you please respect our privacy. I'd also appreciate it if you kept your interrogation tactics to yourselves."

"Autumn, don't be upset at the guys. They don't know about your husband," Frost told her. His voice was soft and understanding. She turned and stared at him, trying to decipher if he was telling the truth. Why wouldn't he tell them? She thought groups like these guys told each other everything.

"You didn't tell them?" She asked, looking him over, but, of course, neither his facial expression nor his body language gave any inkling if he was being honest or not. As she scrutinized him more, his eyes were what gave her the answer. His light brown eyes held nothing but compassion and sympathy. He was totally honest, and her respect for him soared.

He shook his head. "No. It wasn't my place to. What you shared with me was between the both of us. I love these guys like brothers, but there are times that we don't tell each other everything. Autumn, you need to understand; we have an instinct that when we think someone is in trouble, we tend to react. Especially when it involves women and children. We've all seen a lot of bad shit happen in the places we've been. And sitting here listening to Cody telling us that the police were at your house because someone broke in, well, it brought out that protective instinct in all of us, and quite honestly, it scared the shit out of me."

She glanced around the room at the guys. Maybe they were just trying to help, and she was just overreacting? She took a seat in the chair next to Frost's bed and tucked her hair behind her ear.

"I'm sorry if I offended you guys. I don't have much time before Cody gets back, but I think I should clear a few things up."

Frost reached out and covered her hand. "Autumn, you don't have to explain if you don't want to. You are not going to hurt their feelings."

His touch and sincerity grounded her. She now understood these guys were just looking out for her. Over the last two years, people, like her friends back in California and her co-workers here at the hospital, told her all the time she was building a wall, but she denied it. Apparently, they were right, and she needed to work on tearing it down. And now couldn't have been a better time to start working on it.

"No, Frost, I need to. I've been sitting here trying to decide whether you guys were the real deal. I'm not a person who spills their entire life story to others, especially strangers." She took another glance at the men and gave them a small smile. "But, for some reason, I trust all of you." She took a deep breath, and Frost squeezed her hand, giving her the courage. She looked at him, smiled softly, and squeezed his back. A silent thank you for giving her the push and strength she needed. She could definitely do this.

"My husband, Kevin, was a Marine stationed out of Camp Pendleton. Two years ago, while on patrol in Iraq, his unit was ambushed. From the few details I know, his unit was outnumbered. While trying to get his men to safety, he sacrificed himself and was fatally shot. After his death, I was slowly falling down a very dark rabbit hole, and if I didn't get out of there, I don't know if I would've been able to climb back up. But here I am. It took all the strength I had, but I climbed those walls to reach the light at the top. Once I succeeded, I told myself it was time for a change. But I couldn't do that back in California. If I had stayed, the same people would still be around me, and I was afraid I would begin to rely on them again and start the whole process over. So, I started looking for a job out east, and by a stroke of luck, I came across this one."

She hadn't realized while she was talking that a few tears had slipped out. She wiped them away. Stitch walked over, squatted down in front of her, and took her other hand. He used his other hand to wipe away a tear she must have missed. He had gorgeous hazel eyes. She could see tiny specks of gold mixed in with the light green color. The room was quiet, so quiet you could hear a pin drop.

"Wow, honey. Thank you for sharing something that I'm sure is very difficult and upsetting to talk about. And I'm sorry to hear about your husband. I'm sure he was a great man. It took a lot of courage to do what you did. To move away and start over like that. All while raising a son on your own, having to adjust to a whole new environment, and make new friends. See, my instincts were right. You are a strong woman." He winked and squeezed her hand before releasing it.

She snorted a laugh. "I wouldn't go that far. Besides, the ladies here at the hospital are my only friends. My social life isn't what you would call impressive."

"Now, I find that hard to believe with your personality."

She tilted her head sideways, giving him a look like she didn't believe him.

"Don't look at me like that. You are friendly, funny, caring, and patient, considering you can put up with this one." He motioned to Frost, who was attentively listening.

She smiled. "Thank you, Stitch. That is very kind of you to say. As far as being patient, it helps when the patient is cooperative." She gently patted Frost's hand and smiled at him.

"Well, you can consider all of us your friends now, and we don't extend our friendship freely. You will fit in perfectly with our little unit."

She wasn't sure what to say, so she just smiled and said thank you and tried to keep from bursting into tears. These guys really were special, and she was grateful she got to see a glimpse of the real men behind their SEAL facade.

⸙

Frost was proud to be part of a team with the men standing before him. His mind pondered over the woman who'd just confided something very personal, and they came together for Autumn and made her feel empowered despite what she may have thought.

She was strong, for sure. And, the heartbreak and changes she had experienced over the last two years had taken a toll on her. He wanted to know more about her. Hell, he wanted to know everything. Never in his life had a woman affected him the way Autumn had. There was a need inside of him to protect and possess her and Cody. He wanted to help her take those final steps and heal her heart completely. He had a feeling it was going to be an uphill battle, but he was all in. He would make it happen. Well, as soon as he could get out of the hospital.

As they were leaving, Cody went around the room, shaking everyone's hand and thanking them again for the t-shirt and hat. When he got to Frost, he asked. "So, after you go home, I won't see you again, will I?"

Frost swallowed hard. He needed to really think about his words first before speaking them because the way his mind was feeling right now, he wanted to tell Cody he would see him every day, but he couldn't because that would surely scare Autumn. If he wanted to pursue her, he had a feeling he was going to have to tread the waters carefully.

He took a quick glance, and Autumn seemed like she was holding her breath while waiting to hear his answer. He shook Cody's hand and looked him in the eye and made an instant decision. This kid was going to be part of his life, and so was his mom. He just needed to convince her.

"I wouldn't say that, buddy. Like Stitch told your mom, we're all friends now, and friends hang out with one another." He looked up at Autumn, who was staring back at him with those green eyes of hers. He saw how they shimmered, and he knew she was tearing up again and could see the emotion swirling in them. And when she cracked a smile, he knew things were on the right track.

"Really?! You mean I can hang out with you guys?" An overly excited Cody asked the guys, and Frost had to laugh.

"Yeah, buddy. That is as long as it's okay with your mom." He looked up at Autumn again and raised one of his eyebrows in question at her, and she smiled.

"Of course, it's okay, just as long as these 'meet-ups' don't involve any strenuous activities. At least until Frost heals." She raised an eyebrow back at him, and it made Frost laugh. "You got yourself a deal."

"Cool!" Cody exclaimed, and the guys chuckled.

"Well, kiddo, let's say you and I head home and let these gentlemen talk. Plus, I need to stop by the store."

Frost didn't want them to leave. Nor did he want her going home by herself, not after knowing a stranger had been in her home. He needed to know she was okay when she got home. On instinct, he reached out and took her hand before she turned to walk away. His touch obviously surprised her as he heard her breath hitch before she turned back to look at him. When her eyes locked on to his, he felt cupid's arrow hit him square in the heart, and he knew he was done for. He let go to reach over and grabbed his phone from the table.

"Give me your number," he asked, knowing he sounded kind of bossy.

"Why?" She asked with her hands on her hips, hips that he would love to squeeze.

"Because I want to call you later and make sure you got home okay. Please…" He held his breath. He wasn't sure if he was moving too fast. But when she nodded and started giving him the number, he wanted to pump his fist in the air. Her giving him her number was another show of trust.

After saying goodbye, Frost watched her leave the room. The urge to protect both of them overwhelmed him, and the whole break-in at her house didn't sit right with him either. Someone was trying to make a statement. He would talk to her about it later and try to get some more information from her.

"It hits you when you least expect it. Doesn't it?"

"What?" Frost asked, looking up at Potter, who had snuck up on him and now stood towering over his bed.

Potter crossed his arms. "Meeting 'the one'."

Frost thought about denying it, but what good would it do? "Yeah, it does."

Potter grinned, something he didn't often do unless his wife, Tenley, was around, and then the giant couldn't wipe the smile off his face. "She's sweet. A little shy and timid. And Cody seems like a nice kid. He seems to have a good head on his shoulders, especially knowing what happened to his dad. He's only a few years older than Alejandra. If things progress between the two of you, maybe I'll have Tenley reach out to Autumn and see if they want to get the kids together or something. You know those playdate things kids have."

Frost started laughing. Hearing Potter, the biggest and meanest on the team, talk about setting up playdates was hilarious. Potter scowled at Frost.

"What the fuck is so funny?"

"You. You're the meanest looking guy in the teams I know, and here you are talking about kids and playdates." Frost laughed harder as Potter's face took on an even meaner expression. And in no time, he had the others laughing along with him.

Potter glared at the guys with his arms crossed over his chest. "Laugh all you want, assholes. At least I can go home tonight and wrap myself around my woman. What can you all say about that?"

Frost stopped laughing and scrunched his nose up. "Christ, man, I don't need to hear that shit. Tenley is like my sister. But getting back to what you said and all joking aside, I think that would be a great idea. Just from the little time she and I have spent together, I get the impression she's holding back. Like she's scared to let go. I don't know. It might take some time."

"However you decide to woo her, you'd better make it quick. She's a fine-looking woman with brains. I've come to the conclusion that women like that are hard to come by. And I'm sure other men would like to claim her as theirs," Irish said.

Frost scowled at the blonde hair, blue-eyed man. Irish was a total ladies' man. He never had any problem hooking up with a woman.

Although he noticed over the past couple of weeks when they'd been out at the local bar, he left alone. In the past, Irish never went home without a woman on his arm. Shit, he hoped to hell Irish wasn't attracted to Autumn. That thought pissed him off. He gave Irish a mean look. "Don't even think about hitting on her. She's off-limits."

Irish laughed. The fucker. He had a habit of messing with the guys who had women. One of these days, karma was going to come back around and bite him in the ass.

"Look, if you're serious and you really like her, just take your time, and everything will fall into place on its own. Shit, look at Tenley and me. The moment that woman stepped into the bar, she had me," Potter told him.

"Yeah, but I don't know if she feels the attraction to me like I do with her. You felt that pull immediately with Tenley. At times with Autumn, it seems like that pull is there, but then she starts to pull in the opposite direction."

"That's where you just have to convince her to take that chance."

Frost nodded his head.

Just then, a man entered the room, putting an end to their conversation. The guy wore hospital scrubs and had a hospital ID clipped to the front, but Frost had never seen him before and wondered who he was. He didn't like surprises, especially when it involved strangers coming into his hospital room.

The guy looked at Frost. "Sorry, I don't mean to interrupt. If you just give me a quick minute, I just need to check your IV and vitals, and then I'll be out of your hair."

Frost must have given the guy an odd look because the guy introduced himself and shook Frost's hand.

"Sorry, I should've introduced myself. I'm Scott. I'll be the RN assigned to this floor for the night."

"You are?" Frost asked, surprised. Since he'd been in this place, all his nurses had been females.

Scott laughed. "Yeah, sorry, I know I'm not pretty like the other nurses, but I promise you're in good hands."

Frost sat up straighter in the bed. This guy had nothing to be sorry about. This was a good thing. Hell, it was better than good—it was great! "No, it's not that. I'm actually glad you're here. It means I'll at least have a peaceful night. If I'm being honest, I was getting a little annoyed with the 'hands-on' treatment I was getting from the previous nurses, if you know what I'm saying. I was just telling my therapist about it yesterday."

Scott looked surprised. "Autumn must be your therapist?"

"Yeah. Why?" Frost gave the guy a once over. Not that he was judging, but the man nurse was a good-looking guy. He then wondered if he was interested in her. Shit, Irish just might be right. He needed to act quickly if he wanted a shot with her.

"Well, that explains a lot. Autumn apparently spoke with the charge nurse on this floor and explained how some female nurses had been acting a bit unprofessional with a patient. Let me guess, you're supposed to be discharged in two or three days." Frost nodded his head, and Scott smiled. "Well, you can thank Autumn the next time you see her. She must have listened and had your back because I'll be on this floor for the next two nights, and my colleague Patrick will be on day rounds."

He gave Scott a chin lift and smile. "Sounds great. Thanks, man."

"No problem. I'm all finished. I'll be back in a couple of hours to re-check the IV and vitals. In the meantime, if you need anything, just press the button."

Well, I'll be damned. Frost was astounded. She'd actually listened and helped him. Then he wondered if she was a little bit jealous of hearing about the nurses and the way they were coming on to him.

"Well, there you have it. If she didn't care about you, she sure as hell wouldn't have done that."

No, she wouldn't. Frost picked his phone up and sent off a text to Autumn. Thankful, he now had her number.

Frost: *I just had a very interesting conversation with my new nurse SCOTT. Thank you!*

Autumn: *You're welcome.*

He put the phone on the table and leaned back, resting his head on the pillow. He knew he had a silly grin on his face and was sure the guys would rib him about it later, but at least he knew he'd get a decent night's sleep all because of his Irish Beauty.

CHAPTER SIX

Autumn arrived at the hospital about twenty minutes ago. It had been a little over a week since Frost had been discharged from the hospital. Though she hadn't physically seen him, he had texted her a couple of times. Once, asking if she had gotten the lock on the window fixed, which she had. Mr. Voight, the landlord, apparently wasn't keen on being threatened with a lawsuit. The other time he texted was to ask her what her favorite color was. This seemed odd, but two days later, it all made sense when she received a beautiful floral arrangement delivered to her at the hospital. The card attached to the arrangement read, "To a true Irish beauty." With her flaming red hair and green eyes, it was easy to tell she came from Irish heritage. She didn't recognize some of the flowers, so on her way home that evening, she stopped by a florist to see if they could tell her what they were. She had been flattered when she learned the flowers were native to Ireland. It was a very well thought out gift that scored some points for Frost.

She and Nancy were going over the day's schedule, and she was about to ask Nancy about Mr. Pitcher's back therapy when suddenly Nancy's eyes widened, then a shit-eating grin spread across her face. When Nancy got that look, it made Autumn nervous.

"Holy hotness! Isn't that the SEAL who was here a week or two ago?"

Autumn spun around to see the nurse at the reception desk near the end of the hallway, talking to a man. She could only see the back of him. The person resembled Frost, but she couldn't be certain it was him. She didn't tear her eyes away, then watched as the nurse smiled and pointed in her direction. When the man turned around, her breath caught in her throat. *It is him, and oh shit, he is heading straight for me!*

She'd enjoyed working with him during his PT, and Cody still couldn't stop talking about him and his team. She had to admit that when he had been discharged, she was a little sad. He was fun to be around and easy to talk to. But she didn't understand why he was back here. His rehab had been transferred to the outpatient clinic near his home.

He walked with a slight limp toward her. The well-worn blue jeans and grey t-shirt he was wearing gave him a guy next door appeal. He was grinning, which, of course, showed off his dimple. Her heart started to have palpitations. He looked mouthwatering.

"Wow. First flowers, and now a personal visit. I'd say someone's caught the eye of the Chief Petty Officer," Nancy whispered in a low voice.

She swung her head around and looked at Nancy, who gave her a sly grin. Her friend was a nut job.

"What are you talking about?"

"What I'm saying is that sex on a stick walking toward you right now with an adorable grin on his face wants you."

Autumn had to wonder if her boss hadn't slipped earlier in the day and hit her head. Not that she would argue about him being sex on a stick because the man was gorgeous. All six-foot-something of him. And that was just it. He could have any woman he wanted, so why would he want her? She was a widow with a kid. Ever since Kevin died, she considered herself a woman with baggage when it came to dating men. She just shook her head at Nancy, trying to deny everything the woman was saying.

"Oh, honey, believe me, it takes something special to make those types of men smile. Judging from the one plastered on his face, I beg to differ with you. He wants you. It's clearly written all over him. I say go for it."

When he stopped in front of her, she gulped. She had forgotten how tall he was as he stood towering over her. She gave him a soft smile as she tilted her head back to look up at him. It took her a moment to gather her words.

"Frost… What brings you to this side of town?"

He didn't answer her right away; instead, he turned to Nancy before smiling and reached his hand out.

"Hi, I'm Frost."

Nancy shook his hand. "I'm Nancy. It's nice to meet you. And you seem to be making a good recovery."

He squinted his eyes, and Autumn could tell Nancy's comment had caught him off guard. Especially since she was a stranger to him, and he didn't know what her role was at the hospital.

Before he could interrogate Nancy, Autumn spoke up. "Frost, Nancy is my manager here at the hospital."

His shoulders immediately relaxed, and he gave Nancy another smile. "Well, I guess I should thank you for my introduction to this amazing woman." He slid his arm around Autumn's shoulders and pulled her into his side. Oh hell, she was so screwed. Even though she was stiff as a board, she found herself closing her eyes and inhaling his cologne and damn, he smelled good.

Nancy's giggle brought her back to the present. "It was my pleasure. Autumn's one of the best physical therapists I've known, and my most sought-after therapist. She'd have a waiting list if we allowed it. All of the patients simply adore her." She laughed, then winked, and Autumn wished the floor would open up and swallow her now. Could Nancy be any more obvious?

The gentle squeeze on her shoulder had her looking up right into those brown eyes of his. "Well, then, I guess I should be grateful."

"Yes, you should be. Considering all of the men that come through here, it's just a matter of time before one of them sweep her right off her feet." Autumn couldn't help the eye roll. Okay, now Nancy was being ridiculous.

"I guess I'm lucky I stopped in today before someone could make a move before me."

Autumn wanted to fan her face because it was hot. Dear God. What in the hell was Nancy doing? The two of them were talking as if she wasn't even in the room. When Nancy ran her mouth, there was no telling what would come out of it next. She needed to change the subject, stat.

She stepped to the side, causing Frost's arm to fall from her shoulders, and she immediately felt the loss. With a little room between them, she looked up at him. "Are you here for an appointment?"

He cleared his throat and stuck his hands in his front pockets. He grinned again. A groan nearly escaped as she caught sight of his dimple. *What the hell was it with her and dimples?*

"No, I was at the base for some business and decided to drive over here to see if you had some time to grab a coffee at the shop across the street."

She stared at him in shock. Was he seriously asking her out for coffee? Was this a joke or something? She looked at Nancy, who just stood there with a smirk on her face that said 'I told you so.'

She looked back at Frost and pulled her bottom lip between her teeth. She tended to do that when she was nervous. Then Nancy gave her arm a nudge. "She'd love to." She looked at Autumn. "You have about an hour to kill before your next appointment. Take thirty minutes and go have some coffee. Oh, and bring me back one of those cinnamon muffins. Those things are to die for." Before Autumn could argue, Nancy turned and walked away, leaving Autumn staring at her friend's back as she retreated. She totally just set her up. *Bitch!*

She turned back and caught Frost checking her out. He smiled as his eyes met hers. Damn, she couldn't say no to him. What the hell, it was just coffee, right? How bad could it be?

She took a deep breath. "Let me go grab my purse." Before she could turn away, he clutched her hand, stopping her and then smiled again.

"You don't need your purse unless you need it for something other than money. Coffee is on me."

Taking another deep, cleansing breath, she gazed into his eyes. "Lead the way."

Frost held the door open for Autumn. Immediately, the aroma of fresh coffee and freshly baked goods consumed her. Placing his hand on her lower back, he guided her to a table near the back. His innocent touch sent the blood racing to the most delicate places. She smiled to herself when he picked out the table, just like her husband. He always had to sit with his back to the wall and near an exit.

"What would you like?" He asked her with a twinkle in his eye. She wondered what his reaction would be if she told him she'd like an order of him.

Oh. My. God. Stop that! Just tell the man you want a coffee.

She shook those thoughts from her head and cleared her throat. "I'll take a regular hazelnut coffee, one sugar, please." Despite clearing her throat, her voice seemed to squeak. Jesus, could she sound any more nervous.

He winked, then strode toward the counter to order. While he waited in line, she took the time to study him. He had a firm jaw and always wore that serious expression she'd become accustomed to expect when he smiled at her, and his dimple appeared. Most of the time, he looked so in control and intimidating. Her eyes wandered around the bustling little coffee shop, and she spotted numerous women checking him out. Not that she could blame them. But seeing other women swooning over Frost got her a little riled up. They were all beautiful women, and again Autumn had to wonder why he wanted to be here with her. She didn't consider herself beautiful. She felt she was an average woman at her age and with a child. The only trait she was cursed with was her fair skin. If she weren't careful in the sun, she'd look like a fried tomato. She tried to eat healthily and worked out when she could, but with her schedule, she was lucky to make it to the gym once a week. She never let her weight bother her. She was simply happy with who she was.

She must have really been deep in thought because she jerked when a hand landed on her shoulder. When she glanced up and saw a man standing there, she became alarmed. But as she looked closer, she realized it was the man she had practically run over with her shopping cart at the grocery store last week. She had been in one of her daydreaming moods and wasn't paying attention when she ran her cart into his.

"I thought that was you sitting over here," he said to her, removing his hand from her shoulder.

She smiled, but something about him didn't sit right with her. Maybe it was the way his eyes ran over her body.

"Hi," was all she managed to say. She didn't know what else to say to him, and she looked toward the counter. Frost had ordered and was still waiting for the coffees, but his eyes were focused on the guy standing close to her, and he didn't look happy. She gulped.

"Are you sitting alone?" The man asked her, obviously hoping to join her.

"No, she's with me," Frost growled from behind the man. Autumn had to hide her smile when the guy turned around and took in the sight of Frost. Frost had several inches on him in both height and width. Frost looked from the guy to Autumn, silently asking her who this guy was.

"Frost, this is…." Well, shit, she didn't even know the man's name. Before she could think about it any longer, the guy stuck his hand out for Frost to shake.

"The name is Cecil."

Frost had his hands full with the coffees, so he just gave Cecil a chin lift, then maneuvered his large frame around the man and took the seat across from Autumn. In a surprise move, Frost reached across the table and took her hand into his. She looked down at their clasped hands and grinned. His hand was warm from carrying the coffees. When she looked up and saw Frost staring at her, she saw more than jealously. There was a feeling of warmth and caring.

Before she could dwell on Frost's show of possession, Cecil cleared his throat. When she looked up at Cecil, he didn't appear happy as he was shooting daggers at Frost, and Autumn wondered what the guy's problem was. It gave her an uneasy feeling. She didn't even know this guy. All they did at the grocery store was say a few words to one another. But, having Frost holding her hand gave her a sense of protection, and it brought a smile to her face. It felt right. It was as if Frost knew. Frost grinned at her and winked before turning his attention to Cecil.

"How do you two know each other?" Frost asked, taking a sip of his coffee with his free hand.

Autumn spoke first, hoping to get the conversation over with, so the guy would leave. She only had thirty minutes, and she wanted to spend every minute of it talking to Frost.

"I accidentally ran him over in the grocery store the other day. Isn't that right, Cecil?"

Cecil smiled at her though it never really reached his eyes. It reminded her of a slimy used car salesman when he knew he'd got you hooked. She still couldn't put her finger on it, but something just wasn't sitting right with her. Cecil never took his eyes off of her, and Frost began to look annoyed.

"Yes. I tried to find you before you left the store. I wanted to see if you'd like to have dinner with me."

Autumn's mouth gaped open, and her eyes went wide. She seriously started to consider this guy's mental status. Did he have a death wish? She was sitting here with a man who towered over this guy and one who could most likely take him down with one swing, and this fruit cake was hitting on her.

"But it seems I'm a little late." He handed her a business card. "Give me a call if you change your mind," he said before turning around, walking out the door.

Her eyes shot over to Frost, who was glaring at Cecil's back. When he turned back and faced her, his expression was cold, and she gulped. His body was rigid. He just stared at her, seeming to collect his thoughts. Finally, after a couple of seconds, he spoke.

"You are not calling him." He reached for the business card and tore it into little pieces. She should have been pissed off at him for doing that. They weren't dating, she didn't belong to him, but honestly, it was a little funny to see him act this way. It was almost as if watching a little kid throw a temper tantrum because another boy wanted to steal his 'girlfriend.' She started giggling.

"What's so funny?" He asked, sounding insulted, which only made her cover her mouth so that she wouldn't laugh harder.

"You."

"Me?" He asked, pointing at himself.

She shook her head. "Yes, you. Seeing you get all flustered with Cecil." She turned and looked in the direction Cecil went. "He's harmless."

Frost stared at her. "No, he wants you. And I don't know how I feel about that." He said those words with meaning, and Autumn could only swallow the lump in her throat as she looked into his eyes and saw the emotion swirling in those amber orbs. They stayed that way for about a minute, just staring at each other like they were trying to read what one another was thinking. Finally, Frost grinned and moved her coffee in front of her.

"One hazelnut coffee with one sugar, just like you wanted."

"Thank you."

He winked and then thanked her again for agreeing to join him. It was like the interaction with Cecil never even happened.

She opened the lid and inhaled. She loved the smell of hazelnut. Then she made the mistake of glancing over at Frost, who had just happened to take a sip of his coffee and damn if she didn't wish she was the coffee cup as his lips made contact with it. His lips seemed firm but full, and she could just imagine how they would feel pressed against her lips. Holy shit, she was literally staring at the man like she wanted to drink him up. She felt her cheeks blush and looked away, then took the first sip of her coffee. She closed her eyes, relishing the taste. This was one of the best coffee houses in the area. She set her cup down and looked at Frost. He was staring at her, grinning.

"What?" She asked, feeling a little self-conscious. It always made her nervous when people stared at her. She always thought they were judging her, especially during the year that followed her husband's death.

He shrugged his shoulders nonchalantly. "Just admiring you. That's all. I like what I see."

"Okay…" She felt her cheeks flush, and she didn't know what to say. This was so awkward.

He chuckled and set his cup down, making her look at him.

"I have to apologize upfront, Autumn. I didn't really think this through, and to tell you the truth, I don't do this type of thing."

Now she was confused. "You don't have coffee with people?" She asked, taking another sip of her coffee.

He smiled and chuckled. "No, I have coffee with plenty of people. Just never had coffee with a beautiful woman before." His gaze met hers over the rim of his cup as he lifted it to his mouth.

She smiled back. "Well, if you're being honest, I guess I should confess something too."

He arched one of his eyebrows and grinned, looking all sexy. "And, that would be..."

She laughed, and her insides felt like mush by his flirtatious words. "I've never sat in a coffee shop with a good-looking man before. My husband hated coffee."

He threw his back and laughed loudly, drawing attention to them, but she didn't care. Damn, even his deep laugh was sexy.

His eyes met hers. "Well, I don't know if I consider myself good looking or not, but it's good to know that you think I am. I guess I'll have to take your word for it." He winked again.

She snorted a laugh. She was quite sure he and his team probably got hit on every time they stepped out in public, especially when the women found out they were SEALs. "Oh, come on. You know you're good looking. My god, your entire team, is like a walking version of a military calendar of men you see places trying to sell."

He gave her a mischievous look and his signature boyish smile. "So, you're checking out my teammates too." His voice was low and sexy.

She shook her head but was laughing and pointing at him. "No, that's not what I meant, and you know it." She reached over and slapped his forearm. Though she had to admit she had checked them all out. They were all nice-looking men and seemed very genuine.

"What did you mean then?" He asked as his light brown eyes gazed into hers.

"I'm just surprised some beautiful woman hasn't already staked a claim on you."

He gave her a serious look. His eyes penetrated hers. She could feel the intensity. "Never thought about it until recently," he told her, still holding her gaze.

"Why is that?"

"My job," he told her, and she gave him an odd look. "My job is not relationship-friendly, if you get what I mean. There are a lot of sacrifices that have to be made to make the relationship succeed."

She swallowed the hot coffee. She knew what he was referring to. She sacrificed a lot being married to Kevin, and he was just a Marine. Frost was a SEAL. They were like 007 agents, all secretive and whatnot. She was intrigued; why all of a sudden was he interested in pursuing a relationship when he'd avoided it up to now?

"I can understand that, but what happened to make you rethink the whole relationship thing now? I mean, you're still a SEAL." She leaned back in her chair and got more comfortable. She was very curious to hear his answer.

"I'm going to be thirty-one in November, and I'm not going to be a SEAL forever." He shrugged his shoulders and looked out the window. She could tell he was thinking, and when he looked back at her, his brown eyes pierced hers. "I guess seeing two of my teammates each fall head over heels for their women made me start thinking more about my future and what I wanted. I mean, if they make it work, then anyone can. Especially Potter."

Autumn could sense this discussion was getting serious, but she wanted to know more. "And what is it that you think you want?'

"I don't have to think. I know what I want," he said with a firm tone and stared straight into her eyes. She swallowed hard at the intensity. "I'm not getting any younger. I want a family."

She nodded her head. She understood what he was saying. She was glad she had Cody at a young age. Part of her still yearned for at least one more child. Her husband had wanted more children, and they did try when he was home, but the timing wasn't in their favor. She must have been deep in thought because when she looked up from the table, Frost was eyeing her intently.

"I hope I didn't frighten you with all of that," he said as he ran his hand through his hair. The poor guy actually looked a little nervous, and it made her smile. The big bad Navy SEAL gets nervous when talking about his emotions.

She smiled and shook her head no. And, honestly, he hadn't scared her. It was good to hear the truth. She felt compelled to at least contribute to the conversation since the man basically spilled his inner thoughts to her. Something she had a feeling he didn't often do.

"To be honest with you, dating hasn't even been on my radar. Between work and taking care of Cody, I don't really have time. The ladies at work are always trying to set me up on blind dates." She played with the lid of her cup as he watched her.

"How come you've never taken them up on the offer? You have to have some time for yourself. And you are quite beautiful, might I add." He gave her a flirtatious smile, which caused her to blush.

"I don't really know. Now and then, I find myself asking the same question. But honestly, I can't say why. Sitting here, having coffee with you is the closest I've come as far as dating goes."

His eyes lit up, and he raised one of his eyebrows. "So, this is a date?"

She scrunched her nose up. "No, this is what I call two people getting to know one another over a cup of coffee."

"What if I'm hoping for more conversations over coffee? Or, maybe even lunch or dinner? Would you consider the offer?"

Autumn couldn't believe she was having coffee with Frost, and now he wanted to go out with her again?

She was nodding her head without even thinking. "I think it could be arranged. I have a pretty busy week, though. I have some things planned with Cody already. Maybe next weekend? Can I text you?"

"Absolutely. Whenever it's convenient for you." He glanced at his leg. "It's not like I have much I can do. If you want to bring Cody along too, I have no problem with that. I like him. He's a great kid. This may seem a little fast, but I want you to know that I'm here for you and Cody if you need anything, even if it's just to lend an ear. I've been told I'm a great listener."

Her insides were all twisted. This man was slowly weakening her defenses. "Thanks. I appreciate that. It's hard doing the parent thing alone. Being both the mom and dad, you know."

She glanced at her watch. She needed to get back across the street to the hospital. Her next patient would be arriving in about twenty minutes. Although a part of her didn't want this to end.

"Well, I'd better get going before I'm late for my next appointment." They stood up together, and she smiled up at him. "Thank you for the coffee, Frost. I enjoyed this."

He grabbed the bag off the table and guided her out the exit. They stood on the sidewalk, and he was looking down at her with a hungry look in his eyes. She felt her body shake a little under his stare. He leaned down and lightly brushed his lips against her cheek. Before he stood up straight, he whispered in her ear. His warm breath collided with her skin, making her shiver.

"I know we agreed to be friends first. But know I plan on getting a chance to take you out on a real date one of these days."

She nervously smiled at him, and he handed her the bag. "What's this?" She asked, taking it.

He laughed. "It's Nancy's cinnamon muffin. I figured I could at least buy her favorite muffin since she helped persuade you to have coffee with me."

71

Autumn smiled. "I'm sure she will devour it as soon as she sees it." She went to take a step off the sidewalk when Frost reached out and grabbed her elbow, stopping her. She turned back toward him.

"I forgot to ask you, any news on who may have broken into your house?"

It was so kind of him to ask. She shook her head. "No, no other fingerprints were lifted except for mine and Cody's."

"No other problems since then?"

He looked very concerned, so she smiled to try and ease his fears, although she still had sleepless nights since the break-in. "Nope, unless you count the flat tire I had the other day. I've had issues with that tire the past few weeks. The guy at the shop said it must have a slow leak."

He caressed her arm as he looked into her eyes. "You make sure you get that looked at. I don't want you and Cody stranded somewhere."

Her heart lifted a little, knowing he cared. He gave her that smile that she loved. The one that showed his dimple. She felt her heart start to race.

"Don't make me wait too long to hear from you."

She tilted her face up towards his and smiled. "I'll try not to." With a grin on her face and skip in her step, she walked quickly across the street. She put her hand on her stomach as she felt the flutter in her belly. *Oh my god, this is really happening.*

Frost watched Autumn cross the street. He thought their time together was a success. Though he wished he had more time. He was shocked to learn she hadn't dated since her husband's death, but he could understand her reasoning. Being a single parent and juggling everything from work, school, activities was tough. Not to mention time-consuming. Not that he knew firsthand, but some of his friends were single parents, and he'd seen what they went through. It was actually quite commendable how they balanced a home and working life. But if he played his cards right, hopefully, he'd be able to help with those types of things.

He shook his head and grinned. Damn, she'd done a number on him in a matter of two weeks. He couldn't wait to take her out again. He unlocked the door to his Tahoe and jumped in. His next stop was his PT appointment. At least he had something to keep his mind occupied while the therapist he'd been working with put him through the grueling workouts.

Cecil watched the guy lean down and kiss Autumn's cheek. He was furious and wondered who this Frost guy was. The way he carried himself reminded him of the military men around town. He always seemed on guard, looking around at his surroundings.

Through his investigator, he'd found that Autumn was a widow and employed at the Naval Hospital as a physical therapist.

He watched Frost as he walked to his vehicle and noticed the slight limp in his stride. Cecil was going to need to step up his game and make a move, but didn't want to come on too strong because he saw her as a woman who was shy and would need to be pampered. He had the means and money to do a lot of pampering. Watching her walk across the street as her ass swayed had him grinning as a plan started to formulate in his head.

CHAPTER SEVEN

"Good grief, Ace, where in the hell did Alex have all this shit stored?" Frost asked, looking at the long driveway filled with tables packed full of garage sale items. Items were even lying on the ground and leaning up against tables.

Ace looked around and scratched his head. "I have no fucking idea. But you'd think by the amount of stuff out here that the house would be empty."

As Frost took in everything, his eyes hit on something. "Is that your JS Blak Box 2 surfboard?" He asked Ace as he walked over to where it was leaning against a table.

"Yeah. Alex told me to get rid of stuff I didn't use. Hell, it's been collecting dust for the last five or six years."

Frost picked it up and looked it over. It was an awesome board. It could hold its own on a variety of wave types and conditions. "How much are you asking for it?"

Ace raised his eyebrow. "Why? Do you know someone who wants one? You can have it."

Frost knew he wanted it for Cody as soon as he saw it. He wasn't too sure how his mom would feel about it but during one of his visits, Cody had mentioned that he wanted to learn how to surf.

Not many people knew Frost was an avid surfer. He taught himself while he was stationed on the West Coast. Surfing was what he loved to do in his downtime. Anytime he got the chance to ride the swells, he was there. He not only enjoyed it as a sport, but it was also therapeutic. Being alone out in the water where it was just him and the waves calmed his mind. Usually, the beach was his first stop when he returned home from a mission. It was an opportunity to clear his mind, a means to expel all the emotions that came with working a dangerous job. Being in the water like that was the only real place he felt he could let his guard down a little.

Frost looked at Ace. "I do know someone, but I'm going to buy it."

Ace gave him a funny look, and then Alex walked over after getting a break in customers. She'd been up to her ears in people all morning. She wrapped her arms around Frost's waist and gave him a tight squeeze. "Thank you again for helping out today."

He kissed the top of her head and hugged her back. "Glad to help." He shifted the position of his leg. His leg was a little sore, and he knew he had overdone it today, helping Ace and Alex move everything outside.

He noticed Alex step back, and then she glanced down at his leg. She looked back up at him and squinted her eyes at him. Without saying a word to Frost, she turned toward Ace. "Hey, babe, would you mind running inside and grabbing us some waters? It's getting warm." It was early May, but the area was already getting a taste of what temperatures the summer would bring.

Ace shot Alex an annoyed look, raising an eyebrow at her. "Why can't you go get them?"

Alex narrowed her eyes at her fiancé and put her hands on her hips. Frost chuckled because he knew that look, growing up with Alex and having her as a best friend. It was her bitch stance. And if Ace were a smart man, he would just say 'yes dear' and go get the damn waters.

"Well…for one, I can't very well leave when people are here because you scare them off if they try to ask a question."

"Bullshit! I do not," he said, giving her a comical look.

"Yes, you do. You practically bark at them."

"Well, they shouldn't ask stupid questions. And why does everyone assume that they'll get the item cheaper than what the price tag says?"

"Because people like to barter. That's what yard sales are like. I upped the prices on things because I know people do it. So, by the time they 'talk' me down and I agree on their offer, I'm actually getting what I originally wanted for it," she explained, smiling as if she was so proud of herself.

Frost looked on as Ace was glaring at Alex like she had two heads.

"Then what was the effing point of putting price tags on everything when all you had to do was make one sign that said, 'everything is

75

negotiable, make an offer'?" Ace said, spreading his arms out wide to make a point.

Frost had to bite back his laugh when he heard Alex growl, then throw her hands in the air and start to mumble about stupid, muscle headed men. He kinda had to agree with Ace on the subject, but he wasn't about to inject himself into the conversation. Nope, he liked where his balls were attached, thank you very much.

Ace rolled his eyes, then wrapped up Alex in a hug and whispered something in her ear that caused her face to flame a bright red before he walked away and into the house.

Alex was smiling when she turned back to Frost, but that smile quickly morphed into an interrogation look. And with that look, he knew it was time to haul ass out of there. He quickly picked up the surfboard and looked at her. "Well, I'd better get going. Tell Ace I'll bring him cash tomorrow for this."

He turned and got about two steps in when she barked at him. "Oh no, you don't. You aren't getting off that easy."

He turned around. "What are you talking about?"

She glanced down at his leg, and he grimaced. He should've known; the little minx never missed anything.

"Your leg is bothering you." It wasn't a question. It was a statement.

He sighed. "Will you drop it if I tell you it is and that I'm going straight home and putting it up?"

She crossed her arms in front of her chest like she was ready for a fight. "Maybe. You haven't been pushing it have you?"

He grinned. "No, 'Mom,' I haven't."

Alex dropped her arms to her side. "I care about you, that's all. I'm not trying to be overprotective. I just want you to heal. I know it's got to be tough to sit back while the rest of the team does their thing."

He leaned down and kissed her cheek. "I know your intentions are good. And I appreciate your concern, but I promise you I'm good. It's just a little sore right now."

She hugged him. "You know I love you, right?"

76

He smiled and hugged her back, squeezing her. "Yeah. I do. And I love you too."

"Well, I sure as hell hope you love each other like brother and sister." They both looked up and saw Ace standing there, holding the waters, glaring at Frost. Both Frost and Alex burst out laughing.

Alex smiled as she walked over to Ace. "Are you jealous, honey? Do you need a hug too?" She said as she wrapped her little arms around his waist and snuggled close to him. Ace's eyes softened. The love Ace and Alex had for each other was what he hoped to have one day.

"No, I'm not jealous. I just don't know why every guy on the team needs to always put his hands on you." He gave Frost a mean look, and Frost laughed. The guys on the team loved to fuck with Ace because he was so possessive of Alex. So, anytime one of them got the chance, they did so on purpose to get him riled up. Irish was the worst one. How Ace hadn't beaten the shit out of him, Frost didn't know.

Frost cleared his throat. "I'm going to head out, Ace."

Ace reached out and shook his hand. "Thanks again for lending a hand. Potter said he and Tenley should be back around the time the sale is over, so he can help drag anything back in that hasn't been sold. Although I'm hoping most of it goes."

"No worries. Glad to help." He nodded his head toward the surfboard. "I told Alex I'd bring you cash tomorrow morning."

"You never said who the board was for."

No, he hadn't because he didn't want to, but he couldn't keep it from Ace. "It's for Cody. Autumn's boy."

Ace's eyebrows rose. "Autumn? The physical therapist?"

Frost nodded. "That's the one. He mentioned one time when we were talking about how he wanted to learn to surf."

"Are you two dating?"

Frost's eyes widened. "No." *Not yet,* was what he wanted to tell Ace. If Frost had his way, he and Autumn would already be dating, but he knew she needed time. He was almost positive losing her husband to the war made her fearful of getting involved with another man in the military. Especially a SEAL.

Ace ran his hand over his jaw. "Hmm…Well, if it's for him, don't worry about the money. He'll love it."

"Are you sure?"

Ace grinned. "Absolutely. Are you going to teach him?"

Frost smiled. "That's my intention. We'll see."

"So, you're not dating her, but you do like her?" Ace asked with a twinkle in his eye. And Frost was starting to wonder what Ace was up to.

"Yeah, I do. She's different than other women I've met. But like I said, I'm trying to take things slowly. I took your advice and showed up at the hospital last week and asked her out for coffee."

Ace's eyebrows shot up, and he smiled. "And how did it go?"

"Considering we were both nervous as hell, I'd say it went well. Something is holding her back from taking that next step. I'm pretty sure it has to do with my job."

Ace smiled again. "Are you going to ask her out again?"

"That's my plan. She was supposed to text me during the week, but I haven't heard from her. I've been swamped getting all of my paperwork together this past week. As long as the doc says it's okay, I'm scheduled to take the PRT in two weeks, and hopefully, get cleared for active duty."

Ace nodded his head toward the road and then smirked. "Well, I'm sure you'll do just fine on the PRT. And, as for asking Autumn out, here's your next opportunity."

Frost turned around and saw Autumn and Cody walking up the driveway. Her red hair was blowing in the light breeze. When she looked up and met his gaze, he saw the surprised look on her face, but he didn't miss the spark in her eyes, and it made his heart skip a beat. It had been almost two weeks since they had coffee together.

It was a typical Saturday for Autumn. Wake up, make breakfast for herself and Cody, then decide what they wanted to do. She made it a point that every Saturday, she and Cody spend quality time together. That is unless he stayed over at a friend's house.

Being on a tight budget and trying to find things to do with a ten-year-old had its challenges, but somehow she always came through looking like an awesome mom. She was an avid couponer and always looked for discounts on places they could go, like the movies, zoo, aquarium, and the boardwalk.

Today, Cody decided he wanted to go yardsaling with her. They had already been to four sales, but nothing had interested her. Cody was hungry, so they were on their way to lunch when she saw a huge sign with the words "Yard Sale" and an arrow pointing towards a more upscale neighborhood. She loved going to yard sales in these neighborhoods because they always had nice stuff they were selling. More than often, the stuff was brand new, and she could get it for a steal.

She pulled up to the large house and got excited when she saw the set of pots and pans on one of the tables. She'd been searching for a decent set since they moved. She noticed several other people were browsing the sale. She turned the car off and looked over at Cody. "I promise this is the last stop, and then we'll grab some lunch, okay."

Cody looked at his mom and smiled. "Its fine, Mom. I know you love these things, so I don't mind. Plus, if I get too hungry, I have a granola bar that can tide me over until we eat."

She smiled. She knew she had a great kid. Despite losing his dad and then her uprooting him and moving across the country to start a new life, he was still reliable. She was very proud of him.

They both got out of the car and started walking up the driveway when a slight breeze blew her hair into her face. Just as she brushed it back, she looked up and met the eyes of the man who had occupied her mind for the last couple of weeks. She felt kind of stupid because she never texted him last week to set up lunch or dinner. Something went haywire with her phone the latter part of the week, and all of her contacts were deleted, including Frost's.

Her lips parted in surprise, and she knew she was smiling as Frost walked toward her. Damn, the man did a number to her libido. He was wearing tan cargo shorts and a black t-shirt with a skeleton of a frog on it. Even dressed down, the man had appeal. His light brown hair was hidden under a black baseball cap.

"What are you guys doing here?" Frost asked as he leaned down and kissed her cheek. His lips lingered a little longer than they should've, and it sent her heart into overdrive.

"Frost!" Cody all but shouted before giving him some sort of a fist bump that guys do.

"Hey, Cody. How's it going?"

"Good! I can't wait for school to let out for summer break. Only one more week. How's your leg?"

Frost smiled. "It's good. A little sore today, but that's to be expected. Thanks for asking."

Ace and Alex walked up, and when Frost introduced Alex, Autumn felt her face heat up, remembering the last time she saw Alex in the hospital and basically accusing her of trying to get into Frost's bed. And if that wasn't bad enough, her fiancé overheard her.

Autumn shook Alex's hand, and the two of them said hello. Autumn felt the need to apologize for her actions, especially since she didn't know if Ace had told her what had happened.

"I owe you an apology."

Alex gave her an odd look, but she saw the smirks on Frost's and Ace's faces.

"Why on earth would you owe me an apology?" Alex asked her, looking between Ace and Frost, probably to see if they knew what was going on.

Autumn explained, and by the time she was through, Alex was laughing, and it made her feel a little less of an ass.

"Well, apology accepted, and it's very nice to meet you, officially that is. Frost speaks highly of both you and your son. And, if I must say, you are beautiful."

80

Autumn was shocked at Alex's words, and she felt a little flush. She glanced up at Frost.

"Alex!" Frost said through his clenched teeth. Ace started laughing and walked away, pulling Alex with him.

Frost looked back at Autumn, and Autumn noticed Frost's cheeks were a little pink, which was very unusual for him. She smiled to herself, wondering if Frost was blushing about what Alex said. That left her wondering what exactly he had said about her to his friends.

"Sorry about that. Alex tends to meddle in all of the team's lives."

She waved him off. "It's fine. She seems nice."

"Hey, Mom, can Frost come with us to lunch?" Cody asked, interrupting them.

She looked at Cody and saw how happy he was. For some strange reason, Frost had become an important person in Cody's life. She looked at Frost, who was eyeing her cautiously. Hell, if she wanted to get to know him better, now would be a perfect opportunity to start.

"If Frost would like to join us, he is more than welcome to. Plus, I owe him lunch." She peered up at Frost with a grin and winked. "We were going to head over to that little deli on the corner across the street from the base."

Frost smiled wide, showing his straight white teeth. God, the man was beautiful.

"I love that place. They have the best Italian cold cuts in town. If you're sure you don't mind, I'd love to have lunch with you both." Autumn couldn't help but grin like a little schoolgirl. She loved how Frost always made it a point to include Cody in the conversation. She got a little giddy inside.

"Maybe this would lead to a real date. Oh, Jesus, I haven't been on a date in.... God, her last date was with her husband, and that was years ago. Whoa...slow down there, chicky. He might not have those feelings that you're feeling. He could just be having lunch to be nice to Cody. No, that's not right either. You know for a fact he has feelings for you. It's you that's holding back."

She felt her smile fade, and her stomach felt like it was twisted in a knot. She saw him staring at her with an intense look. He reached his hand out and rubbed her upper arm. His touch sent tingles down her body to places she wasn't supposed to be feeling tingly.

"Is something wrong?" He asked her. His eyebrows were scrunched together, and he looked concerned.

"Please don't feel obligated to have lunch with us. If you were hanging out with your friends here, I understand. And, I'm sure Cody will understand." *There I go again, pushing him away. Stop it!*

He gave her an intense look. "First off, I know I'm not obligated to do anything I don't want to do. Well, except when my commander gives an order. And, second, maybe I want to spend more time with you and Cody, so I can get to know you both better. I was getting ready to leave here anyway. Plus, I was beginning to think I wouldn't hear from you again."

She swallowed hard. Now she felt awful for insulting him. "I'm sorry, Frost. It was wrong of me to say that." She twisted her fingers together. How would she tell him that it was her own insecurities causing her to pull away? "The reason I didn't text or call is that I just got a new phone. I'll explain what happened over lunch. That is if you still want to join us?"

His expression softened, and he stepped closer and whispered in her ear. "I never intended not to show up. Like I said. I want to get to know the real Autumn Kauffman." His breath was warm against her ear. His lips were just millimeters from her skin, and she was feeling really hot right now. She needed to put a little space between the two of them before she really did something embarrassing. Like turn her head just a fraction and kiss his inviting lips.

She stepped back, and Frost winked.

She gathered herself. "Let me just pay Alex for this stuff, and I'll be ready to go. If now is a good time for you."

He grinned. "Now is perfect. I'll go say bye to Ace while you settle with Alex."

She watched him walk toward Ace, who was talking to Cody. God, hopefully, the boy wasn't grilling Ace on the SEAL team. Ever since Cody met Frost, he'd had the case of SEAL hero worship. Seeing that Ace was laughing at something Cody said, she breathed a sigh of relief. She made her way to Alex and paid for the items while apologizing again. Alex had told her it was fine, and there were no hard feelings. Then she surprised Autumn when she told her that she hoped to see her around. She wasn't quite sure what to say to that. So instead of giving a direct yes or no answer, she told Alex that it was possible.

She called out to Cody as she was walking to her car. He was still standing with Frost and Ace, talking. She watched and noticed that Cody seemed to fit right in with the two guys. She could so easily see Cody as one of them when he grew up. With that thought, her stomach went into knots. Could she handle her son and only child joining the military and being shipped off to some foreign country to fight the bad guys? Then again, the thoughts crept into her mind; would she be able to handle a relationship with Frost, knowing he was doing the same thing?

She heard Cody call out to her before she could dwell on that question.

"Mom, is it okay if I ride with Frost?"

She smiled again when Cody looked up at Frost. Yep, total case of hero-worship.

"If Frost doesn't mind, then it's okay with me."

She laughed as Cody pumped his fist in the air.

She got into her car, and a nervous feeling hit her. What if something happened to cause an end to her and Frost's friendship? What would that mean for Cody? God, what has she gotten herself into?

She put the car in gear and headed toward the deli. God help her. The man made her feel things she never felt before.

Frost pulled his Tahoe into the parking lot at the deli. He couldn't help but grin as Cody talked. During the ten-minute drive, Frost didn't think he even got a word in. Cody was an awesome kid, full of life, and very intelligent. He was very mature for his age. Frost believed the maturity stemmed from his father's death and his need to feel like he had to grow up—as if it became his responsibility to take care of his mom. Hopefully, in the near future, he could take some of that responsibility off Cody's shoulders.

After he parked, they got out and decided to wait outside until Autumn got there, but after about five minutes of waiting, Frost frowned. She left about a minute after they did; she should have been here by now.

Several thoughts went through his head, though the logical one was that maybe she stopped off somewhere on the way. He looked over at Cody and could tell he was worried by the way he was scanning the roadway and biting his bottom lip. He had to smile; like mother like son. He noticed how Autumn nibbled on her lip when she got nervous.

Cody looked over at Frost and shook his head. "Something's wrong. She should've been here by now."

Hearing Cody confirm the same thing he was thinking put Frost on alert. But again, they had to be logical. "Do you know if she was planning on going anywhere else today? Maybe she stopped off on the way."

Cody shook his head. "No, she never mentioned anything, and she would have texted or called me. Plus, her car has been acting up for the past couple of days, but she was waiting until she got paid next week to have it checked out." Cody pulled his phone out of his pocket. "Let me try calling her."

Frost didn't like hearing her car wasn't running right. Her drive to and from work every day wasn't short, especially during rush hour.

Cody put his phone back in his pocket. "She's not answering."

He squeezed Cody's shoulder. "Let's give her a few more minutes; then we'll backtrack and look for her, okay, buddy?" Cody nodded his head, but Frost could tell the kid was worried. Hell, he was starting to worry.

About two minutes had passed when he saw Autumn's car. She pulled into the parking lot, but the squealing noise coming from her vehicle caused him to frown. He immediately thought about his teammate, Diego. He knew a lot about cars; maybe he'd give him a call and see if he could take a look at it.

He started to walk over to where Autumn had parked next to his Tahoe, and he could see through the windshield that she did not look happy.

Autumn banged her hand against the steering wheel in frustration. Dammit, she was hoping the car would last until she got paid next week. She didn't have the funds right at this moment to have a mechanic look at it. Plus, she needed to make plans for transportation to and from work while her car was in the shop.

She saw Frost and Cody approaching, so she got out to meet them.

"That doesn't sound healthy," Frost said, making a face at her car.

She shut the door and looked at the car herself. She knew her car was a piece of shit, but she wasn't in any position financially to look for another car.

"No, it doesn't, and it stalled at the light about a mile from here. That's why it took me a few extra minutes to get here. I honestly didn't think it was going to start. It's been acting up for a couple of weeks now, in addition to the back-right tire going flat. I was hoping it would make it to next Friday."

Cody wrapped his arms around her waist and hugged her. "We were getting worried about you."

She squeezed him back and leaned down and kissed the top of his head. "I'm sorry, honey. I didn't mean to worry you." She looked at Frost, who was watching her. He had his hands in his shorts pockets. She mouthed the word 'sorry' to him, and he gave her a soft smile.

He motioned to the car. "I can call my teammate Diego and see if he could take a look under the hood. He loves tinkering with cars in his spare time. I'm not sure what his schedule is, but I'll ask."

"Do you know how much he'd charge? I don't know exactly what's wrong with it, so I don't have any sort of estimate or anything."

"There wouldn't be a charge."

She felt a little relief. At least if someone Frost knew looked over the car, she knew she wouldn't get scammed.

"Thank you," she replied, looking up at his handsome face, and he smiled. "No thanks needed. I told you when we had coffee the other day; I'm here for you and Cody."

Autumn and Frost sat in a booth near the back of the deli. They were both finishing up their Italian cold cuts. Cody had spotted a friend of his and was sitting with him while he ate, so that left Autumn and Frost all alone to talk.

Frost set his sandwich down and wiped his hands and mouth with his napkin. He held out his hand. "Hand me your phone."

She was caught off guard by his abrupt request. "What? Why?" She asked, setting her sandwich down.

He wiggled his fingers. "Just give it to me…please."

She took her phone out of her purse and laid it in his waiting hand. She watched as he typed something in it. When he finished, he handed it back to her.

"There, my number is programmed in your new phone now. Use it. The only time I won't answer is if I'm in a team meeting or deployed or training and not reachable. If I'm deployed or training, you'll know. Just not where we are. Most of the time, I'll be unreachable. But leave a message. If we get a chance and have access to a line, we can sometimes make a quick call home.

"I also put Alex's number in there as well. Not only is Alex Ace's fiancé, but she is also my commander's daughter. If, for any reason, you need anything and can't get hold of me, call her, okay?"

She stared at him.

"Promise me." He raised an eyebrow at her trying to look intimidating, but then he grinned, and his adorable dimple was on display, and it made it difficult for her to concentrate on what he was saying.

She shook her head. "I have to ask, why are you doing this? We barely know each other."

"Which I am trying to change. Autumn, I'm normally a very hard man. I don't have or show a lot of emotions. I've been trained to be that way.

It's a part of me. I don't do relationships. I never have since I joined the Navy."

Hearing his last statement about relationships made her heart drop, and it must have shown on her face as well because he was quick to follow-up on his statement.

"Shit, I'm fucking this up." He took a deep breath. "What I'm trying to say is that I like you, Autumn. I like you a lot, and I'd like to get to know you better. And that includes Cody as well. I want to spend more time with the both of you. You have gotten so far under my skin that I don't even know how to act. I get so freaking nervous when I'm around you." He smiled at her.

Her heart was saying yes, but her brain was telling her no. She didn't want to go down that path again. Falling in love with someone who put their life on the line every day. Could she handle it if something went wrong?

"I don't know, Frost." She nibbled her bottom lip and looked over where Cody was talking to his friend.

"Just give it some time, okay? Like I told you over coffee, friends first. How about I take you and Cody out for dinner Friday night, and we can spend some more time getting to know each other? What does he like?"

He wasn't really giving her an out here, but at the same time, she couldn't deny her attraction to him. Deep down, she wanted what he wanted. What would it hurt to have dinner? As friends. For now, at least.

She surrendered and gave her shoulders a shrug, giving him a faint smile. "What does any kid crave? Pizza."

"Then, pizza it is. I know a great place. It's not far from here. I didn't ask where you live. I can pick you guys up."

"No, that's not necessary," she said a little too quickly, and she knew he picked up on her quick answer by the way he squinted his eyes as he looked at her. She didn't want him to know where she lived. She was embarrassed at her current living arrangements, but it was the only place she could afford at the moment. "I work until 6:00 pm on Friday. How about if Cody and I just meet you there? We live not far from the base. Say around 7:00 pm? Or is that too late?"

Frost eyed her for a second, but then he nodded his head. "Seven is good. Will Cody be at the hospital after school?"

"Yeah. Most days, he's there unless he has an afterschool activity. One of the nurses at the hospital, her son goes to the same school, and she normally picks Cody up for me and drops him off at the hospital on her way home since she has to drive past the hospital."

"What school does he attend?"

"St. Joseph's Academy. I was hoping he could attend the public school by our house, but with me working at the hospital in Norfolk and the schedule I have, there was no way I could coordinate getting him home from school, plus I don't have anyone to watch him."

Frost nodded, knowing the school since he grew up around here. He also knew the cost of tuition at the private school was astronomical, though she most likely received a life insurance payout left by her late husband and probably could afford it. But that wasn't any of his business.

"What time does he get out of school?"

"Around 2:00 pm. Why?" She took a sip of her iced tea and eyed him cautiously over the rim of her glass.

"Well, I was thinking, I have therapy on Friday and then a meeting with the team in the afternoon, but we should be finished up by 1:00 pm. Why don't I swing by his school and pick him up and take him over to the base? I can show him around. You know, some of the areas where we train, like our obstacle course, things like that. Then afterward, he and I can meet you at the restaurant. If that's okay with you."

"You don't have to do that."

He reached across the table and put a reassuring hand over hers. "Are we going to do this again?" He asked, smiling. "I know I don't have to, but I want to." When she didn't pull away, he smiled inside and knew he was headed in the right direction. *Baby steps*, he thought to himself.

"I'll talk to him tonight and let you know, okay?" Frost wondered who she was trying to kid. Cody would be ecstatic to tour the SEAL base with him.

They spent another thirty minutes just talking. Frost told her a little about his family. His mom, Marie, his dad Hal, a former SEAL, and his brother, Trey. Trey was three years older than Frost and married with two kids; a one-year-old little girl named Gracie and a four-year-old boy named Cortland. He showed her pictures of them.

When the topic shifted in her direction, Frost was stunned to learn she didn't have any family. Well, she had a mother and father, but they had disowned her. They were very religious and very traditional individuals. They lived in a small town in New Mexico, just outside of Albuquerque. She was homeschooled and was never allowed to date. She had met her husband when she was seventeen at a job fair with a friend of hers where she went to school. Kevin was helping a friend of his who was a Marine recruiter. She explained how he had accidentally spilled his drink on her, and from there, they immediately hit it off. He kept in touch with her, and she would sneak out to see him. When she turned eighteen, she finally told her parents about him, and they told her they didn't approve and gave her an ultimatum. So, she followed her heart and moved out two days later and moved in with Kevin. They married the following year when he was transferred to Camp Pendleton. She explained how she tried reaching out to them when Cody was born. She left several messages but never got a return call. So, she eventually gave up trying.

Kevin's parents were the complete opposite. They were immensely supportive of both Kevin and Autumn. She became like another daughter to them. Unfortunately, they were both killed in an automobile accident three years ago. She told Frost a little about Kevin's younger sister, Carlie. From Autumn's facial expression and the way she spoke about Kevin's sister, he got the feeling the two of them weren't exactly close.

"Damn, sugar. So you had no family at all to fall back on when you were dealing with the loss of your husband?"

She shook her head. "No. If it wasn't for Nathan, I don't know where Cody and I would be right now. I wasn't in a good place during those ten months. But he was my rock at the time. He helped me through a lot. I don't think I could ever repay him for everything he did.

Like I said, Kevin had a sister, Carlie. But she and I never really hit it off from the start. She took Kevin's death hard." Autumn paused and scrunched her nose up. "You know, I never understood why, though. I mean, yes, she was his sister, but they rarely spoke to one another. Especially after their parents' accident. She became even more distant with Kevin. Kevin had been upset with her for the way she handled their parents' estate."

"Why is that? If you don't mind me asking."

She grinned at him. "I don't mind. It's actually nice being able to talk to someone about all of this."

Frost still had his hand over hers on the table. He liked the connection. It felt right.

"Carlie did some things behind Kevin's back. She hid some valuables that had been left to him and me, along with half of the money from their life insurance policy and half of the money from when she sold their home."

Frost noticed the way she turned up her nose like she was disgusted, and it intrigued him. From the little time he'd spent with Autumn, she always seemed upbeat and smiling. But right now, that wasn't the case. Her usual bubbly self was gone, and in its place was a woman who looked irritated and somewhat sad at the same time.

"How much money are you talking about?"

She stared at Frost across the table, and Frost could see the malice in those green eyes. She definitely did not like her sister-in-law.

"Three-hundred-thousand dollars."

"Three-hundred-thousand, total?"

Autumn shook her head. "No, three-hundred-thousand each. She walked away with six-hundred-thousand. And that was after taxes, and attorney's fees and jewelry and whatever else she found in the house that she wanted.

Frost let out a whistle.

"Why did Kevin let her get away with it?"

Autumn gave her shoulders a slight shrug. She had the same question but didn't want to badger Kevin about it when he was always being deployed.

"During that time, he was deployed a lot. Our front door was a constant revolving door with him."

"Remind me what division was he was in, again?" Frost asked as he took a bite of his sandwich.

"1st Marine Division. His deployments started out six to eight months long. Then a couple of years later, things started to change. He was gone for just weeks or sometimes even just days at a time. However, there were some instances when he was gone for months at a time. It just didn't seem like he was home much."

That didn't sound right to Frost. What she was explaining sounded like Kevin may have been involved in some special operations unit. Like the Navy had the SEALs and the Army had the Rangers, Green Berets, and Delta Force, the Marines had a few "secret" units of their own. And, now, he wondered if her husband was part of one of those units. He wouldn't say anything, but he made a mental note to ask his commander about it. Maybe he could look into it.

"Nathan was there for her as well. He actually took a couple of weeks of leave and flew out to North Dakota to be with her and help her with some stuff. She had some stuff she had to sort out with the government, so Nathan helped her out."

Again, Frost saw that same look cross her face when talking about Carlie, but she quickly masked it. If he were a betting man, he'd say there was some animosity between the two of them.

Frost ran his fingers through his hair. She made this Nathan guy sound like he was a god. And, now, he was starting to wonder if there were any intimate feelings between the two of them. Not that there was anything wrong with it. He'd seen it happen several times in his career when a wife loses her husband to war, and then the best friend steps in to help take care of her and the family if there are children involved. Then the next thing you know, they fall in love. Damn, he really hoped that wasn't the case with her. But if it was, why did she leave California? Why not stay with him?

"So, anyway, that is my story in a nutshell. I know it's not that impressive, and I don't have much, but all that matters is Cody," she told him with a twinkle in her eye.

He wanted to ask her more about Nathan, but now wasn't the time to press the issue. He was grateful for everything she'd shared with him.

They spent the next hour just talking. When they parted ways in the parking lot, Frost offered to follow her to make sure she made it home safely, but she politely turned him down, saying she didn't live too far, and they'd be okay. Just like he did when he took her out for coffee, he leaned down and kissed her cheek.

After making sure they both got into the car, and the car started okay, he waved, then walked to his vehicle. He pulled out his cell phone. He needed to call Alex and let her know he'd given Autumn her phone number.

Pulling her up in his contacts, he dialed. It rang twice before he heard his friend's chipper voice.

"Hey! To what do I owe the pleasure of your call?"

"Damn, can't a friend just call to say hi?"

"Guys don't call their friends to say hi. Plus, you hate talking on the phone. And you were just at my house about two hours ago. What gives?"

She had him there. And he did hate talking on the phone. And why did she sound out of breath?

"Are you okay? You sound out of breath."

"Oh yeah. I was just showing Ace some new moves I learned in my kickboxing class the other day."

"Sure…Is that what you kids are calling it now?" He asked with laughter in his voice, and he heard her snicker.

"No, but some of the moves I could probably incorporate into the bedroom."

Frost rolled his eyes. "Ew. Alex stop right there. I don't want to hear about you and Ace's bedroom antics."

She giggled. Damn, he loved her and was so glad to have her back in town.

Her soft voice through the phone had him focusing. "Anyway, you called me. What's up? Potter just got here to help Ace move the tables back into the garage."

"I wanted to give you a heads up, and I hope you don't mind, but I gave your number to a friend of mine."

"Uh, you do remember that I'm engaged, right?" She teased him.

He laughed. "Sorry. The friend is actually a she, and I wanted her to have an emergency contact should she need something and I'm not around."

There was silence over the line, then Alex blurted out, "Holy shit! Are you dating Autumn?"

"No."

"Frost? Are you fibbing? You would never give my number to someone unless you really cared about this person," Alex goaded him.

"Damn you, Alex." She giggled, and he loved it. "Let's just say we're taking it slow, you know, a friends first kind of thing. She has some reservations about getting involved with someone right now. Plus, she has a son, remember? So, we need to be mindful of him."

"Well, she seems very sweet, though I only got to spend a little bit of time with her, and her son is very well mannered. Even Ace talked about him. I'm happy for you. You deserve to have someone special in your life."

"So then, you're not pissed I gave out your number without asking?"

"Of course not. I know you would've only done something like that with good reason. And, please let her know if she needs anything, even if it's just a girlfriend to talk to, she can give me a call."

"Thanks, Alex. That means a lot. I love you, sugar."

"I love you too. Ouch! What the hell, Ace? It's only Frost for Christ's sake."

Frost chuckled as he hung up, knowing that Ace probably slapped her on the ass for flirting. That man was so possessive and protective of Alex, it was hilarious. Then he wondered to himself if he would be that way with Autumn. That was a no brainer…Of course, he would. He hopped up into his Tahoe and headed to his apartment, knowing that he'd be seeing her again in less than a week.

CHAPTER EIGHT

"So, tell me, how is that man of yours?"

Autumn rolled her eyes at Nancy. "He isn't my man."

"Really?" Nancy questioned as she took a bite of her Caesar salad. She and Autumn were having an early lunch because one of the other therapists called in sick, and the afternoon schedule was jammed packed with patients.

"Really," Autumn stated, trying to downplay her feelings for Frost. Nancy raised one of her perfectly shaped eyebrows at her in question. "So, you haven't seen or spoken to him since your coffee date? Autumn didn't overlook the way Nancy emphasized the word 'date.'

"We had lunch over the weekend, and he is taking Cody and me out to dinner tonight."

Nancy put her fork down. "And you are saying he's not your man? Autumn, what's stopping you?"

Autumn set her sandwich down and took a drink of her sweet tea. "I'm really trying, Nancy. But every time I seem to let that wall down a little I can't help but feel I'm setting myself up for heartbreak all over again."

"Is it because of his job?" Nancy asked, covering Autumn's hand.

"Yeah. I mean, look what happened to Kevin, and his job wasn't even a close comparison to Frost's. He's a freaking Navy SEAL. You've been around here long enough to know what those men go through. Yeah, most of their missions are classified, but we all hear the stories. I met him because he was in here for a gunshot to his leg for Pete's sake. That has to be a sign, doesn't it?"

"Oh, honey. You can't compare the two."

"I don't know," Autumn said, shaking her head.

"Let me ask you this. Are you attracted to him? Do you enjoy spending time with him? Does he make you happy when he's around?"

"I am very attracted to him, and not just because of his looks. He's easy to talk to, and the couple of times we have talked, I find myself opening up like it's natural to share my thoughts and concerns with him."

"What is your heart telling you to do?"

"My heart is saying to let him."

Nancy smiled softly. "Then follow your heart, sweetie. Take a leap of faith. You might surprise yourself."

Autumn sighed. She had a few hours to ponder this before her dinner with Frost.

Frost walked into his apartment. He stopped by to shower and change before he went and picked Cody up from school. He was excited to spend time with him. He was planning to take him to the base and show him some of the areas where he worked. Maybe let him run parts of the famed "O" course. His commander even got it cleared to take Cody out in one of the SEAL Delivery Vehicles. After that, the two of them would meet up with Autumn at Bartelli's for dinner.

He walked into the living room and found Stitch sitting on the couch with his bare feet propped up on the coffee table, watching some medical show on the TV. He gave Frost a chin lift.

"Hey, man. I thought you were taking Cody to the base for a tour this afternoon."

"I am. I just stopped home to shower and change. Got any plans tonight?"

"No. Why? What's up?"

"Would you like to come along to Bartelli's with Autumn, Cody, and I?"

"Aww…Feeling a little insecure, and you need a wingman?" Stitch chuckled, and Frost picked up his Guns and Ammo magazine from the table and threw it at Stitch's head.

"Fuck you!"

"I don't understand. I thought you'd want to spend some alone with them."

"I do, but I think it might be good if I start incorporating some of the team into some of the outings. You know, to get her used to everyone. And also let her see that we live a normal life when we are home."

Stitch nodded his head. "I get it. And, sure, I'll meet up with you guys. But you're paying, and I get my own buffalo chicken pizza. Just text me when you're heading that way, and I'll meet you there. Does Autumn know I'm coming?"

"No, but I'll text her and let her know."

Stitch gave him a serious look. "You really like her, don't you?"

Frost set his hands on his hips and let out a deep sigh. "Yeah, I do. I just wish she'd let me in. I'm going to keep trying, though."

"She's been hurt before, Frost. Give her time; I'm sure she'll come around. Look at it this way. Would she really be letting her son spend time with you alone if she didn't at least trust you?"

He thought about that, and Stitch had a point. "Yeah, I guess you're right."

"On another note, how's the leg? You ready for the PRT next week?"

"It's good. I only have some slight discomfort where the incision was. The doc said that was to be expected, and it wouldn't cause any delay to return to the team as long as I passed the required tests. This sitting around shit is driving me fucking crazy."

"I'm sure. I'm just glad we didn't have to pull another guy in. Not that I mind other team members, but it just messes with the team's dynamic when someone new comes on board. I know Ace will be thrilled to have you back."

"Speaking of Ace, he mentioned Mia was coming for a visit in a few weeks."

"Really? I didn't know that." Frost noticed Stitch seemed to sit up a little straighter and pay more attention to him than the TV.

"You didn't know? Huh, the way you two have been talking lately, I thought she would've mentioned it to you."

"Why? It's not like we're dating or anything. Plus, it's been a few weeks since I last spoke with her. She's been studying for her boards. I think her exam is coming up in the next month or two." He shrugged his shoulders like he was trying to play it off that he wasn't 'that' interested, but Frost knew better.

"So, you don't have any feelings for her?"

Stitch shook his head no. "Even if I did, she's Ace's sister. Team members don't poach family members. Plus, she's dating some guy, remember? The fucking former Green Beret. She must have been pissed off at Ace to date an Army dude."

"I don't think she's dating him anymore. At least that's what I heard anyway," Frost said, shrugging his shoulders as he walked into the kitchen to grab a drink.

"When did you hear that?" Stitch shouted loud enough for Frost to hear, and it made Frost smile. Apparently, his best friend had more of an interest in Mia than he'd let on, although he had a feeling; Stitch had the hots for her since Christmas last year. They spent a lot of time together over the holidays and kept in touch quite frequently. But according to Stitch, it was to help with her medical studies.

He walked back into the living room and took a swig from his bottle of water. "A couple of weeks ago. Alex mentioned something about it. She caught him in bed with another woman."

Stitch dropped his feet to the floor. "What?"

"Yeah, major asshole. Alex said Mia had to convince Ace not to travel to New York to teach the guy a lesson."

Stitch ran his fingers through his hair and stared at the television. Frost stood up. He needed to get in the shower now if he didn't want to be late getting to Cody's school. He looked back at his friend. He wouldn't be surprised if Stitch was on the phone calling Mia the second he walked out the door.

"Hey, but it's not your problem, right? She's still young, beautiful, and brilliant. She'll have no problem landing a great guy. Hell, working in New York City, she's probably got men flaunting themselves all over her."

Stitch mumbled something under his breath, and Frost chuckled to himself as he walked to his bedroom to get ready. It was so easy to mess with him. Most of the guys had a feeling Stitch had a thing for Mia. If he were going to make a move, now would be the perfect opportunity.

CHAPTER NINE

Autumn was laughing so hard. "Oh my gosh! You two are hilarious. It's like you know exactly what each other is going to say, so you finish each other's sentences," Autumn said as she took a bite of her pizza. Frost and Stitch had been entertaining her for the last hour with their stories from when they were younger and wilder. Although Autumn had to disagree on the wilder part because she would imagine being a SEAL most likely put "wild" to shame with the things they probably got into.

"So, Autumn, what do you do when you're not working? Do you have any hobbies?" Stitch asked in-between shoving another slice of pizza in his mouth. Autumn looked down and noticed there was only one slice of the large buffalo chicken left. She couldn't believe Stitch had eaten the entire pizza himself.

Trying not to think about how her body would feel if she ate that much food, she focused on Stitch. "Honestly, between work and taking care of Cody, I feel like I'm always working. I mean, on the weekends, I try to do some fun things with Cody, like going to the movies, walking the boardwalk, visiting some of the parks. Back in California, I did a lot with the other wives on base. We had girls' nights out, scrapbook days, things like that."

Frost listened as the two spoke. Autumn seemed very comfortable talking and being around Stitch. He told her a little about his background and about being the medic on the team. He also noticed everything that Autumn ticked off that she did with Cody didn't cost much money or was free, and he got a funny feeling in his gut. He looked over to where Cody was playing a video game in the adjoining arcade. When Cody asked if he could play some games, he saw her hesitation at first but then dug into her purse and handed him a five-dollar bill. He wasn't going to tell Autumn, but a few minutes ago, when he walked over to check on Cody, he slipped him another ten dollars but made him promise not to tell his mom. He had a feeling that would embarrass her if she truly didn't have spare money to do things she and Cody would enjoy.

"You should hang out with Alex and Tenley when they do their girls' nights out. Those two are wild. Well, now that Tenley is pregnant and can't drink, they've tamped down their wildness. But don't let it fool you. They still get in trouble. But seriously, they like to do all that women stuff on the weekends, like getting their toenails painted, shopping, shit like that. Trust me, you would have a lot of fun with them."

From what Frost had gathered from his "dates" with Autumn, she wasn't the type to go and hang out. She would much rather just hang with her kid. Not that it was a bad thing, but she needed to have some fun herself.

As Stitch went on and on, Frost sensed Autumn was starting to get a little uncomfortable talking about doing things and going out to various places. Again, his gut told him she didn't have much. He decided to change the subject.

An hour later, Frost found himself walking Autumn to her car. He placed his hands on her hips and pulled her into a hug. He could smell the citrus shampoo she used. He liked it. He knew he had to let her go, but dammit, she felt good in his arms. He pulled back slightly and could see her cheeks looked a little flush. He grinned, and she smiled back at him. He leaned forward and kissed her forehead. He needed to get her into her car before he took her lips right there in the parking lot.

He opened her door, and she moved to get in, but he placed his hand on her arm, stopping her.

"I'll give you a call in a few days. Maybe you, Cody, and I can make some plans to get together again."

"I'd like that," she told him, her voice sounding a little husky, and he could only hope she felt what he felt.

"Okay." He couldn't resist. She was just too damn tempting. He leaned down and kissed her cheek. "Drive safe," he told her before shutting the door and climbing into his own vehicle to make the drive back to his and Stitch's apartment.

CHAPTER TEN

Autumn was sitting in the living room, folding the last load of laundry. It was Saturday, and she had the morning to herself. She had dropped Cody off at his Sea Cadets drill meeting about an hour ago. She didn't need to pick him up for another five hours, so she was using the alone time to get some chores done around the house, though there wasn't really much to do since the house was small and she and Cody were good at picking up after themselves and keeping the place neat. All that needed to be done was to give the bathrooms a good scrub down, vacuum, dust, and change the bed sheets.

She picked up the laundry basket with Cody's clothes and entered his room. One of her rules was Cody had to put his own clothes away. She set the basket down on his neatly made bed. Of course, it was made to military standards. He had sat there one Saturday making, then remaking his bed until he got it down perfect and could bounce a quarter on it.

She started toward the door when she looked down at the desk and saw the picture of Cody with Frost and the other guys on his SEAL team. She walked over and picked up the picture. She smiled, remembering how excited Cody was that day. Just meeting Frost's teammates was an experience to watch. But she thought Cody was going to pass out when they handed him the t-shirt with the SEAL Team 2 logo on it and the hat.

Looking at Frost in the picture, she thought about their dinner last night. And she had to admit, she was beginning to have deeper feelings for him as much as she was trying to avoid it. Getting to know the real him and not the SEAL that most people know has been moving. Under all of the armor, he was just a normal guy living a normal life, and she really liked that.

His job, though, was what was holding her back. The thought that he could be deployed at a moment's notice and not knowing where he was going seemed a little hard to handle.

She knew from experience how it felt to worry all the time when someone you loved was deployed. It was an emotional rollercoaster. She remembered some of her late husband's deployments earlier in their marriage. She knew where he was, but then she'd hear and see on the news that there were attacks on US forces in that same area. She went through a lot of sleepless nights, lying there wondering if the next knock on the door was going to be the Chaplain and NCO coming to notify her that her husband had been killed.

She swallowed the large lump in her throat. She remembered all too well the day that knock became a reality.

It was a warm sunny California day. She had just gotten home from the grocery store and was just starting to put away the groceries when she heard the knock on the door. She opened the door, expecting to see one of her neighbors but, instead, saw the two Marines. She fell to the floor in a puddle of tears. It was the worst day of her life.

She didn't realize she was crying until she saw a tear splash onto the picture she was holding.

The thought hit her hard. If she opened up her heart again, would she be able to handle the pain if history repeated itself?

Before she could dwell on it anymore, there was a knock at the front door. She set the picture back down and wiped her face.

She walked to the front door, wondering who it might be. She wasn't expecting anyone; perhaps it was Mrs. Higdon from next door. But then she remembered that when she saw Mrs. Higdon last night, she mentioned she was going to be attending a show up in Richmond with a friend of hers from her sewing class.

Making sure she was attentive before opening the door, she pulled the curtain to the front window back, and as soon as she saw who was standing on her porch, she couldn't hold back her smile. She fumbled with the chain and deadbolt in a rush to open the door. She swung the door open and leaped into his arms.

"Oh, my god! Nathan!"

❧

Nathan laughed as he squeezed her tight.

"What are you doing here? Why didn't you call and tell me you were in town?" Autumn asked him as she took his hand and led him into the house. He already wasn't a fan of the neighborhood she was living in. He would ask her about that later. More importantly, he wanted to know why she looked like she had been crying.

She led him to the living room, which was pretty much right inside the door. He looked around and smiled, seeing all of her and Cody's pictures adorned through the home. She had a beautiful smile, and Cody held the features of both his mom and dad.

They sat down on the sofa. She was beaming now, and he took in the sight of her. She looked good, really good. But he could see some sadness in her eyes. She had never been good at hiding her emotions from anyone. Her eyes always gave her away. He reached out and took her hand. He could feel her shaking.

"I've missed you," he told her, and she squeezed his hand.

"I've missed you too," she spoke as tears started rolling down her face.

He wrapped his arms around her and pulled her into him. He could tell she had lost some weight in the year he hadn't seen her. But, overall, she looked good. She looked healthy.

"What are the tears for, honey? Since we've been talking on the phone, you've been telling me everything was good."

She pulled back, wiping her face, and looked up at him and smiled. "I am good, Nathan. But some days are not so good, and today just happens to be one of them. But, now that you're here, it's starting to turn around."

He smiled at her. "You want to talk about it?"

She wrinkled her nose up in a cute way and shook her head. "No, I'll be fine. I'm already feeling better seeing your handsome face."

They sat on the sofa and talked. He explained he was in town for two days for some meetings in Norfolk and thought it would be nice to surprise her and Cody and maybe take them out to dinner and catch up. He listened while she talked about work and then about Cody and what he had been up to. He was happy to hear that he'd joined the Sea Cadets. He'd heard nothing but great things about the program for kids.

He glanced down at his watch and saw it was almost 2:00 pm. He had a meeting he needed to get to. He stood up and stretched.

"I need to get going to make it to my meeting on time."

Autumn stood as well. "Oh, okay."

"Are you and Cody free for dinner tonight? I can swing by and pick you guys up. There's a place near-by that I heard about from some of the guys. They told me it was a must place to go to eat. Apparently, it's off the beaten path, and mainly only locals frequent it."

"Sure, sounds like a plan. Why don't you just text us when you're close, and we'll be ready."

"Great, we can catch up more at dinner." He leaned forward and kissed her cheek. He couldn't wait to tell her about his new girlfriend, Tessa. That was going to surprise the hell out of her.

Autumn walked him out to his car. He glanced at her car parked next to his, and he cringed. He hated that damn car. He was surprised it was still even running.

"Your car holding up okay?" By the frown on her face, he knew the answer.

"Define holding up?" She asked, and his gut clenched.

"Is it safe?"

She waved her hand in the air. "It's fine. It's just been acting up a little, but someone is coming by to look at it."

He didn't like the sound of that and wanted to know who this someone was. "I hope it's someone you know and trust. There are a lot of shady mechanics out there."

She gave him a smirk. "Of course, it is someone I know. It's a friend of a friend."

He looked her over and knew she was withholding information. He'd find out more about it later.

"Okay. We'll discuss it more at dinner, along with why you are living in this complex." She stuck her tongue out at him, and he laughed. As long as he'd known her, she always had a sassy side. She wouldn't be Autumn Kauffman without it. It was a trait that her husband had loved about her.

"No! No, no, no! He's mine, you bitch!" Carlie shouted as she threw the pair of binoculars she was using to watch from across the street. The binoculars hit the wall putting a dent into the moldy sheetrock.

Nathan was meant to be with her. How dare he kiss her, even though it was only a kiss on the whore's cheek, it was still intimate. She remembered Nathan's words to her when he visited her in North Dakota a few weeks ago. He told her he was planning on coming here to see Autumn and Cody. But he also told her that they were only friends when she asked, and he was coming here just to check on them.

But from the way he smiled at Autumn and touched her, there was more there than just being friends. That meant he lied to her. Liars had to be punished. She squinted her eyes as she watched Nathan back out of the parking spot and Autumn wave to him with a big smile on her face.

"We'll see who's smiling, bitch, when you're at the bottom of the ocean."

Initially, she just planned to pay off some guy who needed some quick cash to destroy Autumn. That way, her hands stayed clean. However, those plans changed when Nathan told her he was coming here to visit Autumn and her bratty son.

Ever since her brother, Kevin, had brought Autumn home to meet their family twelve years ago, her life had been was turned upside down. She was pushed aside by both Kevin and her parents. She was tired of always hearing Autumn this and Autumn that. Autumn was the golden child, and she was tired of always being compared to her. Sure, she wasn't the greatest kid and had her issues, but who didn't. She knew Autumn had tried to be the nice sister-in-law, but it hurt knowing her own parents and brother could love that bitch more than her. She missed her parents, but in the back of her sick and twisted mind, she knew they got what they had coming to them.

She had convinced Kevin that she should hold onto his share of their parents' estate and life insurance money, which made her feel empowered. Then she paid off the young girl in the VA office to "misplace" Kevin's paperwork. What an ingenious idea that was and because of that, she was still the sole beneficiary listed on Kevin's life insurance policy. When he was killed, she found herself four-hundred-thousand dollars richer.

Carlie picked up her backpack and pulled out a picture of her and Nathan. It was taken when her brother had first brought Nathan home to meet the family. She had fallen in love with him instantly. She knew he liked her, as well. Over the years, he'd always sent her flowers and called her. She wished he would make a move on her. She was tempted to make the first move, but she didn't want to come across as being pushy. But then her brother had to go and get himself killed, fucking up her plans to seduce Nathan.

Of course, it was Autumn everyone was concerned about. Nathan even let her move in with him. She smiled, staring at the picture. "That's okay, my love. I'll forgive you."

She took a peek out the front window of the dilapidated house she was going to be working out of for the next few weeks. She also had a room at an extended stay joint just north in Hampton Roads under an alias name. She hadn't realized how easy it was to get fake IDs.

Autumn wasn't going to take Nathan from her. She would eliminate her before she even had a chance. And, of course, Nathan would be so upset and distraught over her death that he would turn to her to console him.

She smiled…as she thought of all the different ways she could end Autumn's life. She pulled out her phone and dialed her contact here in town. On the second ring, he answered.

"Yeah?"

"I have another assignment for you. Come to the abandoned house directly across from the woman's house," she told the guy.

She was shocked at the guy's response. "Sorry, no can do."

"What do you mean you can't? I have cash, and I'll pay you in person," she screeched.

"I don't care. I'm not for hire any longer." The guy hung up.

Carlie slammed the phone down on the counter in a rage. "Fuck!" She was furious. Finding another person to do her dirty work was going to set her back on her timing. She needed to locate someone fast. She had equipment that needed to be set up. She wanted eyes on Autumn. This was a seedy neighborhood, so she shouldn't have a problem finding a criminal who wanted to make some quick cash.

Skinny set his phone down on the table next to the chair he was sitting in. He was in the middle of a meeting with Cecil when the crazy bitch called. He almost wanted to laugh at the way she screeched when he told her he wasn't for hire anymore. It's not like he needed the money because Cecil paid him extremely well. He just liked the challenges that criminal activity can bring. It was an adrenalin rush for him. Since Cecil wanted the redhead, his plans had changed. Now instead of terrorizing the woman, he would be helping Cecil behind the scenes.

"Was that the woman trying to hurt Autumn?" Cecil asked as he sat behind his custom stainless-steel desk with a glass tabletop. He had an angry expression on his face.

"Yep. Said she had another assignment for me."

"Did she say what it was?"

"No. But, I swear the woman is crazy obsessed with your woman." Cecil's lips twitched up at the mention of Autumn being referred to his woman. Skinny knew the right things to say to his boss.

"Where does this woman live?"

Skinny shrugged his shoulders. "I honestly don't know. She's always wired the money through Western Union. But now that I think about it, she mentioned on the phone just now that she would pay me cash in person. She might be in town."

Skinny watched as Cecil's face went flat.

"You've been watching Autumn for a couple of days now. Have you noticed anyone following her?"

"No, but she has been hanging out with that guy you saw her with at the coffee shop." Cecil tapped his fingers on the desk, and Skinny knew that was a sign that his boss was annoyed. "Do you want me to continue following her?"

"Yes, but I also want you to be on the lookout for this mystery woman who's after Autumn. I don't want to take any chances; if you see her, take her out. I don't want any harm to come to my future wife."

Skinny swallowed hard. Jesus, he'd never seen his boss this strung up. Especially over a broad. However, he knew how important this upcoming deal was for Cecil and what he needed in terms of presenting himself as a family man.

"I have some business that's going to occupy my time for the next two or three weeks. And, unfortunately, it's going to pull me out of town. I'm going to rely on you to keep watch over things around here while I'm gone. That includes making sure Autumn stays safe. When I return, I'll put some pressure on her. She won't be able to say no to me," he grinned.

CHAPTER ELEVEN

Frost was laughing at a joke Stitch was telling the group. He, Ace, Alex, Stitch, and Irish were sitting at Bayside. Potter and Tenley were supposed to join them for dinner; however, Tenley wasn't feeling well. She'd been having a bout of morning sickness the last few weeks since she found out she was expecting her and Potter's first child. Well, technically, their second since they had adopted Alejandra. Tenley had cared for the cute little girl during the aftermath of the major earthquake that struck the northern coast of Ecuador last Christmas.

Frost was grateful that Ace and Alex had invited him tonight. It had turned out to be an enjoyable evening with friends, plus it had taken his mind off the dynamic redhead who'd been invading his thoughts twenty-four hours a day, seven days a week.

He wondered what she was up to this evening. He had enjoyed their evening together the other night. While they ate, Cody told Frost about his upcoming trip to Washington, D.C., with his Sea Cadet division. Frost knew all about the program. He and Stitch were part of the local division when they were in middle and high school. His SEAL team even hosted one of the training sessions that were offered to the older cadets. Frost was surprised to learn that Autumn wasn't going on the trip with him. When he asked why she told him it wasn't financially possible at the time. But if he remembered correctly, the cadets' portion was paid for, so only the adults had to pay. And, it still wasn't much as they got a group discount, maybe two hundred dollars. But he could tell it wasn't a subject she wanted to discuss, so he let it drop.

Slowly but surely, the more they talked, he was lowering her defenses and making progress on taking their relationship to the next level. He had to admit; he was falling hard for her and the funny part was they hadn't even shared a kiss yet. But if things progressed the way he hoped, they would, and that would be happening very soon. He couldn't wait to feel her lush pink lips pressed against his.

"Hey, Frost…Isn't that Autumn's son, Cody?" Alex asked, pointing toward the patio. Frost turned around and damned if it wasn't him. He was leaning against the deck railing, staring out at the water. Frost thought he looked deep in thought but looked as if something was bothering him.

Frost glanced around the restaurant, knowing that if Cody was here, Autumn most likely was too, but he didn't see her, and that concerned him because if he knew Autumn like he thought he did, she wouldn't let him come here alone.

He excused himself from the table and made his way outside. As he got closer, he could hear Cody mumbling something about a person named Nathan. Frost wondered if he was referring to Autumn's friend Nathan from California. If that was indeed who he was referring to, he didn't sound happy about him. Thanks to his SEAL training, he waited quietly and patiently, listening to Cody speak his thoughts out loud. He felt kind of bad for invading his privacy, but so far, he didn't like the information he'd heard coming from Cody. Something about someone stopping by or maybe them going to visit.

After another couple of minutes of torturing himself, only hearing bits and pieces, let alone feeling like a giant ass for sneaking up and listening, Frost finally announced himself.

"Hey, Cody!"

When Cody turned around, Frost became worried because Cody definitely looked upset. The poor kid looked to have tears in his eyes. But at the sight of seeing Frost, he perked up.

"Hi, Frost. What are you doing here?" Cody asked him as he glanced around. Almost like he was looking for someone specifically and wondered what was going on. Cody's expression looked like he was worried or guilty of something.

Frost eyed him. The kid was definitely acting funny, but he wasn't worried because he knew how to get anyone to talk if he wanted to. But, for now, he would play it cool. He motioned toward the inside. "I'm having dinner with some of the guys and Alex. How about you? Is your mom here with you?"

Frost watched as Cody's eyes widened, and then his face turned almost green-like. Frost was now alarmed, especially when Cody lowered his head and wouldn't answer him. Frost wondered what the hell was going on because the kid standing in front of him now was not the free-spirited kid he'd been hanging out with the last couple of weeks. This kid was genuinely upset, and Frost had no fucking clue why or what to do.

He took Cody gently by the elbow and pulled him over to one of the tables nearby and sat him down. There were no other people near them.

Christ, where did he start? Give him an enemy to interrogate, and he knew what to do. But a kid? Nope, he had not a fucking clue. He wished Potter and Tenley had not canceled tonight. Tenley would know what to say. But since she wasn't, he was going to have to wing it.

"What's got you looking upset, buddy?"

Cody shrugged his shoulders. "It's nothing."

"Come on now. I wasn't born yesterday. It sure didn't sound like nothing when you were standing over there talking to yourself."

Cody's eyes went wide. "You heard everything I said?"

Shit, now he really felt like an ass.

"I didn't hear everything, but I heard enough to know something or someone is bothering you."

Cody sat there for a few seconds, not saying anything. He was just starring off towards the water again. Finally, Cody took a deep breath, then looked back at Frost.

"My mom's friend from California showed up today."

Okay, that was nowhere near what he was expecting Cody to say. He kept silent, knowing he wasn't finished.

"It's a guy friend." Well, that got his attention. So, Nathan, who Cody was referring to, must be Autumn's "guy" friend. Now, he wondered exactly what type of "friend" he was. Several questions were forming in his head. Was there something going on between them? Jesus, if that was the case, he didn't know if he could ever speak to her again. But he wouldn't do that. Cody was too important to him already.

"Cody, does this guy friend have a name?"

"Nathan. He was my dad's best friend. He was with him when my dad was killed. He helped my mom and I after dad died. When Mom and I had to move out of our house, he let us live with him. After a few months, that's when Mom decided we needed to…what did she call it…start a new chapter. Nathan didn't seem very happy when Mom told him about her plans. They don't know, but I overheard them arguing about it the night Mom told him."

Damn. Frost knew most times, best friends and teammates always took care of a surviving spouse, especially ones with children. They always tried to keep in touch with the family just to check up on them and make sure they were surviving okay. A buddy of his back on the West Coast lost his best friend and teammate, and he took care of the spouse. Eventually, they fell in love and married. He wondered if Autumn had started to fall for Nathan and that was why she decided to leave, and if that was why she was hesitant about starting a relationship with him. He had a lot of questions he needed to ask her. The first being if these past few weeks of spending time with her and Cody were for nothing. Shit, did Nathan come here to woo her back? Right now, though, he needed to be here for Cody because obviously, he was having a hard time with Nathan being around.

"Why would a 'friend' visiting your mom upset you? Your mom actually told me a little about Nathan last week. He sounds like a nice guy." Cody shrugged his shoulders. "Come on now, you can talk to me. I'm fairly good at keeping secrets." He smiled and winked, and it made Cody laugh.

"I'll tell you, but you have to promise me you won't think I'm a loser?"

He gave Cody a stern look, and Cody dropped his eyes. "Cody, look at me." When Cody raised his eyes, Frost could see the timid boy lying beneath the armor he showed on the outside. "I will never think of you as a loser. You copy?"

Cody swallowed hard and slightly nodded his head. "Yes, sir. I understand."

"Good, now tell me why Nathan being here upsets you."

113

"It brings back memories of my dad. I mean, it's not like I forget about my dad, but seeing Nathan, and him being my dad's best friend, just makes me think about dad more. I try not to let it bother me, but I can't help it. I know Mom was surprised and happy to see him, and I want to be happy too, but it's hard. He's always telling me stories about my dad, and as much as I want to hear them, a part of me doesn't." He looked up at Frost with tears in his eyes. "Does that make me a bad person, Frost?"

Frost felt like his heart was being squeezed. He couldn't imagine the anguish and pain this brilliant young man sitting in front of him was going through. He had never lost a parent, but he'd seen what it did to kids who lost one at a young age. Being a military brat growing up, he'd had plenty of friends who lost a parent to war. A lot of those kids got into a lot of trouble because they took their anger out doing stupid shit. Some got help and turned their lives around, while others ended up taking a hard route into adult life and never really fully recovered. But this kid sitting in front of him, the kid who felt foolish because he felt he would be considered a loser because of what he was feeling, was the prime example of a courageous individual. Frost held a lot of respect for the kid.

"No, Cody. What you just told me doesn't make you a bad person. It just proves that you're human. I've lost friends to war. I know it's not easy. I can't imagine what you and your mom went through losing your dad. But take it from me, I know it may be hard to hear someone, especially your dad's best friend, tell you stories about your dad, but listen to what he has to say. One day, you're going to be thankful that you did. Especially one day in the far future when you have kids of your own and you tell them stories about their grandpa."

"Frost, would it be okay if I called you when I'm having a bad day and just need to talk?"

Frost smiled and ruffled Cody's hair. "I'd be disappointed if you didn't. I'll always be there for you, Cody."

"Thanks, Frost."

Now for the important question.

"Cody, where's your mom?"

Cody's eyes widened. "Oh, no! I told her I was just going to the bathroom. She's probably worried."

Frost chuckled. "That's okay. Come on, let's go find her."

Cody stood and looked way up at Frost. "Umm, Frost?"

"Yeah, buddy?"

"Don't be upset, but Nathan is here with us."

Okay, again, he wasn't expecting that. His stomach clenched. Frost hoped this was just a friendly and quick visit for Nathan. He was starting to think he took too long to make his move, but Autumn knew what his intentions were. He made them quite clear over their coffee a couple of weeks ago, and their lunch and dinner this past week, and she was starting to open up more. God, he prayed she wasn't just taking him on some cruise to emotional torture. He guided Cody back inside the restaurant. He followed behind as Cody led them to a table on the other side where his mom was sitting.

As they approached the table, the man he assumed was Nathan had his arm around Autumn as they looked at something on his phone. He stopped in front of the table, and he felt sick. They looked cozy sitting together; a little too cozy for just friends.

"Mom, look who I found!" Cody stated as he sat down at the table across from Autumn and Nathan.

She glanced up, and Frost knew the moment it registered with her, who Cody was referring to. Her face turned the same sickly green color that Cody's had just a few minutes ago. He just raised his eyebrows up in question.

"Frost! What are you doing here?" She asked, then looked back towards Nathan, who still had his arm around her and pulled her even closer to his side, which had Frost biting the inside of his cheek. Frost did a quick mental rundown on the guy. Definitely could tell he was a Marine by the 'high and tight' haircut. By the lines on his face, he was older, maybe early forties. However, he looked to be in good physical shape. If he remembered correctly, Autumn's husband was older.

"Autumn. Are you going to introduce me to your friend?" Frost could see how uncomfortable she was as she sat there, staring between the two of them. Frost wanted so badly to rip the guy's hands off. He was angry, but he wouldn't cause a scene, at least not here and not in front of Cody. What he did want to know was exactly how important this guy was to Autumn. And, as if she was reading his mind, Autumn straightened in the chair, causing Nathan's arm to fall to his side. Okay, that was possibly a good sign. Or was she playing it off?

She pulled her lip between her teeth, and Frost knew she was contemplating how to explain who he was to Nathan. But, before she could get a word out, Cody answered for her.

"This is Frost. He's a friend of Mom's. And he's in the Navy."

Frost knew Nathan was sizing him up as well. "Ah...a sailor, are ya?"

Frost gave the man a sarcastic smirk. "Yeah, something like that." Then he looked at Cody and winked, and Cody smiled. He knew Cody wouldn't tell Nathan he was a SEAL, and, he definitely didn't plan on getting into a pissing contest with this guy.

"Yea, he and Mom have been hanging out, right Mom? And he took me to see some of the ships on the base in Norfolk and some other things." The other things being the SEAL base.

Go, Cody! Obviously, the kid was in his corner, although he probably didn't even realize what was transpiring right now. Frost had to hide his chuckle, watching Autumn's mouth gape open. But then his smile quickly disappeared when she finally was able to respond.

She turned toward Nathan. "Frost and I are good friends, Nathan."

Whether or not Autumn had romantic feelings for this guy, Frost knew Nathan and her were important to each other. He could see it in their eyes by the way they looked at each other. But after her comment of Frost just being her friend, he wasn't going to stick around any longer. He had his 'real' friends back inside, waiting for him.

"Well, I better get back over to my *friends*." He made sure to put some emphasis on the word 'friends.' But what almost made him turn around was the sadness that immediately filled her eyes. No longer were her green eyes bright and cheery looking; no, they were replaced with a dark, dull green color. "Don't let me interrupt your date." He turned to Cody. "I'll see ya around, buddy."

"Frost," Autumn called after him. He had only gotten a few steps away from the table. He stopped and closed his eyes. His hands were fisted by his sides. He wanted to turn around and drop to his knees and beg her to give him a chance. But he wouldn't. He turned one last time to look at her. She was gorgeous. His Irish beauty, but she wasn't his. She never was. If Nathan was the man she wanted to be with, then he had to let her go, and he himself needed to move on, even if it killed him to do so. All he wanted was to see her happy.

She went to say something, but he just held his hand up and gave her a painful smile. "Autumn, I understand now why you held back and couldn't take a chance on us. If he is what makes you happy, don't let me stand in the way. However, I sure as hell wished you would've said something before I went and fell for you."

Those were his final parting words before he turned and walked back to his friends. Shit, he wasn't even hungry anymore. He stopped by the table, told everyone he was leaving and dropped some cash on the table to cover his drinks and food. Of course, they wanted to know what happened. He just told them that he wasn't great company right now. Once outside, he hopped into his Tahoe and took off towards a beach just down the road. This area of the beach was desolate and quiet this time of the night. He needed to be alone to process what the hell just happened. He slid his fingers through his hair. Christ, did he just make the biggest mistake of his life and let the woman he loved slip away?

He shook his head. Love? He didn't know what love felt like. But if it was the pain he was feeling in his chest right now, then yeah, he loved her.

He had some PT clothes in his go bag; maybe a nighttime run would help clear his head. This would be a good test for his leg. He was due to take the PRT next week, and if everything went accordingly, he'd be placed back on active duty.

ᔕ

Autumn was fuming as she, Nathan, and Cody made their way out of the restaurant. She was pissed at both men; Nathan, for acting like an overly protective brother and Frost for jumping to conclusions and not giving her a moment to talk to him.

She tried going after him when she saw him exit the restaurant, but he was already in his Tahoe and turning out of the parking lot.

"Autumn, will you please stop for a minute?" Nathan asked as he walked behind her to the car.

She turned and glared at him.

"Why in the hell didn't you say something this morning? It's obvious you like the guy, and he likes you."

"I wasn't ready yet to say anything to anyone. We've only been out a few times as friends."

Nathan gave her a sympathetic look. "Honey, you need to let the past go and move on. Kevin would want you to be happy. If this guy Frost is what makes you happy, then go for it. Don't hold back."

She took a deep breath. "But I'm scared to open my heart up and go down that road again."

"Honey, he's in the Navy and most likely works aboard a ship. It's not like he's in a ground unit like Kevin was." Oh, God, if only Nathan knew what Frost was really involved in within the Navy. "You need to put yourself first for once. Look, if it makes it any better, I'll talk to the guy and let him know I'm not interested in you romantically."

"You would do that for me?"

"Yeah, I would because I care about you and Cody. And I can tell you both really like him. I just want to see you both happy and know you're being taken care of. Come on." He wrapped his arm around her shoulders and walked her the rest of the way to the car.

CHAPTER TWELVE

Autumn arrived late for work. It had been three days since Frost turned his back and walked away from her. Since then, she'd tried reaching out, but each time she got his voicemail. She opted not to leave a message. What she had to tell him wasn't something she wanted to leave in a message.

She walked into the employee lounge and stashed her bags in her locker. She was a little sweaty from walking from the bus stop. Her car wouldn't start this morning, and she had missed the first bus, so she had to wait for the next one, which made her late. At least she could call and give Nancy a heads up, which Nancy was okay with since her 9:00 am appointment had canceled.

She looked down at her watch. She had about fifteen minutes before her next patient arrived. She pulled her phone from her pants pocket and dialed Frost's number. After the fifth ring, she got his voicemail. This time she left a quick message, asking him to please give her a call.

Nathan was still apologizing for the other night. He had planned on staying a few extra days, but he was called back to California. She had hoped that he and Frost could've officially met. She shook her head; there was nothing she could do about it right now. She just hoped her day would get better.

ॐ

Seven hours later, Autumn's day wasn't any better. In fact, it was worse. Much worse as she sat in the ER of the local hospital.

She received a phone call from Cody's school about two hours ago, saying he had fallen outside and hit his head on the sidewalk. It was a hard-enough hit that it had knocked him out. They told her an ambulance had been called, and they were transporting him to the hospital. She had freaked out and was a nervous wreck, and of course, it had to have happened when she didn't have a car. A couple of the nurses offered to drive her, but she knew it would mess up the schedule if they did. She did try to call Frost again, but again, received no answer, just his voicemail.

Knowing it would take longer to take the bus, she decided to grab a cab at the taxi stand outside the main entrance of the hospital. There were always a few on stand-by.

By the time she arrived at the hospital, Cody had regained consciousness and was being evaluated. Now they were waiting for the doctor to hear the results of his CT scan. She reached over and brushed his hair off his forehead. He blinked his eyes open, and she could see the pain in his eyes. God, she hated to see him suffering.

"Hey, sweetie. How ya feeling?"

He mumbled an okay, then cleared his throat. "My head hurts here." He pointed to the left side near his temple.

She smiled. "I'm sure it does. Ms. Morgan saw you fall, and she said you hit pretty hard. Do you feel dizzy or queasy?"

He slowly shook his head. "No, just tired."

"Remember what the doctor said; if you start to have any symptoms that he told you about, you need to let me know as soon as possible."

He whispered an okay and closed his eyes again, and she knew he was asleep.

A few minutes later, the doctor knocked lightly on the door and entered. He explained that Cody had a concussion, and the CT scan came back clean. He wanted to keep him in the ER for another hour before discharging him.

After thanking the doctor and thanking the lord that her son was going to be okay, she started debating how they were going to get home. It was almost a quarter to five, and now they had to wait at least another hour before Cody could be discharged; it was going to be getting dark by the time they left. She hated taking the bus at night, plus she wanted to get Cody home as soon as possible. With all of the stops and then having to walk the quarter-mile from the bus stop to their house, that option was thrown out of the window. She thought about taking a cab, but after spending a fortune for the cab ride to the hospital, she didn't have the money.

She picked up her phone and tried calling Frost again, and for the third time today, she got his voicemail. This time, she opted not to leave a message.

She set her phone on her lap and rubbed her temples. She had about given up on who she could call, and then she remembered…She scrolled through her contacts until she found the person Frost had told her to call if she ever needed anything and couldn't get a hold of him.

She hit the green button, and the line started to ring.

"Hello?"

"Hi. Is this Alex?"

"Who's calling?"

"I'm sorry. This is Autumn, Frost's friend."

"Oh. Hi, Autumn! How are you?"

"Well, at the moment, I'm in a little bit of a pickle. Frost mentioned that if I couldn't get hold of him that I could call you." She paused, realizing how ridiculous this probably was. He probably told her about what happened. She wouldn't want to help. "God, this is so embarrassing. You know what? I'm sorry I bothered you. Please just forget I called."

She went to disconnect, but she heard Alex's plea. "Wait! Autumn?"

"Yeah?"

"You sound frazzled. What's going on? Obviously, it was important enough to call Frost." The woman had a point.

Autumn took a deep breath and started to explain the day's events to Alex. Alex was very understanding and concerned and told her she was just getting ready to leave work herself and to give her about fifteen to twenty minutes. She'd meet her at the hospital.

Autumn disconnected the call, and her body slumped in the chair. She felt like a ton of bricks had been lifted off her. Tears stung her eyes. Alex hadn't even questioned her; just told her that she understood, and she was on her way. She was a saint.

121

She sat there in the chair with her head cradled in her hands. She heard a faint knock on the door. A beautiful brunette, wearing hot pink hospital scrubs, walked in. She smiled. "Hi, are you Autumn?"

Autumn looked at the woman. "Yes."

The woman looked at Cody, who was snoring, then she walked closer and sat in the empty chair next to Autumn. She stuck her hand out. "My name is Tenley. I'm one of the RNs in the emergency room. I'm a friend of Alex's. She called me and asked me to come and check on you."

Autumn stared at this Tenley woman. Were these women for real? Two acts of kindness from complete strangers in a matter of minutes was completely unheard of in this day and age.

"I'm sorry, how is it that you know, Alex?"

Tenley laughed and patted Autumn's leg like they'd been friends for years. And, for some reason, Autumn felt completely comfortable being in her company.

"Alex is my best friend. She and I grew up together here in Virginia Beach. As you know, Alex is engaged to Ace. Potter, who I know you met a few weeks ago when Frost was in the hospital, is my husband. Oh, and Frost is also one of my best friends. He and Stitch, one of the others you met, grew up with Alex and me."

Holy shit…Talk about a small world. Tenley's calm and soothing voice helped tame Autumn's nerves.

"So, you are all like a little family?"

Tenley smiled wide. "We sure are, and when one of us is in trouble or in a little bind, we are always there for one another. No questions asked. Well, most of the time." She winked, and Autumn had to laugh.

After talking a little more, Autumn learned that Tenley recently found out she and her husband were expecting a baby and adopted a seven-year-old girl from Ecuador. Tenley's sincerity truly touched Autumn. She seemed like a wonderful woman and a great mother. She was even more shocked when Tenley wanted to exchange cell numbers with her and introduce Cody to her daughter Alejandra.

Tenley was getting ready to go and check the discharge papers for Cody when Alex walked in. She was wearing dark navy-blue dress pants, and a crisp white three-quarters sleeve button up blouse that was unbuttoned at the top just enough to look classy and sexy. Her three-inch Calvin Klein Pointed-Toe Pumps rounded out her outfit. The woman screamed class and confidence. She looked absolutely stunning and so professional.

She smiled at both Autumn and Tenley. "Oh, good, you got to meet one another."

Tenley grinned. "Yep. We were just having a little girl talk while we waited. I was going to see if Cody's paperwork is ready, so we can get that sweet little boy home and in his own bed. He needs to take it easy and rest for a couple of days."

Alex looked at Autumn. "Well, that is good news. What did the doctor say?" Alex asked as she walked over to the bed and gently touched Cody's arm. Autumn tried not to let her emotions get the best of her, but these two women were just too amazing. She was a complete stranger to them both, but here they were, talking and acting like they'd all been best friends for life.

She tried dislodging the huge lump that had formed in her throat. "The doctor believes he has a mild concussion. I just need to monitor him for the next twenty-four hours."

Alex shook her head in understanding and came to sit down in the chair Tenley had vacated. She reached out and covered Autumn's hand with hers. "How are you holding up?"

Autumn couldn't hold back the tears any longer, and as soon as she blinked, they began to fall. "I think I'm okay now. About an hour ago was a different story." She looked at Alex. "I was so scared when I got that call. I feel so exhausted right now."

Alex smiled softly and squeezed her hand. Just that little bit of reinsurance made Autumn feel a bit better.

"I'm sure you are, but Autumn, you did the right thing by calling me."

Autumn wanted to respond because, honestly, she wasn't really sure if it was the right thing to do, but Tenley came in at that moment with Cody's paperwork.

ॐ

An hour later and Autumn and Cody were in Alex's SUV on their way home.

"Alex, I can't thank you enough for doing this for us. I would like to repay the favor somehow."

Alex waved her off, but Autumn knew she was probably taking her away from her plans for the evening. She glanced in the back seat, where Cody was once again asleep. For the next twenty-four hours, the doctor instructed her to wake him every thirty minutes, and bring him back to the hospital quickly if he developed any severe concussive symptoms, such as dizziness or nausea.

"Has Frost called you back?" Alex asked. The question surprised her, and so did the annoyed tone Alex spoke with.

"No, not yet. I figured he was busy since he said the only time he won't answer is if he was deployed or was working and couldn't answer. I think he was supposed to take his PRT this morning."

"I don't know why he hasn't called you back, though. That doesn't make sense. He's seemed a little off ever since the night he saw Cody at Bayside."

It made perfect sense why he hadn't called and why he was upset that night. She was now afraid she had blown any chance at a relationship with him. But, on the other hand, it kind of pissed her off that he was acting like a child and giving her the silent treatment. Pissed or not, he could be a man and at least allow her to explain. Obviously, Alex wasn't aware of what went down at the restaurant.

"I think it's my fault." She sighed. "Hell, I don't know."

"Your fault?" Alex questioned as she turned on her left turn signal to pull into the housing complex.

Autumn shook her head. "Yes." Autumn wasn't sure if she wanted to get Alex caught up in her and Frost's issues. She seemed to be close to him, so she knew Alex's loyalty would lie with her friend.

"Does this have to do with Frost seeing you with that other man? And before you ask, Frost and I are best friends. He, Tenley, and Stitch, one of the other SEALs I believe you met in the hospital, all grew up with each other. So, we kind of tell each other everything."

Autumn's stomach churned. Yep, Alex was loyal to her friends, and Frost had told them.

"Don't look so defeated. Frost might be my friend and all, but I know perfectly well he can sometimes get his head up his ass." She smiled, and Autumn had to chuckle. "Now, it's obvious you have feelings for Frost, and he has them for you. I don't have anywhere pressing I need to be right now, so why don't I help you get Cody inside the house and situated? Then you can explain to me what exactly happened."

Autumn smiled with tears forming in her eyes again. "I think I'd like that very much."

Once Cody was tucked into bed and comfortable, Autumn joined Alex at the kitchen table. It wasn't much of a kitchen table per se. It was just a small round table with two chairs. It wasn't even a matching set, but she couldn't pass them up for the price at a yard sale, and she needed something that she and Cody could eat on instead of sitting on the floor at the coffee table or the breakfast bar.

She pulled a bottle of wine out and offered a glass to Alex, which she happily accepted. She brought the glasses over to the table and sat down, handing one to Alex.

She took a large sip savoring the taste. She wasn't a big drinker. She'd have a glass of wine here and there, but she never drank when Cody was home. Today however called for a drink, and she was thankful to have someone join her.

She looked across the table at Alex and started to unravel the details from the fiasco at Bayside.

Autumn began by telling Alex about Kevin and how he was killed in action during a tour overseas and how Nathan, the guy from last night had been her lifeline back in California for the months afterward and how it took her having a 'come to Jesus moment,' before she realized and decided she needed to move on with her life and be on her own.

Then she told her about Nathan showing up out of the blue the other day for a surprise visit.

"Do you think Nathan may have stronger feelings for you?"

Autumn gave Alex a funny look. "You mean like he, likes me?"

"Yeah. I've seen it numerous times, having been raised in a military community. When someone loses somebody they care about, a best friend, teammate, or someone along those lines steps in to help out and fill that void, but then it leads to that person becoming attached to the individual in mourning, and next thing you know, they both find love."

Autumn took another sip of wine and considered what Alex was saying. She didn't think so because Nathan had never made any move or said anything that would insinuate he had feelings for her other than a friend. Plus, he mentioned the other night at dinner that he had a girlfriend, and it seemed pretty serious.

"I don't think so. I mean, he was there for Cody and me. He helped me with everything from the funeral to all of the paperwork needing to be filed, considering I was the spouse of a deceased soldier. Even though it's not like it did any good." She scrunched her face up.

Alex placed her wine glass down on the table and asked, "What happened with the paperwork?"

Autumn sighed. "What didn't happen? Cody and I were on a separate health insurance plan than my husband. The hospital I worked for had a great insurance plan. When Cody was born, my husband was on tour overseas, so I put Cody on my health insurance policy. Over the years, we decided that it was silly to have two insurance policies when his military policy could cover all of us.

When he received his orders that he was being deployed again, we hurried to fill out all of the necessary forms and submit them before his departure. That was when we both realized his sister was still listed as his sole beneficiary on his life insurance policy. So, while we were there, we killed two birds with one stone, and he updated his life insurance policy, removing his sister from the policy entirely and naming me as the sole beneficiary with Cody as the contingent."

"I hear a 'but' coming?" Alex stated.

Autumn took a deep breath. "Yeah, there is a big 'but.' Somehow, the paperwork was misplaced."

"What about the life insurance? Please stop me if I'm being too nosey, but did he have the max? I think it's around four-hundred-thousand dollars. Most soldiers select that."

"Yeah, he did, but without the updated paperwork, there was no proof Kevin filed anything, so all the money from the policy was given to his sister. Who, by the way, hates me. She always had, so, of course, she took every penny and ran with it, and didn't even offer anything for Cody. That's the part that really irritates me."

"What about your health coverage and your spouse survivor benefits?"

"The insurance was a nightmare. Trying to deal with the VA is like running around in a circle. I eventually got tired of the lies, excuses, and then the wait in trying to deal with them, so I just gave up. Thankfully, Cody and I still had my insurance to fall back on. I did receive the survivor's benefit, which is about $1,400, but that pretty much pays for Cody's school tuition."

Alex was stunned. Autumn was amazing, not to mention a fabulous mom. Her courage to give her son the life her husband wanted with limited resources was commendable. She deserved a damn medal of her own, and Alex completely understood Autumn's frustration with the VA. What Autumn went through was just a tiny example of why she started her foundation.

"Autumn, have you heard about the new clinic and foundation opening up in town for Veterans?"

Autumn nodded. "I have. I was speaking with a few of my colleagues at work the other day about it. A couple of us were trying to find a contact there to offer our services if they were needed. The higher-ups at the naval hospital said they would cover our pay if we wanted to volunteer one day a week there. Do you by chance know who I could contact? I think I heard they were going to open in October."

Alex chuckled, and her respect for Autumn skyrocketed. "I'm actually really, really close to the founder."

Autumn's eyes got big. "That's great! Let me grab a pen and piece of paper, so I can write down their contact information."

She went to get up, but Alex reached over, grabbing her arm, stilling Autumn's movements. "Autumn, the founder of the Jacob Hardesty Foundation, is me."

Autumn stared at her. "Come again?"

This time Alex full-out laughed at Autumn's expression. "I'm the CEO and Founder of the foundation and clinic. My full name is Alex Hardesty. My dad is...was Jacob Hardesty, US Navy SEAL killed in action."

Autumn covered her mouth. "Oh, my god, Alex! I can't tell you how many people admire what you're doing and accomplishing, including myself. And I'm sorry about your dad. But what a wonderful thing to do in memory of him."

Alex laughed and knew in just the short amount of time she'd spent with Autumn that she had made a new friend, and if Frost had a problem with it, then tough shit.

The two new friends spent another hour talking until Alex told her she'd better head home. She was surprised Ace hadn't called to track her down. She did tell him she had an errand to run on her way home. Then she remembered the team was coming over to watch the MMA fights. Shit! She was supposed to cook dinner for them. She looked down at her watch. Damn, almost eight o'clock. Well, that wasn't going to happen. They would just have to settle for pizza and wings.

After saying good-bye to Autumn and promising to get together soon, she headed home. And boy was she itching to get there because Frost would be there, and he had some major explaining to do.

CHAPTER THIRTEEN

"So, Ace…What is Alex fixing for dinner?" Skittles asked, taking a seat on the large sectional sofa in the media room. Everyone was there to watch the MMA fights. As a bonus, they were celebrating Frost's return to the team. He had passed his PRT, making it official. Well, his first official day would be in about a week. He had to go through all the paperwork first. They didn't have PT tomorrow, so they were ready to unwind with some beers and a nice home-cooked meal. That was a treat for a lot of the guys, as most were bachelors and didn't know jack shit about cooking unless it involved a microwave or opening an MRE.

Ace glanced at his watch and frowned. "I'm not sure, but she should've been home by now. She called when she was leaving work and said she had an errand to run. But that was like two and a half hours ago."

Frost watched as Ace pulled his phone from the pocket of his shorts, then walked out of the room. He looked down at his phone that was lying on the table in front of him. He glanced at the blue blinking light on it that indicated he had a voicemail. He knew who the voicemails were from, but he was still too pissed off to listen to them.

For the past couple of weeks, he'd gotten to know Autumn, and he liked everything he'd learned about her. He had made it quite clear he wanted a relationship with her. So, why hadn't she just said she had a boyfriend instead of making him look like a complete ass?

Before he could think another thought, Ace walked back into the room. And, boy, he did not look happy.

"What's with the look, Ace?" Stitch asked, walking over to the bar and pouring a beer from the tap.

"Something's wrong with Alex." Making that vague statement had all of the guys turning their immediate attention to him. Before any of them could question him further, he was quick to expand on his comment, realizing what he had said. Ever since the whole terrorist debacle with

Alex a year ago, the entire team had been protective of her and went to extreme measures to keep her safe from any harm.

"She's not in trouble…" He winced as he rubbed the back of his neck. "She sounds pissed off." Ace glanced at Frost. "She specifically asked if you were here."

Frost's eyes widened. "Me?" He pointed to himself.

Stitch laughed. "What'd you do to piss her off?"

"I didn't do anything. The last time I spoke to her was at dinner the other night. Everything was fine." *Everything was fine until he had to leave.*

Ace scrunched his eyebrows together. "She seemed fine then, and she seemed fine this morning when she left for work."

They all heard the front door slam, followed by the sound of Alex's heels clicking on the hardwood floor as she marched down the hall toward the room. Frost sat up straight as Alex walked into the room, carrying five pizza boxes and bags that smelled like wings.

She plopped everything down on the bar top and not so gently. It was silent as everyone watched her, waiting for her to make her next move. When she finally looked up and met Frost's eyes with a hard glare, he knew he was in deep shit. As for why, he wasn't so sure, but apparently, he'd fucked up somewhere, and he was getting ready to get his ass handed to him.

"Babe? Are you okay?" Ace asked in a low, calm voice as he walked over and hugged her.

While Ace had Alex occupied for a moment, Stitch moved next to Frost and nudged his arm and whispered. "What in the hell did you do, man? If looks could kill, you'd be six feet under."

Frost quickly tried to think back to between dinner the other night and now. He couldn't come up with anything. He shrugged. "I honestly have no idea."

Skittles decided to kill the silence as he grabbed himself some pizza and wings. "Man, I was craving a home-cooked meal, but I'll take it."

Alex poked her head around Ace. "I'm sorry, Skittles. I had all intentions of coming home and cooking a delicious meal for you guys, but, because asshole over there," she pointed to Frost, "can't seem to answer his phone, I had to handle something important after work, which kept me occupied longer than I expected, so you guys get pizza and wings tonight instead."

She shot her daggers back to Frost. Damn, the way the light hit her face, her green eyes almost looked like they were glowing. Frost picked up his phone and scrolled through his calls, making sure he hadn't missed a call from her. Nope, just the three missed calls from Autumn and a couple from the guys from earlier today.

"Alex, I have no idea why you seem pissed off at me. I didn't miss any important calls." Well, that was a total lie because Autumn was important to him, whether she knew it or not. He just needed a few more days to cool off.

Alex crossed her arms as she stood her ground in front of them. Frost had to give her credit. The five-foot-four woman rarely got intimidated. Most people pulling a stunt like she was right now in front of a group of SEALs wouldn't last long. Hell, he had killed enemy combatants for less.

"You didn't miss anything important today?" She said, raising one of her eyebrows. Oh, he knew that look. She did have something on his ass. But what? "How about explaining first why you missed your PT appointment this morning. Don't you need that to get cleared to take the PRT on Thursday?"

Well, shit...He did cancel the appointment, but he had a perfectly good excuse. He opened his mouth to respond, but Ace intervened. "Alex, he took his PRT this morning."

Alex seemed surprised by Ace's confirmation. He owed him a drink for saving his ass from his best friend's fierce claws, but then the wheels started turning in his head. How in the hell did she even know he was a no show for PT? Had the little wench been spying on him? She'd been on his ass like flies on shit since he was discharged from the hospital.

He looked over at Alex and gave her the evil eye right back. "How did you even know about my appointment?"

Instead of answering his question, she asked. "Have you checked your voicemail today?"

He looked at his phone again, and the indicator said he had two voicemails. He knew they were from Autumn. Wait a minute. How the fuck did she know about the voicemails? Alex was a smart woman, but unless she gained ESP in the last few days, someone was giving her inside information.

"I'll take your silence as a no. Why don't you listen to them now?"

"I'll listen to my voicemail when I'm damn well ready to." He loved his best friend dearly, but she was really starting to piss him off.

"No, you'll listen to them NOW!"

Jesus, he knew he'd lose this battle, so he might as well get it over with and appease her highness before she blew a gasket, and then they could all get on with the rest of the night.

He hit the button to listen. "No, put it on speaker," she said.

"What?"

"You heard me. Put the damn phone on speaker."

What the hell? Was she serious? She narrowed her eyes and raised her eyebrows. Fuck! She was serious.

He mumbled 'fine' and hit the speaker button and the first message.

"Hey, Frost...It's umm Autumn. Listen, please give me a call. I need to explain the other night. It's not what you think. Bye."

O-okay...he thought to himself. What was so special about that? It was what he was expecting. He looked up at Alex. "You know I could have listened to that privately without an audience, Alex." He was a little pissed off at his friend's meddling.

Ace looked over at Alex. "Sweetheart, what's this all about?"

She gave Ace a nasty look, and Frost could have sworn he heard her growl at Ace. He actually wanted to laugh until Alex shot him a look and demanded he listen to the next one. So, once again, he pressed the button to get to the next message. This time, though, he heard a completely different tone in Autumn's voice, and the panic he heard made his heart stop.

"Frost, it's Autumn. I'm so sorry to call you, but I didn't know who else to call." He heard her sniffling. Was she crying? He glanced up to look at Alex and saw her eyes were a little glassy. What the fuck was going on? *"I don't have my car today, and Cody was involved in an accident at school, and he's been taken to the hospital by ambulance."* There was a pause for a few seconds, and he could hear her breathing deeply. *"God...this is so stupid. You're not answering your phone, so you obviously can't help me."* There was another pause, then a click sound, indicating she disconnected the call.

Fuck! Cody was hurt, and she called him when she needed help, and because of his childlike actions, he now felt like a first-class ass.

He stood and looked at Alex. "How did you know?" He put his phone in his pocket and pulled out his car keys. He was going to see her. Jesus, he didn't know if she was at home or was still at the hospital. How did she get to the hospital? Nathan? *No. Don't even go there. Now is not the time to even think about that prick.* Cody was who was most important right now.

Alex sighed. "I know because I've been with her and Cody for the past two hours."

Frost stood speechless as he stared at his best friend. "What?" He asked, clearly confused.

"You gave her my phone number, remember? The good news is, she follows orders well."

She smirked at him, and then it dawned on him. "She called you when she couldn't get a hold of me," he stated.

The guys looked like they were watching a tennis match with all the back and forth he and Alex were doing.

"Yeah, she did. But she didn't call me until she was trying to find a ride home from the hospital. She ended up taking a cab from the Naval Hospital to the local one." Frost knew how far of a drive that was, and cabs weren't cheap. That must have had to cost a fortune. He listened as Alex continued. "She was embarrassed to have to call me, but she was desperate. She didn't want to have to take the bus since it was getting late."

Frost mumbled to himself as he started to pace the room. "Is Cody okay? I mean, what happened?"

"He's okay. He fell at school and hit the side of his head pretty good. Initially, he was knocked out, but he regained consciousness in the ambulance on the way to the hospital. All of the scans were clean. He has a concussion and will probably have a pretty good headache for the next couple of days. When I left their house, he was sleeping. Autumn has to wake him every thirty minutes throughout the night and monitor his symptoms."

"How is Autumn?"

Alex took a deep breath. "With everything she's been put through today, I'd say she's doing pretty damn good. She's, of course, exhausted, plus she's pissed off about her car."

"Shit. Her car was acting up last week, but then she told me it was fine."

"Yeah. Well, it wouldn't start this morning, not to mention her right front tire was flat."

Frost walked over to Alex and hugged her and kissed her cheek. "Thank you."

She tilted her head back to look up at him. "Don't fuck this up. She's a keeper."

"She's seeing someone, Alex. I already fucked up and waited too long."

Alex shook her head, her long chestnut brown hair swinging back and forth as she did. "No, she's not. And you would've known this if you hadn't acted like a child and ignored her calls. Nathan is just a good friend. Anyway, he's involved with someone else back in California. He's in town for business over at the base in Norfolk and stopped by to surprise Autumn and Cody."

135

Oh, shit. Did he ruin his chance with Autumn because he was being a stubborn, jealous jerk? "I need to see her, Alex. You've been to her place. Where is it?"

"That depends." Frost arched an eyebrow at her. "Are you done acting like an asshole?"

"Alex!" Ace growled. But the others, including Frost, all chuckled. Alex had a habit of calling out the team members when they were, in fact, being assholes.

Alex looked at Ace and stuck her tongue out at him, then turned back to Frost. "Fine. But I need to warn you; you aren't going to be happy where she lives. She lives in that complex of duplexes about two miles from the base. You know the one that all of the drug dealers hang out at."

"Why in the hell would she choose to live there? Surely she had enough money from her husband's life insurance plus the supplement the government gives her for spousal support."

He gave Alex a pleading look. "It's not my story to tell, but I will tell you she opened up to me tonight as a friend. And I am telling you that she is my friend now. Whether or not you two patch things up, there will be times you will see her because there is no way I'm turning my back on her now. Tenley met her as well at the hospital, and she feels the same."

Was there anything Alex didn't fix? Frost gave her another hug and kiss. "Thank you. I owe you."

She grinned and squeezed him back. "Damn straight, you do. I'll collect later, now go get your girl."

CHAPTER FOURTEEN

Autumn stepped out of the steaming hot shower. She wished she had a bathroom that had a big Jacuzzi tub that she could soak in. That was an amenity she'd wished for all her life but one she'd never had. Her house in California was base housing. Those houses were nothing fancy. Though at least with that house, she had a normal tub that if she needed to soak, she could. Here, all she had was a tiny shower stall in her bathroom. Cody's bathroom had the same set-up. She was lucky she even found a house she could afford that had two bathrooms.

She toweled off and looked at her reflection in the mirror. Her red hair was what garnered her a lot of attention. She had a decent figure for mom standards. At least that was what she thought. Of course, certain parts of her body were never going to be the way they used to be pre-pregnancy. Cody was worth the stretch marks. He was her life and what had kept her breathing. Anyway, she was never really the type of person who was always worried about how they looked, probably because she had met her husband at such an early age. She tried to get in a few workouts during the week at the gym the hospital had made available to the employees. Most of the time, it was walking and jogging on one of the treadmills.

Her mind floated to Frost. He would probably consider her body chunky and soft compared to the women who normally threw themselves at him. Nope, she wasn't going to think about him. He'd obviously made his choice since she hadn't heard from him. She shook those thoughts away, stepped out of the bathroom, strode over to her dresser and pulled out a thin black V-neck t-shirt and grey lounge pants. She was in for a long night with Cody, so she might as well as get comfortable. The cool air from the air conditioner caused goosebumps along her skin.

As she brushed her hair out, she couldn't get Frost out of her head. She knew damn well that Frost assumed she and Nathan were dating. But if the tables were turned and she had seen Frost out with another woman even though they were just friends, she would probably assume the same.

But damn Nathan and his possessiveness. She knew he meant well and felt responsible for looking after her and Cody because her husband had asked him to do so. But she needed to be strong, not only for herself but for Cody as well. That was why she chose to leave California and move across the country in the first place. She needed to gain control of her life and start living again.

She thought back to what Alex had said about Nathan. Was it possible he had feelings for her? But he mentioned he was dating someone back in California. She supposed it was always possible, but why hadn't he ever said anything to her or acted on those feelings? Not that she would've accepted his advances. She just didn't have those types of feelings toward him. He would always be her husband's best friend and a close friend of the family.

She glanced at the clock. It was almost ten. Another couple of minutes and she would need to go and wake Cody again. He had taken about ten years off her life with his accident today. Hearing from a school nurse that her son was knocked unconscious and on his way to the hospital was not a phone call any parent wanted to receive.

She shook off the shiver that traveled through her body. She pulled on her t-shirt and pants. She had just stepped out into the small hallway and was heading into Cody's room when she heard a knock at the door.

She froze, wondering who would be at her house at this time of the night. She thought about Mrs. Higdon next door. That woman was always looking for someone to talk to, and it didn't matter what time it was. Mrs. Higdon had lost her husband a few years ago, and neither she nor her husband had any family. Autumn thought that because she and Cody didn't have any family either, it was why she and Mrs. Higdon became close within the year she had lived here. The older woman was very motherly and great with Cody. Cody had even stayed with her a few times when she'd had to run out for a quick errand.

Mrs. Higdon knew that Autumn was up if she saw lights on in the house and she would stop by. She probably had been watching the house earlier and saw Alex and now wanted to know who she was. Mrs. Higdon was nosey like that, but Autumn loved the older woman anyway.

She thought back to what Alex had said about getting together this coming Saturday. She hoped it was a start to a friendship. She liked Alex a lot and was looking forward to spending next Saturday with her and Tenley. They were planning a spa day with facials, manicures, and pedicures. Not that she should be spending her well-earned money on something that materialistic, but it had been years since she had done something for herself. So, yeah, she was going to splurge a little.

Another knock sounded, this time louder and more forceful. She walked to the door and opened it, not bothering to look through the peephole, knowing it was Mrs. Higdon being impatient. However, swinging the door open, she came face-to-face with Frost. Her mouth gaped open, and she felt her nipples harden. What in the hell was that all about? Her body betrayed her.

Frost was a bundle of nerves as he pulled into Autumn's housing complex. Using the directions Alex gave him, he parked his Tahoe in the guest parking spot in front of Autumn's duplex. As he got out, he scanned the area. It was a habit considering his line of work. Always know your surroundings. It was ingrained in his head during BUD/S training.

Other than a lady who looked to be in her seventies standing outside of the house next door to Autumn's, everything seemed calm and quiet. He wasn't a fan of the complex she was living in, though. Everyone knew it was a known hangout for drug dealers and prostitutes. He bit the inside of his cheek at the thought.

As he walked up to Autumn's front door, he felt eyes on him. When he looked next door, the same lady was watching him intently. He nodded his head in her direction, and she gave him a faint smile. She seemed innocent, but there was something else he was feeling. His sixth sense was at work again. He scanned the area once more as he approached the door. Some people were hanging out in front of a house a few doors down, and the house across the street was dark, but he noticed the curtain in the front window moved. He turned around, chalking it up to neighbors just being nosy. If he lived in a complex like this, he would want to know who was coming and going, so he couldn't really blame the person for looking.

He knocked on the door and frowned. The damn door was the cheapest door made to man. That didn't sit well with him, knowing the kind of activities taking place in this area. He'd have to rectify that quickly. As he waited, he thought to himself he probably should've called Autumn first before just showing up on her doorstep late at night. Then again, he didn't want to allow her to reject him. Nope, surprising her is better.

It seemed like a couple of minutes went by, so he knocked again, this time with a little more force behind it. He saw a light flick on behind the blinds. He ran his sweaty palms down his cargo shorts. Fuck, he was nervous. He wasn't sure how she was going to react to seeing him. He was getting ready to pull his phone out to call her when the door opened.

His breath hitched in his throat. She stood there wearing what looked to be her pajamas, and he bit the inside of his cheek again. The thin material of her black t-shirt didn't hide her hard nipples. Instantly, he felt his cock harden beneath his cargo shorts. His attraction to her was strong, and he wanted to ravish her body, but he knew he had a lot of making up to do. They needed to iron out a lot of details. And it started with him needing to apologize for being an ass.

"Frost?"

He nodded his head. "Hey, Autumn. May I come in?" He prayed she wouldn't shut the door in his face. Not that he would blame her if she did because he totally deserved it.

But she didn't, nor did she say anything further. She just stepped back and opened the door wider and gestured with her hand for him to come in.

Step one, conquered. He'd made it through the door with ease. The next step was to grovel.

She shut the door behind him and crossed her arms in front of her chest. She didn't make a move toward him. Her body language read she was being cautious. Shit, he'd feel that way too if the roles were reversed.

140

He took the few seconds of silence to look around. There wasn't much to the inside of the place. It was small. And by small, it was tiny—a small living room connected to a tiny kitchen. And a hallway that probably led to the bedrooms. In all brutal honesty, the apartment he shared with Stitch was bigger than this place. She had it decorated nicely in a beachy theme. She also had pictures of her and Cody scattered around the room in frames. It felt homey considering the size.

When his eyes landed back on his Irish beauty, she was still watching him cautiously. She was probably wondering if she should throw him out. Not that he would blame her. One of them needed to break the ice, so he decided it would be him. Clearing his throat, he asked her, "How is Cody?"

Autumn didn't answer, but her eyes grew wide. Dropping her arms to her side, she started walking toward the hallway quickly. Her quick actions had Frost moving in behind her. When he got to the hall, he realized he was right. There was a bathroom and a bedroom on each side of it. Again, the house was like a crackerjack box; it was so small.

He followed on her heels to the bedroom on the right. His eyes wandered down to her ass as she walked in front of him. Yeah, bad timing, but he was a man, and the way her ass swayed as she walked in those lounge pants had him adjusting himself.

Standing taller than Autumn, he was able to see over her head when they entered the room. The room, like the rest of the house, was tiny. It was painted in a light grey color and seemed like a typical ten-year-old boy's room. However, this boy's room was impeccably clean and organized. There were posters on the walls of sports teams and music groups—some military paraphernalia, presumably given to him by his dad. But what also caught his eye on a shelf above his desk that made him grin was the SEAL Team 2 cap he had given Cody. Next to it was a framed picture of Cody with him and the guys from that day.

He watched as Autumn sat down on the bed with Cody and gently ran her fingers through his brown hair. She said something, but Frost couldn't make out what it was because her voice was so low, but Cody began to shift his body, and then his eyes opened.

141

"Mommy?" Frost could hear the pain and exhaustion in Cody's sleepy voice. When Autumn shifted her body, Frost caught a glimpse of the side of Cody's head. The skin by his temple was bruised and swollen, and the road rash along his cheekbone looked nasty.

"Hey, sleepyhead. How ya doing? Not feeling sick or anything, are ya?" Her sweet voice saturating through the room.

"No, just tired. Can I go back to sleep?"

She laughed and leaned over and kissed his forehead. "Sure, honey. Do you need anything? Some water, maybe, or do you need to use the bathroom?"

"No, I'm good," he said as his eyes started drifting closed again.

"Okay, sweetie. I'll be back to check on you."

Frost watched silently from the doorway as Autumn tended and cared for her son. The gentle touches and the whispers she gave him reminded Frost of his mom when he was younger. She cared for him and his brother the same way when they were hurt or sick. It was apparent her son always came first, and Frost admired her for it.

After giving Cody another kiss on the head, she got up and turned toward Frost, and his gut clenched, seeing the strain and exhaustion on her face. She was hanging on by a thread.

She walked toward him, and he backed out into the small hallway. She shut the bedroom door and tried to move past him, but his body took up most of it, blocking her from moving by him. He reached out and grabbed her hand. "Autumn?" He spoke in a low tone as to not disturb Cody.

She kept her head down, but he heard the deep unsteady breath she took. Taking his other hand, he touched her chin lightly, making her head tilt back, so she was looking at him. When her watery green eyes met his, he wasn't surprised to see the tears silently rolling down her cheeks.

"Aw, babe. Come here." He pulled her into his chest, securing his arms around her as he leaned his back against the wall. Her slender arms went around his waist instantly, and her hands clutched the back of his t-shirt. She felt so petite in his arms. With her face tucked against the side of his neck, he could feel the wetness from her tears on his skin. She was breathing heavily, probably trying to keep from sobbing out loud. He placed a kiss on the side of her head, then scooped her up and carried her out to the kitchen.

He set her feet down on the tiled floor. Keeping one arm around her waist, he pulled a paper towel from the holder on the counter and gently wiped the tears from her red, splotchy face. He laughed to himself. She was not a pretty crier, but most people weren't. She tried to lower her head again, but he wasn't having that. They were going to straighten a few things out.

He made himself at home, not caring the least. He reached into the tiny refrigerator that wasn't even full size and pulled out a bottle of water for her. What he didn't like seeing were the bare shelves in the fridge. He would add that to his list of things to talk to her about, later. By the time he left her house, she was going to understand that they should give this thing a shot.

He handed her the bottle of water and got himself one. Taking her hand, he brought her around the counter to the two bar stools at the small breakfast bar. If you even wanted to call it that. Jesus, this house was like being inside a damn dollhouse. He felt like a giant in it.

He took a seat on one of the stools and pulled her in-between his splayed thighs. Her body felt so good pressed against him. He nudged her chin up, and the sad look she had in her eyes made him feel like a big pile of shit. Knowing he was partially responsible for it hit him deep inside. She needed him, and he needed her.

"Frost…"

"Jack," he barked, interrupting her.

"Huh?"

He grinned, holding onto her waist. "My name is Jack. I want you to call me Jack."

"Oh….O-okay, Jack." She smiled. "I like Jack."

He laughed. "Well, that's good because I'd hate to have to change it. I hear the process is a royal pain in the ass."

She slapped his chest playfully and smiled, which was what Frost was hoping for, to make her smile. He didn't like seeing her upset and crying. "You know what I meant….*Jack*." She said his name, emphasizing it, but he had to admit, he loved hearing his name roll off her lips. Lips that he couldn't wait to kiss.

He grabbed her hand before she could pull it away and held it to his chest. The warmth from her palm seeped through his shirt and into his skin. He took his other arm and wrapped it around her waist and pulled her even closer to him. With her body wedged in-between his thighs, his heart beat rapidly at the feel of her body pressed against his. She brought her free hand up to his chest, where her other hand rested and looked up at him. Even sitting on the stool, he was still slightly taller than her.

"I owe you an apology for the other night." Her voice sounded shaky and nervous.

He released her hand and put his index finger over her pink lips. God, he wanted to nibble and taste those lips. "Shhh…If anyone needs to apologize; it's me."

He could tell he shocked her by the way she scrunched her eyebrows together. "Why would you owe me an apology? I'm the one who led you to believe there was something between Nathan and me, though that wasn't my intention at all. Nathan showed up out of the blue that morning, wanting to surprise Cody and me, and he asked if he could take us to dinner. Then when I caught your expression after you saw Nathan and me together, I knew you felt betrayed. But to tell you the truth, I panicked. I didn't want Nathan to know about you. At least not yet. I mean, gosh, what are we?" She asked him as her green eyes focused on him. She rambled on and was starting to get herself worked up again. She probably hadn't even realized she was fisting his t-shirt, and she was staring at the stove.

"Autumn…" He said in a deep, commanding voice.

She snapped her shamrock green eyes back to Frost, and he had to bite his lip. Christ, what he would do to have her on her knees, looking up at him like she was right at this moment with her lips wrapped around his cock.

Not the time, asshole. You're here to apologize and make things right. Not scare her off.

He closed his eyes for a quick second and released a small groan.

"Are you okay?" She asked, running her hands up and down his chest. Her touch sent a fire through his veins. He grabbed her hands to stop her movement before she could do any more damage to him.

She gave him a look, then tried to pull her hands away, but he gripped them tighter, holding them still against his chest.

Shit! Now she thinks I insulted her and don't want her touching me.

He grinned. "Sorry, sugar, but I'm trying really hard here to be a gentleman like my mother taught me to be and take things slow, but the feel of your hands touching me right now is like waving a red flag in front of a bull. You don't know how much the alpha male in me wants to throw you over my shoulder right now and march you into your bedroom, spread your body out on your bed and ravish it from head to toe. But I won't because I know you need things to go slow. Plus, I'd never have sex with you, knowing Cody is practically right next door. I'd never disrespect him or you for that matter like that. Like I've told you before, I want to know everything about you. I want to know everything that makes you function." He lowered his head, so they were eye level, and he looked into her eyes.

"And to answer your question about what we are. You. Are. Mine. Let's call the other night a failure in communication on both sides. Tell me you want to be with me as much as I want to be with you, Autumn. Agree to go out on a 'real' date with me this weekend. Just you and I. I'll come and pick you up, and we'll go someplace nice for dinner, and maybe if it's nice outside, we can go for a walk on the beach. What do you say? Please just put me out of my misery and be with me."

He sat there as she stared back into his eyes. It was like she was trying to see past all of the negatives. He saw her eyes soften, and then she swallowed hard, then whispered so softly, her voice was full of emotion.

"I want to be with you too. And, yes, I would love to go on a 'real' date with you."

145

"Good. Now even though I said sex is off the table, at least for tonight, that is," he smiled and winked, causing her fair skin cheeks to turn crimson. "There is one thing that's been driving me crazy since the moment you walked into my hospital room weeks ago."

She pulled away and gave him a questionable look. "And what would that be?"

He widened his legs further and pulled her even closer, making her tilt her head way back to look up at him. One arm held her around the waist while his other hand cupped her chin. He ran this thumb over her bottom lip as he looked her in the eyes. "I've been dying to taste you." He didn't wait for a response before pressing his lips gently against hers. He started out slow, but when he felt her kissing him back, he ran his tongue along the seam of her lips, testing the waters further. She parted her lips, inviting him in, and he felt her silky tongue meet his as her arms went around his neck. His hand at her waist slid down over her ass and squeezed it. The move made her moan, causing his cock to beg for release from the confinement of his shorts. She ran her hands through his short hair. Her nails scraped lightly against his scalp, sending vibrations through his body. He was so turned on right now. He needed to put the brakes on before he went against what he promised her he wouldn't do.

He pulled back from the kiss and looked her over. She was panting and looked flushed. Her lips were swollen and red. He cupped the back of her neck and pressed his forehead against hers and gazed into her lust-filled eyes. "What have you done to me, woman?" She smiled, and he kissed her nose.

"Taking things slow is going to be fucking torture."

He slid his sleek body off the stool but didn't let go of her hand. If he could have his way, he'd find a way to attach himself to her permanently. He guided her to the small periwinkle-colored sofa a few feet away. He sat down and pulled her down next to him. The house was quiet except for the slight hum of the window air conditioning unit.

She laid her head on his shoulder and looked up at him. "Jack, what are you doing?"

He leaned forward, pulled over the little ottoman that matched the sofa, and propped his feet up, getting himself comfortable. Taking his arm closest to her, he wrapped it around her shoulders and pulled her towards him, until she was once again resting her head on his shoulder and snuggled up against him.

He looked down into her inquisitive green eyes. "You said you had to wake Cody every thirty minutes. I'm going to sit with you, so you're not alone." There was no way in hell he was going to sit by and let her burn herself out. Now that he was involved in their lives, he would do his damnedest to take some of the burden off her, starting now.

"Thank you, Jack," she whispered as she pulled her legs and feet up onto the sofa and tucked them under her.

He kissed the top of her head. The smell of her fruity shampoo infiltrated his nose. "I'd do anything for you, Autumn," he whispered back as he held her.

They sat there for a while, neither one of them saying a word. Frost actually had thought she had fallen asleep until she spoke.

"I'm scared, Jack." She kept her head against his chest, and he rubbed her back.

"What are you afraid of? My job?"

Rubbing her nose against his shirt, she answered. "Yes. I already lost one person I loved to a war. I don't know if my heart could take it if I gave it to another man, and history repeats itself."

Frost could understand where she was coming from, but he needed to make her understand.

"You can't think about it that way, babe. You can't predict the future. Hell, I could get hit by a bus tomorrow just walking down the street."

"Don't say that." She lifted her head and glared at him. He used his hand to move her hair out of her face.

"I'm just trying to make you see that not all bad things that happen to military personnel are the result of the war. Take my leg injury, for example."

"You were shot. You were injured in battle. I don't know the circumstances surrounding it, as I'm sure it's classified."

He took her face into her hands and looked deeply into her eyes. "You see, that's where you're wrong. I wasn't deployed when I was shot, nor was I involved in any type of training mission. I wasn't even on the job when this occurred."

"You weren't?" She asked, looking confused, although Frost thought she looked adorable with her forehead scrunched up.

"Nope. Long story short. Tenley, who I heard you met today, got into some trouble, though it wasn't her fault. I had been protecting her and her daughter when one of the guys after her ambushed us outside of a store. The guy tried to shoot at Tenley's daughter, but I made it to her in time and took the bullet instead."

"Oh, my god. What happened? Did they catch the guys who did it? And was Tenley and her daughter okay?"

"Eventually, he was caught and killed. But not before he had kidnapped Tenley and beat her up pretty bad. She's okay now. She and Potter are expecting their first child."

"I know, Tenley told me."

"They adopted Alejandra from Ecuador. When that earthquake struck that region back at Christmas, Alejandra was unfortunately left as an orphan. Both of her parents were killed, and she had no other family. Tenley was a volunteer with the humanitarian aid group down there. She was there for about a month. When she met Alejandra, they bonded from the get-go, and the rest was history. Same goes for Potter."

"Wow! I had no idea. Tenley and I talked a little bit, but she didn't mention any of that. What an amazing woman. Just like Alex. You know, Alex didn't even question me when I asked her about needing a ride home tonight. She told me she understood and would be at the hospital in twenty minutes."

"Well, Alex has her own story of survival. Most of her story is classified, though, but what I can tell you is that she survived being held captive by a terrorist who wanted revenge against her. She was working

148

with me and the team on a mission in a place that tourists would be stupid to go. That is actually where she and Ace met. But she was kidnapped right under our noses. It was amazing we were even able to locate her, but we did. Her condition when we found her is something I don't think I will ever get out of my head." His mind flashed back to that day when Bear carried her out of the building to the awaiting helicopter—seeing her shot with blood oozing from her upper chest. Practically every inch of her body was black and blue from the beatings she sustained at the hands of a mad man and his men.

Autumn cupped his cheek, bringing his attention back to her.

"Jack, I can tell whatever happened still haunts you. You don't have to tell me anymore if you don't want to. I understand."

He smiled and kissed the palm of her hand. Autumn was too sweet, and he loved that she wasn't the type of person who pushed for answers. It would be very helpful for when he was on the job.

"You saying that means a whole hell of a lot, sugar. But you should know some of it because with the amount of time you'll be spending with the team, you are bound to see some of her scars. I just want you to be prepared, so you're not shocked or wonder what they were."

"Okay."

He took a deep breath. "She was tortured. Tortured to the point that when we found her, we thought she was dead. Everything that happened between her and the men who were holding her was caught on film. And all I will say is that she fought to survive. That included killing five of her captors. She has some scarring along her back from what they did to her." He chuckled. "But in the end, she kicked ass just like her uncles had taught her, and she survived and won the battle. I don't know if Alex told you this, but our commander raised her when her father was killed in action. He and the rest of the team that is."

He looked down and saw the emotion in Autumn's eyes.

"Alex and Tenley sound like wonderful women who you are very proud of."

149

"Yeah, they both hold a special place in my heart. But you know what?"

"What?" She whispered.

"I still have room in there for another amazing woman who I'd love to care for and protect along with her son."

She smiled up at him. "You do, huh?"

He grinned and dropped his head down, "Yeah, I do," right before his mouth covered hers and kissed her deeply. He ended the kiss and pulled her closer to his side.

"Take a nap. I'll take first watch." She curled up next to him and laid her hand on his chest, and he swore he felt his heart skip a beat.

CHAPTER FIFTEEN

Mmmm...Hazelnut coffee. Autumn lifted her head and sniffed the air. She wasn't dreaming; she really was smelling hazelnut coffee. The problem with that was she didn't have a coffee maker in her house. Mrs. Higdon next door did and always brought over coffee. That was how she got addicted to hazelnut. Some mornings, Cody would wake up before she did and run next door and bring her back a coffee, surprising her in bed with it.

Her eyes suddenly sprung open as a major thought hit her. *Cody!* Crap, she had fallen asleep on the couch last night when she was supposed to wake Cody every thirty minutes. Then memories of last night came flooding back. She hadn't just fallen asleep on the couch. No, she fell asleep on Jack. And she kissed him! Oh, God, he was such a great kisser. And the way he had spoken to her, made her insides melt. She must have been exhausted, not even to hear him leave.

She'd worry about that later. Right now, she needed to make sure that Cody was okay. She jumped up from her tiny couch and went to take a step but tripped on a pair of shoes. With her brain not yet firing on all cylinders, she didn't catch herself, and she ended up face planting on the floor. Thank goodness, the living room had carpet. As she lay there, a thought hit her. She didn't leave any shoes in the living room, and she took Cody's off him before she got him into bed in his room. She turned her head and saw a pair of tennis shoes. And not just any tennis shoes. They were men's tennis shoes. What the hell?

She heard his voice. "Shit, Autumn!" No, it couldn't be. Did he stay here at her place last night? She put her head back down. She thought she was still dreaming until she felt the strong hands go around her arms and lift her. She tilted her head back, so she was looking up at him. His light brown eyes held a twinkle to them this morning, and he had that sexy morning gruff on his face. God, he was an absolute eye-catcher.

"Am I dreaming, or are you really standing in my living room?" His laughter made her grin. "I guess that answers my question."

He rubbed his hands up and down her arms. "Are you okay? I didn't mean to leave my shoes where you could trip on them."

"Yeah, I'll be okay. Why are you still here?" She asked, running a hand through her hair to tame the mess. She wasn't one of those women who could wake up and look like a million dollars.

"I told you last night I was staying with you."

"I remember, but I fell asleep. You didn't wake me. What about Cody? Nobody checked on him."

He leaned down and kissed her. It was just a quick kiss, and when he pulled back, he had that adorable grin on his face, the one that made his dimple show.

"Cody's fine." He gestured to the breakfast bar behind her, where Cody was sitting eating pancakes.

Cody turned around with a mouth full of food.

"Mom! You gotta try Frost's pancakes. They're awesome."

She looked up at Frost. "You made pancakes?" He smiled and nodded.

"But…How?"

He started to walk back to the stove and spoke over his shoulder. "Well, it's simple. You open the box of pancake mix, put it in the bowl, and then add eggs – Ow!" He jumped and rubbed his side as he laughed. "You pinched me?"

"And you are a smart-ass." He laughed even harder. "Now you know that was not what I meant. I didn't have any pancake mix, so how are you making them?" She looked at the pan on the stove, and the site of the pancakes made her mouth water. They were golden, cooked perfectly, and looked so fluffy.

"While you were sleeping, Cody and I got ourselves ready, and we went to the store and did some grocery shopping."

"You went grocery shopping?" He nodded.

"Cody wanted pancakes and sausage for breakfast." She stood next to him as he flipped pancakes. He took one of the pancakes and broke a piece off, and held it for her to take. She leaned forward, opened her mouth, and he slipped the fluffy morsel into her mouth. Damn, it may just be pancakes, but the man knew how to make them perfectly.

"These are delicious."

He placed two on a plate and handed it to her and gave her a quick kiss. "Go sit with Cody and eat."

"What about you? Aren't you going to eat with us?"

He smiled. "Yep. As soon as these last two are finished cooking."

She walked around and sat on the other stool. She leaned over and kissed Cody on the cheek. Then her eye caught the three bags of groceries sitting on the small table in the kitchen. Tomorrow was her grocery shopping day, but from the looks of it, she could cross that errand off the list. She'd pay Frost back later.

"Thanks for going to the store. That was on my list of things to do for tomorrow."

He smiled. "No problem. Glad I could help."

She looked at Cody. The side of his head looked bad. It was purple and red from the bruising. "How are you feeling, sweetie? Any symptoms the doctor said you needed to watch for?"

He wiped his mouth with his napkin. "No, just my head hurts a little."

"Well, I imagine it's going to hurt a little for a few days." She took another bite and set her fork down. Frost had joined them now. He was standing on the other side of the breakfast bar. "You know, with all of the chaos yesterday, I never asked, how did you fall down?"

"Some lady..." Cody's forehead scrunched up. "I think she was a parent picking up her kid. Anyway, she knocked into me, and I lost my balance, and my foot slipped off the curb."

Frost had a fork full of pancakes and stopped mid-way to his mouth and set it back down on his plate. Now he had a scowl on his face. "You mean to tell me that an adult knocked you down?" Cody bobbed his head up and down. "Did she help you? At least say she was sorry?"

"I don't think so. But I'm not positive. I passed out a few seconds after I hit the ground, and I didn't wake up until I was in the ambulance."

Frost looked at Autumn. "Somebody should've seen what happened. You should ask the school on Monday."

"I plan to. I'm surprised they didn't even call to check up on him. After all, it happened on their property."

"Yeah, well, that school has a reputation for only caring about the flow of money coming in and not much about the students. There are a lot of people who don't care much for that school. That is unless you are filthy rich, and all you care about is your status within the community, and then if you had children and didn't send them there, you were frowned upon for doing so."

"Trust me. I wish I could send Cody to public school. Not to mention, it would help financially."

"Why don't you?"

"Yeah, Mom. Why don't I go to the school with my friends Justin and Caden?"

"Basically, it's because of logistics. I don't have anyone to watch Cody while I'm at work. His school is right near the hospital, and Corrine sends her son there, and she's able to pick him up for me and drop him off at the hospital. Believe me, if I could send him to a public school, we certainly wouldn't be living here."

She could tell Frost wanted to question her more, but she was grateful he chose not to.

Instead, she decided to divert the conversation.

"Speaking of next week, are you excited to get back in all of the fray with the guys? Your leg is feeling up to it."

"Actually, that's what I wanted to see. Do you guys have plans today?"

"Not really, I just need to make sure I get a few hours of work in today. But I can do that anytime. Why?"

"You have to work? Today? It's Saturday."

She remembered she hadn't told him everything about her life and how she needed to work a second job.

"It's not the work you're thinking of. I do some side work for some of the doctors at the hospital."

"What kind of side work?"

"Transcribing their notes. Some doctors still like to record their notes by voice, then go back and put them on paper into the patients' charts."

"Doesn't the hospital have the staff to handle that?"

"No. Believe it or not, they're short-staffed. You know, with funding and budgeting. Anyway, I don't mind doing it. It's additional income."

"Huh…" He rubbed a hand over his jaw.

Then he remembered what Alex had said last night when he mentioned Autumn's income. Alex's words to him were that it wasn't her story to tell. He wasn't going to question her about it now. Not with Cody in the room. But it was at the top of his list of things he wanted to discuss with her. She and Cody were now his responsibility, which included making sure they were well taken care of.

"Anyway, like I said, I can do that anytime. Why? Did you have something in mind?"

He picked up her empty plate and put it in the sink.

"Ace called this morning, and he and Alex invited us over for lunch. Potter and Tenley will be there along with their daughter Alejandra. They have a pool, and I thought maybe the kids could meet one another and go swimming.

"Please, Mom? Can we go?" Cody's eyes lit up. He loved meeting new kids.

Autumn laughed. Cody would go anywhere with Frost and his teammates. As she considered the offer, she felt different. It was hard to explain, but it was a feeling of acceptance. These people whom she just met who were pretty much welcoming her with open arms. She'd be stupid not to accept. Plus, she owed Alex for last night. She looked back at Frost and smiled.

"Could you call Alex and ask her what I can bring?"

"You all set?" Frost asked Autumn as she emerged from her bedroom, looking fresh and ready to have some fun. She was wearing a pair of black shorts and a purple sleeveless top and black flip flops. She smiled and

155

nodded her head. He hoped she would enjoy hanging out with some of his friends. Originally, Ace was planning on inviting the entire team, but he nixed that after Alex suggested that it may be too overwhelming for Autumn. A lot of times, the guys would bring dates with them. This way, Alex and Tenley could bond with Autumn without having to play nice with other women who weren't technically part of their unit. Plus, Cody still needed to take it easy. He was surprised Autumn had agreed to let him go swimming, though she did lay down some rules on keeping the roughhousing to a minimum.

They gathered everything up. Cody grabbed the swim bag with the towels and a change of clothes, Autumn grabbed her purse, and Frost carried the buffalo chicken dip Autumn had made. He inhaled the aroma from the buffalo sauce as he carried the dish, and it made his mouth water. He kept trying to sneak some while she was making it, and she kept slapping his hand.

He was the last one to step out of the house, closing the front door and making sure it was locked. Not like the door could keep anyone out. He scanned the street, and again, he got that uneasy feeling. He looked to the right where the elderly lady was last night, and he caught sight of her. She was sitting in a rocking chair doing some sort of sewing. Autumn had walked over and was speaking with her, so he decided to join her.

"Mrs. Higdon, I'd like you to meet Jack. Jack, this is Mrs. Higdon, my neighbor, and friend," Autumn said as Frost approached.

He shook her hand. "It's nice to meet you, ma'am."

"Likewise," she said as she eyed him up and down and then gave Autumn a sly grin. "You done good, girl."

Frost threw his back and laughed as Autumn's mouth gaped open at the woman's words.

"You're in the military," she said, more as a statement than a question.

"Yes, ma'am. Navy."

She gave him a soft smile. "I thought so. You all look like you're on your way out, so don't let me make you late. You take good care of our girl and her boy. I hope to see you around more, Jack."

He smiled back at her. Meeting her and exchanging a few words with her, Frost already liked Mrs. Higdon. The way he saw it, Mrs. Higdon was a lot closer to Autumn than just a neighbor.

"I'm sure you will."

"Good to hear. Now you all get on out of here."

Autumn leaned down and hugged Mrs. Higdon, but to his surprise, when he went to shake her hand again, she pulled him down and hugged him too. She reminded him of his grandmother. Before she let him go, she whispered something.

"I mean it, Jack. She and that boy are special. You treat her well, and she'll make you very happy."

"She already makes me happy, ma'am. And, I don't plan on letting her go."

She patted his hand and gave him a wink. He couldn't help himself. She was a special lady, and he kissed her cheek.

After their goodbyes, he grasped Autumn's hand as they walked to his Tahoe with Cody on his other side. This feeling of being a family was something he could get used to.

"I like her," he said, referring to Mrs. Higdon.

Autumn smiled up at him and squeezed his hand. "I do too. She's special. She took a liking to Cody and me as soon as we moved here. It was like gaining an instant mom."

Autumn went to step up into the car when she looked down and scowled. Frost looked down as well and saw the cigarette butts on the ground, between his car and hers.

"I'd love to know who keeps emptying their ashtray right next to my car," she growled as she hopped up into the car. Cody was getting in the back and buckling up, and Frost stood there, holding the door, looking at the cigarette butts.

"Does that happen often?" He asked, looking at the pile of butts again. There had to be like eight or so lying there.

She turned her nose up in disgust. "Yeah, a couple of times a week at least. It started about a month ago. And each time, I have to pick them up. It's disgusting. Not to mention rude."

Frost started to get that spidey feeling. It was the same feeling he would get when danger lurked while they were on missions. The hairs on the back of his neck were tingling. He scanned the area as he closed the door and walked around to get in. Nothing seemed out of sorts, and he didn't see anyone, but something kept pulling his attention to the house across the street. Now that it was light out, he could see it better. The small front yard required a desperate trim. And the house itself looked to be falling apart. Shutters were either missing or broken. Even a couple of the windows were broken. The paint on the side of the house was chipping away. The house looked abandoned, but he wondered if someone lived there because he saw them last night. Well, he didn't exactly see a physical person, but he knew he saw the curtain move in the front window.

"What are you looking at?" Autumn asked, noticing his interest in the house. Maybe she knew if someone was living there.

"Does anybody live in that house?"

She pointed to the house in question. "That one?" He nodded, but she shook her head and wrinkled her forehead. "No. Nobody has lived there since we moved in. And we've been here a little over a year. Now and then, someone comes and cuts the grass. Mrs. Higdon said she's spotted some homeless people coming and going from it, but she hasn't said anything lately. Why?"

He didn't want to alarm her.

"Just wondering. I thought I saw someone in there last night when I pulled in." He shrugged his shoulders. "Who knows, maybe it was just an animal in there?" She agreed, but something told him it wasn't an animal. His gut was telling him someone was living there. He just hoped it was an innocent person looking to get out of the elements. He'd need to keep his eyes open.

CHAPTER SIXTEEN

"Autumn seems to be enjoying herself."

"She does, and so does Cody. Thanks for hanging out today, Potter, and bringing Alejandra."

"My pleasure, just as long as your boy knows to keep his dick away from my little girl, everything will be just fine," Potter said bluntly as he took a drink from his beer.

Ace started laughing, but Frost looked at Potter with an unbelievable expression. "Oh, for fuck sakes, Potter. He's ten."

Potter pointed his finger at Frost and grinned. "Exactly! I remember the thoughts I started having when I was that age. And, isn't he close to eleven?"

"So, I'm guessing you worked everything out with her last night," Ace asked.

"Yeah, we came to the conclusion that we were both somewhat at fault. It was a breakdown in communication, and she has some reservations about my job. I understand where she's coming from. She lost her husband to the war. We talked, and I explained that anything could happen at any given time. I used the situation with Tenley as an example." Frost took a drink of his beer. "I think she's good now, though. I'm hoping that a little time with Alex and Tenley will also help."

"Yeah, that has to be hard losing a spouse to war. And then when you finally start to date again, and you wind up with another person serving, but to make matters even more intense, this person has an even more dangerous role in the military."

Frost thought back to what Autumn was telling him about her husband's deployments. He wanted to get Ace and Potter's take on it and see if they had the same thought he did.

"Actually, I wanted to get your opinion on something. Autumn told me a little about her husband's military career, and something doesn't sit right with me." He explained how Autumn told him about the last couple of years before her husband's death, how his deployments were more spontaneous.

"Shit…are you thinking he may have been Special Forces?"

Frost shook his head. "It crossed my mind. If he were truly in the Infantry unit as Autumn said, he would have had a start and end date for deployments. According to her, the last few years weren't like that. She called it a revolving door. He'd leave at a moment's notice and wouldn't know when he'd be back. Sometimes, he was gone for weeks; sometimes, it was months."

Potter let out a low whistle. Then Ace spoke. "Talk to the commander. Maybe he could ask his buddy Tink to look into it. That's if you want to know."

Frost looked over at where Autumn was sitting down by the pool with Alex and Tenley. She was smiling at something Alex was saying. "It's not that I want to know. I just think it would be nice for Autumn and Cody to know exactly what Kevin was into. Special Forces…that's something to be proud of."

"Did you find out why she's living in that shithole of a complex? Because after you left last night, the guys and I were talking some, and none of us like the fact or feel comfortable with her and Cody living there alone. That is a terrible area of town."

"Yeah, I know what you mean. As soon as I pulled into the parking spot, my danger vibe was going off. I didn't like the feeling I was getting."

"You see any of her neighbors?"

"Yeah, I met the lady who lives next door. She's a sweet elderly lady who lives alone. Autumn seems to like her a lot. A couple of houses down, though; I'm not so sure about. When I got there last night, there were a lot of people hanging out outside of it and flowing into the parking areas. Then there's the abandoned house across the street. I swear I saw the curtain in the front window move. I mentioned it to Autumn, and she said, sometimes homeless people go in there to sleep."

"Her place is tiny. Stitch and mine's apartment is twice the size of her place. She has it decorated nicely and all, but Jesus, everything in there is like miniature. I get a sense that she doesn't have much money, but I don't understand that. I mean she has a good steady job, she should be receiving survivor benefits, and I would like to think she got a nice sized check from her husband's life insurance policy."

"Not to mention, she sends her son to that Academy by the hospital. I've heard the tuition for that place is outrageous," Potter chimed in.

"She mentioned this morning that she would prefer to send Cody to public school, but logistically she can't with work."

"Why is that?"

"She doesn't have anybody to watch him after school."

"Shit, Juliette could pick him up if you or Autumn couldn't. She picks up Alejandra.

Frost watched Ace take a sip of his beer and set it down. He had a look on his face that told Frost he knew something.

"What?"

Ace rubbed the back of his neck. "I probably shouldn't say anything because Alex spoke with me in confidence, but if you're concerned, you should know and make a plan to ask Autumn about it. Alex was still wound up after you left last night, and she mentioned something about the government screwing Autumn over and something about a sister-in-law. I believe Alex called her a bitch."

Frost thought back to his conversation with Autumn the other week when she was talking about her life back in California and leading up to her moving here. She mentioned a sister-in-law a couple of times, and each time her facial expression had a look of disgust.

"She's mentioned a sister-in-law before in conversation, but she didn't elaborate too much on it. She did mention how she swindled money away from Kevin and her after Kevin's parents were killed in a car accident. I'll talk with her because I sure as hell don't want her living there anymore."

They all agreed and then started talking about the baseball scores.

"Look at those two. You would think they've known each other for years." Autumn said, referring to Cody and Alejandra. She, Tenley and

Alex were sitting next to the pool talking while the kids splashed around in the pool playfully and giggling. Even Alex's chocolate lab, Zuma, was enjoying the pool with the kids. The dog was amazing. He would actually dive down to the bottom of the pool to retrieve his toy when the kids threw it. Cody had always wanted a dog, but it had never been the right time.

She was a little worried about Cody's head since he still had a slight headache, but he seemed to be having fun. She had given him some medicine before they left their house.

"She's a sweet girl, Tenley. Frost shared with me her story. It's such a sad situation she had to go through, but thank goodness you were there and were able to turn her life around."

Tenley looked at Alejandra and smiled. "Yeah, it was tough at first. I don't know if Frost told you that Alejandra had to stay behind when I came back from Ecuador because of all of the legalities."

"No, he didn't mention that." She took a sip of her iced tea.

"Yeah, I was also going through some bad times as well. Some deep personal issues. At the time, things were complicated between Potter and me. I think I fell in love with that beast of man the moment I met him." Autumn saw her glance at Potter with such admiration and love in her eyes.

"I think he fell in love with you as well that day," Alex said, chiming in.

"Anyway, with everything going on, I was a hot mess, and I kind of hit rock bottom. I was hiding a lot from my friends and Potter." Autumn saw the way Tenley looked over at Alex. It was almost like she was saying she was sorry again. "One night, I snapped. I ended up on a beach here in town, though at the time I didn't know Potter's condo was directly behind where I was. I was so deep in my head, not to mention drunk on about half a bottle of rum and ended up passing out on the beach as the high tide was coming in."

Autumn gasped and touched Tenley's hand. "Who found you?"

"Thankfully, Potter had just gotten home and happened to be out on his balcony and spotted me. He got to me and brought me up to his condo.

162

The next day, he and I talked a lot. I opened up and finally let him in on everything going on. The following week, we were married, and he surprised me by flying Alejandra up for the wedding. While she was here, all of my friends and family helped out with the legal issues, and we were able to adopt her. She's Potter's little princess. From what I heard, she had him wrapped around her little finger the moment they met."

"So, Potter met her in Ecuador, too? Was he there with you?"

"Yes, but he was there with the team."

"Oh, I understand their travels are classified."

"No, they were there because of me. A few days before I was supposed to fly back home, I was attacked at the medical tent I'd been working at. I was alone, and some guys tried stealing stuff, and one thing led to another, but some guys had been passing by and saw what was happening and stopped the bad guys from hurting me further."

"Holy shit, Tenley!"

Tenley finished telling her everything about how the guys who stopped the attack actually worked with her biological dad, whom she had never met, and how he had always kept a watchful eye on her. She then explained about her ex-boyfriend and the drug cartel leader he was working with and how they were trying to use her to get to her father. By the time she finished the story, Autumn's head was spinning.

"Did any of that have to do with the guy who shot Frost?"

"Yeah, if it wasn't for Frost, I don't know if Alejandra would be with us. He saved her life that day." Tenley wiped her eyes, and Autumn noticed Potter was looking directly at Tenley with a concerned expression. The man was definitely in tune with his wife.

"Honey, I think your man is worried."

Autumn saw Potter pointing at Frost and saying something. From where she sat, it looked as if Potter was upset about something. But then she saw the smirk on Frost's face, and Ace was roaring with laughter, so she knew it couldn't be that bad.

The guys made their way over to where she and the girls were sitting.

"What was Potter saying that was so funny, babe?" Alex asked Ace as he picked her up and sat in her seat and pulled her on his lap. Alex snuggled against his chest.

Frost placed his hands on Autumn's shoulders and squeezed gently. She looked up at him, and he gave her a wink.

"Potter's got the case of protective daddy syndrome."

"Speaking of the kids, where did they go anyway?" Ace asked.

Alex looked up at him. "Inside to change and then play air hockey. Zuma went in with them."

"Oh, I hope they know to change in separate rooms," Tenley said and winked at Autumn and then started giggling when Potter's face paled. She pulled on his hand, and he bent down, and Tenley kissed him. "I'm just teasing, honey. You need to stop being such a Papa Bear. I'm sure Cody will take good care of our little girl." He caressed her belly, and the move almost made Autumn shed a tear.

Frost leaned down and asked Autumn how Cody was feeling. She smiled up at him. Happy that he thought to ask.

"He seems to be okay. He's having fun. He and Alejandra really hit it off. Tenley and I are going to schedule some more playdates for the two of them, especially now that summer break is just around the corner."

"What is Cody going to do this summer?"

Autumn thought about it and then realized she hadn't planned anything except for his Sea Cadets trip to Washington, DC. Last year, they were still in California for most of the summer before moving.

"Shoot. I'm not sure. I wasn't even thinking about that. I'll get on online and look for some camps. I know there are two Sea Cadets summer trainings he wanted to do. They are each a week and overnight. The plus side is they are right in Norfolk, so I won't have to spend money on travel expenses. And there is the DC trip he is going on, but their unit raised enough money to cover all of the kids' travel expenses."

"That sounds like fun. If you want, I can see if my mom will watch him the weeks he doesn't have anything planned. I mean, she watches

Alejandra for us. She already has activities lined up, like taking her bowling, to the movies, things like that."

"Oh, I couldn't ask her to do that. I'm sure I can find something."

"Nonsense. She'd be happy to. She loves kids, and now that she isn't working, she needs things to do."

Autumn nibbled on her lip, and she felt Frost squeeze her shoulders again.

"Are you sure?"

Tenley smiled and nodded her head. "I can talk to her later tonight and let you know. But trust me when I say she will say yes."

"Okay, I guess so. I'd pay her, though."

"Oh, honey," Tenley said, reaching over and grabbing Autumn's hand. "You don't understand. You're with Frost now, which means you're now a part of our unit. We all take care of one another. My mom is dating their commander, Derek, who is Alex's dad."

Autumn looked at Alex, who had a big smile on her face, and she nodded. "It's true. We're a unique little unit, and as Tenley said, we take care of each other, and we're there for one another no matter what."

Ace squeezed Alex a little tighter against him. "The way you ladies like to venture into things, us guys have to be on our toes at all time." Alex slapped Ace's chest. "We aren't that bad," she said, snuggling close to him with a big smile on her face. The sight of the two of them warmed Autumn's heart.

All the guys started snickering, then started telling Autumn stories about Tenley and Alex and the trouble they'd gotten into. Autumn was having so much fun she lost track of time until Frost's watch caught her attention. They'd been sitting out here talking for about two hours since the kids went inside. Not that she was concerned they would get into anything, but she was still worried about Cody's head.

She went to get up, and Frost grabbed her hand and gave her a curious look.

"You okay?"

165

"Yeah, I'm just going to check on the kids. I didn't realize it's been over two hours since they went inside, and I haven't seen nor heard anything from them."

Potter looked at Tenley and patted her leg.

"We need to get going. Your mom and Derek will be at the house shortly."

Everyone got up and started gathering everything, then went inside in search of the kids.

"Look at them! They look so adorable," Alex whispered as she took out her phone to take a picture. Autumn and Tenley were getting their phones out to take pictures as well.

Frost and Ace stood there, watching Potter biting the inside of his cheek. It was just too easy to mess with the big guy. Frost felt sorry for the poor bastard who had the balls to ask Alejandra out on a date once she was old enough.

Frost had to admit the sight of the two kids was cute. The two were curled up on the floor in front of the massive TV, fast asleep. They were both on their sides facing each other, snuggled under the blanket and sharing a pillow. Zuma was out cold at their feet.

"Potter...you okay over there?" Ace asked with laughter in his voice. Potter shot him the finger, and Frost started laughing.

"Fuck you two. You just wait until you have kids. I hope you have twin girls. Then you'll know exactly how I feel."

Everyone laughed. Frost looked at Cody, and a thought hit him, making his chest tighten a little. He already had a kid. He may not be blood, but he considered Cody his son. Then he glanced over at Autumn, who was watching him. He glanced at her belly and envisioned her belly round with a baby growing inside. His baby. A little brother or sister for Cody. He felt his cock start to grow as he thought about taking Autumn home and burying himself in her. He shook his head. Holy shit, he was seriously getting a hard-on standing in front of his friends.

166

CHAPTER SEVENTEEN

"Wow, Mom. You look hot!" Cody told his mom, smiling at her as she stepped out into the living room. She and Frost were finally going on their first official date. She wanted to look nice and also wanted to be comfortable since it was supposed to be a warm evening, so she decided on a simple jade green strapless dress that came to just above her knees and hugged her shapely figure.

The restaurant Frost was taking her to had outside seating. He made reservations for a table on the patio, which overlooked the beach. Her friend Eileen at work told her the place had a very romantic atmosphere and was known for its excellent seafood menu.

She ran her hands down the dress. "Are you sure it looks okay?"

"Seriously, Mom. You look great. I'm sure Frost would see it too!"

She smiled. "You think so?"

"I know so."

Just then, there was a knock at the door, and Cody said he'd answer it. She knew it was Frost. They were going to drop Cody off at his friend's house on their way to the restaurant, and he was staying the night, which meant Autumn had the house all to herself tonight. Would tonight be the night she let go of all of her fears and let Frost in completely?

Before she could answer her own question, the voices of Cody and Frost had her looking toward the front door where Frost stood. His eyes were locked on her as she took in the sight of him. Dressed in a pair of black dress pants and a light blue button-up dress shirt tucked neatly into his trousers, the man looked edible, especially with the top two buttons of his shirt undone, showing off his tan skin.

"Hey," he said, taking a step toward her.

"Doesn't she look great, Frost?" Cody asked, smiling.

Frost kept his powerful gaze pinned on her eyes as he answered Cody in a low but deep voice. "She sure does."

She shyly looked down, but Frost used his finger to tilt her face up towards his. He placed his other hand on her hip, and that simple contact sent her heart racing. "You look absolutely stunning, sugar." He leaned forward and kissed her cheek.

She whispered a thank you as she looked into his eyes. What she saw should've had her running for cover. All she could see was a look of hunger in his eye.

"We'd better get going, so we're not late for our reservation," he stated.

She was still staring at him when he leaned down and whispered in her ear. "You keep staring at me that way, and we are going to skip our dinner reservation." He nipped her ear lobe and she was sure it caused her pussy to contract.

Autumn took an unsteady breath and felt a little moisture between her legs. *Holy handbags! I don't think a man has ever had this effect on me.*

They arrived at the restaurant and were seated on the patio. It was a gorgeous night. Not a cloud in the sky, and the crescent moon was shining brightly. A few minutes later, their drinks were delivered. Autumn had white wine while Frost took a beer.

They sat at the two-person table in silence, just staring at one another. Frost loved how the light from the candle on the table illuminated Autumn's face. It was a very intimate setting. He reached over and took her hand and brought it to his lips.

"Thank you for taking the chance with me, Autumn."

"Well, you were pretty persistent, that's for sure," she said with a sparkle in her eye.

They talked a little more, and then the waiter came and took their order. They both ordered the filet with shrimp and clams.

After dinner, they decided to walk down to the beach. As they walked hand in hand in their bare feet, they talked more while stealing a few kisses in-between. Frost told her how Nathan had called him the other day to apologize for overreacting the other night. Frost wasn't really one to hold a grudge, so he simply accepted the apology and moved on. Since Nathan was a big part of Autumn and Cody's lives, he didn't want secrets between them, so Frost had confided in Nathan about him being a SEAL, something he rarely did. Then Nathan confirmed what Frost had been guessing. Both he and Autumn's late husband were part of MARSOC, a.k.a. Marine Special Forces. Nathan told Frost he'd been wanting to tell Autumn but had his reservations. Frost told him it was his decision and that he wouldn't say anything, but he did tell him he thought she should know the truth.

As they made their way back to Autumn's house, Frost made a note to start looking at homes. He didn't want Autumn and Cody living in this neighborhood any longer than they had to.

Autumn was a nervous wreck. She and Frost had a wonderful evening. Between dinner and the romantic walk on the beach under the moon and stars, it was perfect.

She was trying to get her house key out of her clutch, and, at the same time, she tried getting out of the Tahoe and ended up stumbling in her heels. Thankfully, Frost had been standing there and was quick to catch her. He wrapped his long, protective arms around her waist and pulled her close to him. She placed her hands against his chest. Even through his clothes, she could feel the muscle definition.

"D-Do you want to come in? I could make some coffee or something," she asked. God, could she sound any lamer. She hadn't been out on a date since she was eighteen years old.

He smirked at her. "You don't have a coffee machine."

"Shit." She mumbled under her breath. She was already screwing this up. He chuckled, and his warm breath hit her skin, making it come alive.

Frost grabbed hold of her shaking hand. He took the key from her and unlocked the door, and she took a deep breath.

He guided her inside and shut the door, securing all three locks. Okay, she guessed he was planning to stay awhile. She went to turn her back to him, and he gently grasped her shoulders and turned her back around, so she faced him. He took her face in the palms of his hands.

"Autumn. I want you to relax."

She licked her dry lips. "I want to relax, but I'm so damn nervous." Her green eyes looked deep into his. She could do this. She wanted to do this. She wanted to feel free and alive again. "I don't want to hold back anymore, Jack. But I don't want to screw up what we have with my insecurities about your career."

Frost held off saying anything until she finished. She clutched his wrists as he still held her head between his hands. He used his thumbs to caress her cheeks gently.

"Are there going to be days when I'm going to hate your job? Absolutely. Just like there will be days that I love your job. But know that no matter how I feel each day, I will always respect you and your career." She took a deep breath. Frost could tell this was difficult for her to say but damn, he was proud. "Your bravery and commitment to your country are commendable. Someone has to be brave and take care of the bad guys, and you and your team took an oath to serve and protect. I'm so proud of who you are and what you stand for, Jack. And I promise to always be by your side no matter what kind of day I'm having."

Frost's heart felt like it was going to burst from his chest. If he weren't already in love with her, her little speech just now would have sealed the deal. She was one amazing woman, and she was his.

He wrapped his arms around her waist and pulled her close to his body. She held onto his biceps as she stared up at him, her green eyes filled with lust and desire. Oh yeah, his woman wanted him just as bad as he wanted to claim her.

In a low deep voice, he asked, "Sugar, what are you saying?"

Her little pink tongue darted out to moisten her lips, lips that he wanted to kiss and nibble on.

She drew in a deep breath and gazed into his eyes. "I'm saying that I want you, Jack. I want all of you."

That was all he needed to hear. He couldn't help the big ass smile on his face. "I want all of you too." Those were the last words out of his mouth before he leaned down, capturing her mouth. His tongue delved deep, and he explored every inch. He felt her fingers popping the buttons on his shirt, and it drove him wild. He only pulled back when he needed to breathe.

He took her hands and brought them to his lips, kissing each knuckle while never looking away. Her chest heaved with aroused breaths, and he wanted nothing more than to rip his pants open, lift her dress, and bury his aching cock deep in her.

Without saying a word and never letting go of her hand, he guided her to her bedroom. Tonight, he was claiming her officially.

Autumn took Frost's lead and walked into her bedroom. He stopped her right at the bottom of the bed. Her blood was pumping. Frost towered over her, and she was very so aroused.

"Do I need protection?" He asked, and she shook her head no.

"Good, because I don't want anything between us. And just for the record, I've never slept with another woman without protection."

That was good to hear, although she didn't need the visual of him with any other woman. Then she started to think about all of the talk about having and keeping a relationship going with a SEAL, and how the divorce rate was high. SEALs were highly sought after by women who just wanted a hookup to say they'd been with a SEAL. She put her hand on her stomach.

As if Frost knew what she was thinking, he tipped her chin up, so she was looking at him as his other hand rested on her hip. "Autumn, look at me. Baby, it's just you and me." She saw the emotion in his eyes.

"What are you thinking about?"

Geeze, now she felt embarrassed for letting her insecurities get the best of her, but she couldn't lie to him.

"I'm nervous, Jack. Before we go down this path, I need to be sure you're in this for the long-haul. Cody already adores you and has a serious case of SEAL hero worship. But I also need to protect my heart. I know most relationships don't last in the SEALs."

"Sugar, look at me. Do you think that I would have spent the past month trying to convince you to give me a chance if I wasn't invested in this? Baby, I'm in this until you say it's over, which is something I never hope to hear coming from these beautiful lips." He traced her lips with his finger. "Are there guys who are unfaithful to their significant other? Yes, I won't lie. It happens, but I swear to you, Autumn, I would never do that to you." He grinned, showing off his dimple as he cupped her cheek. She moved into his hold, loving his touch. "I've waited too long to find my soulmate, and by god, I would never do anything to fuck it up." He leaned down and kissed her deeply. He took her breath away. He explored her mouth, and she explored his. Their tongues tangled with one another's. When Frost finally pulled away, he pressed his forehead against hers. "I've wanted you since the moment I heard your voice." He kissed her nose.

Autumn absorbed everything Frost was telling her, and she believed every word out of his mouth. She was ready to do this. She was absolutely ready to give herself fully to this man. A man who had shown her that it was okay to love again. *"Holy shit! I'm in love with Jack."*

Frost wondered what thought had just gone through Autumn's head because the expression on her face looked as if she just had an epiphany. She reached upward and wound her slender arms around his neck. He ran his hands up and down her arms. He knew she was nervous because he could feel her body trembling.

As his hands made another pass up her arms, they traveled up her shoulders and continued upward, caressing her delicate neck until his palms cupped her cheeks. He used his thumbs to caress her flushed cheeks. Her skin was so soft.

She locked gazes with him, then her hands slid down his chest and spread open his shirt. She ran her hands up and down his ribs, grazing his abs and arousing him even more. Before she could go any further in her quest to undo him, he turned her around and pressed his chest to her back. As soon as he heard her gasp, he smiled because he knew she had felt his erection. He bent down and whispered in her ear.

"You feel what you do to me?" He nibbled on her ear, and she moaned. Christ, he couldn't wait any longer. He needed to be inside her.

He took hold of her zipper on the back of her dress and pulled it down slowly, his knuckles grazing her spine as he did. Her breathing grew rapid. With a slight shove, her dress fell and pooled around her feet, and he lost his breath at the sight before him.

Autumn was all woman. She wasn't wearing a bra, and she looked gorgeous; her creamy skin had a little glow from being out in the sun. And her long red hair flowed over one shoulder. He removed his shirt and then turned her around. Her head was down, and her hands were clasped together in front of her. He used his finger to tilt her head up. Her shamrock eyes met his, and he was done for. He undid his belt and pants and pushed them down along with his boxers and kicked them to the side. When Autumn took in the size of him, her eyes widened, and he grinned.

She took a step forward, reaching for him, and he met her halfway. Their upper bodies were touching. The skin-to-skin contact was driving him insane. She reached up and placed her hands on his shoulders and stood on her tippy toes to kiss him. He lowered his head, making it easier for her. When their lips touched, it was gentle at first, but then quickly turned carnal as they both battled for control of the kiss. They were both rocking their hips. Frost lowered himself and gripped under her thighs and lifted her up. She squealed and wrapped her legs around his waist. He smashed his mouth down onto hers again. She was a drug that he was addicted to.

"I need you now."

"I need you, too," she panted.

He turned toward the bed, laying her down gently on the soft grey comforter. Starting at her ankle, he kissed and caressed her skin until he reached her breasts. With one thigh positioned between her legs, he hovered over her and stared into her eyes. Using his thumb, he lightly swiped over her nipple, and she gasped. She reached for his face and cupped his cheeks.

"Jack...enough teasing. I really need you now," she told him.

He lifted his head and grinned at her before lifting his body and positioning himself between her thighs. She reached around and ran her nails up and down his back and rocked her hips. Each time her pussy grazed his cock, he swore it got harder. He was literally going to blow his load if he didn't get inside.

He leaned down and kissed her. Knowing she hadn't had sex in over two years, he didn't want to hurt her, so he nudged his cock slowly into her and pulled out, helping to stretch her sensitive tissues. After about the third pass, she let out a sigh.

"Jack, you know I'm not made of glass, right?" He almost laughed at her frustration.

"I know that, but I know it's been a while, and I don't want to hurt you."

She ran her hands through his hair. "I appreciate the thought, but if you don't get inside me right now, I think I might die."

"Well, we wouldn't want that." In one thrust, he seated himself fully inside her. She moaned and threw her head back. Her hips moved in sync with his. She was trying to meet him thrust for thrust.

"Oh, God, Jack. I need more. Harder…"

He sat up a little and gripped her hips, hoping like hell he wouldn't leave finger marks as he pumped his hips faster and harder. In no time at all, he was there. He felt the tingling sensation going down his spine straight to his balls. But he wasn't going over the edge until she was there with him. Another two thrusts, and he felt her tighten around him and knew she was close. Her nails dug into his shoulders as she moaned in ecstasy as she shook and came. He followed right behind her, shooting his seed into her.

They both lay there breathless and sweaty. Frost felt the wetness on his skin and knew she had shed a tear. He had a pretty good idea that taking this step with him was going to be mentally difficult for her, considering it was her first time being intimate with another man since her husband. He then wondered if maybe she wasn't ready. That couldn't be it, because she was asking for it. But his conscience had to know for sure.

He rolled her onto her back and positioned one of his thighs between her legs. He was hovering over her, and he could see the tear tracks.

"Autumn, if I pushed you and you weren't ready, I'm so sorry." He placed a kiss on her nose, and she opened her teary eyes and shook her head as she brought her hands up and cupped his cheeks.

"No, Jack. You did nothing wrong. In fact, everything was perfect. You're perfect." She lifted her head slightly and brushed her lips against his.

"Then why the tears? I don't like seeing you upset." He pushed her dampened hair from her face, and she smiled up at him.

She spoke in a low whisper. "I may be in over my head, but I love you, Jack. I love everything about you. Your personality, the way you care about your friends and family, and especially the way you care for Cody."

Frost felt the huge lump form in his throat. He was expecting a lot of things, but her saying those three powerful words hadn't even made the list.

"I love you, too. So damn much it hurts."

She lifted her hips, and when her hot wet pussy rubbed against his hard cock, he had to have her again.

"I need you again. You drive me insane." He leaned down and suckled the side of her neck down to her collarbone, then glanced up at her as she watched him with nothing but love shining in her eyes.

She grinned before whispering to him. "Then take me. I'm yours, Jack."

He didn't need any further directive as he positioned himself fully between her legs and thrust into her in one deep stroke. The feeling was pure heaven. Nothing would tear him apart from her.

He flipped over with her positioned perfectly on top of him. She was now in control. Frost was ready to come undone at the sight of Autumn on top of him. Her breasts were round and her nipples hard. What a magnificent sight. He reached up, grabbing her nipples between his thumb and index finger. He gently squeezed and tugged. The feel of her velvet walls squeezing him as she raised and lowered herself on his length. She took all of him, moaning every time he consumed her. She leaned back with her hands on his knees, arching her back and exposing her clit. She quickened the pace. He took his thumb and gently rubbed her clit. She cried out for more until she came, moaning his name. The sensation sent him over, and he followed her, spilling himself into her. "I love you so much, baby." And he did. He would love her forever. He leaned down and kissed her tenderly as she ran her soft hands up and down his back. He could get used to this very easily, and right at this moment as they gazed into each other's eyes, he concluded that he was going to marry her. And the sooner it happened, the better.

CHAPTER EIGHTEEN

Frost heard his phone vibrating on the nightstand next to the bed. He released his hold on the warm naked body he was entwined with.

He grabbed the phone and noted the time, 5:23 am, then saw who was calling, Ace. Shit, this wasn't going to be a good call.

He answered as he carefully slid out of bed so as not to wake Autumn, who was curled up on his side of the bed, sharing his pillow. Her flaming red hair was a deep contrast to the white pillowcase. He pulled on his boxers and walked silently out of the bedroom into the living room.

"Hey man, what's up?" Although if Ace was calling at this time in the morning, it wasn't good news.

"Hey, sorry for the early morning call, but the Commander is calling us in. He wants us there within the hour.

"Shit…"

"Yeah, exactly what I said when I heard my phone this morning, and especially when Alex was just giving me the best…" Frost interrupted him. "Christ, man, how many times do I have to tell you I don't need to hear about your escapades with my best friend?"

Ace's laughter boomed over the phone.

"Well, just think we'll have something to talk about on our way to wherever the hell we're headed."

"Yeah, I don't think so." Frost had no intention of sharing details of his night with Autumn. Hell no!

Ace laughed. "Oh, come on. We can exchange stories. Did you or did you not take Autumn out on your first official date last night?"

Frost glanced into the bedroom. His Irish Beauty was sleeping soundly.

"Yeah, and your point?"

"Didn't Cody stay at a friend's house?"

"I'm not talking about this shit with you. I'll see you on base in thirty." Frost clicked off the phone as Ace was laughing.

He walked back into the room and got back in bed even though he told himself that was the wrong move. Autumn stirred and rolled into him. She was still naked, and her warm body felt like heaven against his skin. He ran his hands through her red tresses. Slowly she blinked her eyes open. When she made eye contact, she smiled.

"Hi," she whispered in her morning, husky voice that he loved hearing.

"Hi." He smiled but knew it didn't reach his eyes, and, of course, she noticed and sat up, so she was resting on her elbow.

"What's wrong?"

Well, hell...Now he knew what Ace and Potter went through when they were leaving. It sucked!

"Ace just called. I need to report to the base."

Her eyes widened, and he immediately saw the fear. He pulled her against him and hugged her.

"Don't get upset, sugar. It was bound to happen sooner or later. This is my job."

She was trying to wipe a tear before it fell, and his heart broke. He knew this was going to be extremely hard for her, and he worried. He would make sure to call Alex and have her keep in contact with Autumn.

"I know, Jack. But it just happened out of the blue. It just caught me off guard."

"Unfortunately, that's the way our job works. There are times we may know in advance, and sometimes, it's a fire drill." He brushed her hair from her face. "Are you going to be okay?"

She nodded her head, yes. "Just promise me when you can, you'll call. Please."

He grinned. "You'll be the first person I'd call. But, know there are going to be times when I'll be gone for weeks if not months without any communication."

She swallowed hard. "I understand."

He hugged her. "I know you do. You're a strong woman, and you are my woman. You be sure to keep my side of the bed warm for me."

She laughed, which was what he intended. "Come here and give me some loving before I need to go. I need to get my fill of you." She started laughing when he started tickling her before the fun turned serious, and he made slow passionate love to her.

⁓

On the way to the base, Frost pulled his phone out and dialed his mom. It may be early, but if he knew his mom, she was already up and starting the day. Christ, she was going to be surprised when she found out the reason for his call. He'd never asked to bring a woman to family dinner at their house. He never met anyone he wanted to introduce to his family until now. He couldn't wait to introduce Autumn and Cody to his family.

"Hi, honey!" She answered, sounding like the cheery woman she'd always been known for.

"Hey, Mom."

"Jack, you're not calling to cancel on dinner this Sunday, are you? Well, unless you and the boys are heading out." He smiled. She always referred to the team as her boys.

"As of right now, I'm planning to be there. But we were just called in. If we end up leaving, I'll let you know."

"Good, because I am making your favorite—stuffed cabbage with poor man's bread."

Damn, his mouth was already watering thinking about his mom's stuffed cabbage. It was a Syrian recipe she got from one of her women's monthly club meetings she went to.

"Trey and Sammie will be here as well with the kids. It's been a few weeks since you've seen them. I swear those babies get bigger every day. Oh, good heavens, here I go rambling on. I'm sorry, honey, you called me, so you must have had a reason."

He smiled. God, he loved her, and he made it a point to tell her every time he had the chance to.

"Actually, I wanted to talk to you about Sunday's dinner. Do you have room for two more spots at the table?"

179

"Which two boys will I be feeding this week? I swear if it weren't for Alex and me, you boys would live off frozen meals and take-out."

Frost chuckled. She was one hundred percent right.

"Actually, it isn't any of the guys. It's my girlfriend, Autumn, and her son, Cody. I wanted you and dad to meet them."

He heard his mom gasp, then heard something drop. It sounded like a pot or pan. He heard his dad asking what was wrong. Christ, did she just faint?

"Mom?"

Her stuttering made him chuckle. "Y-y-you have a girlfriend? Since when?"

He laughed again. "Since last week. But she and I have been talking for a couple of weeks."

"Where did you meet? How old is her son? The dad isn't going to be a problem, is he? Have the guys met her yet?"

Oh, my god! "Mom!" He shouted, interrupting her. She'd keep going if he let her.

"I'm sorry, Jack." They were getting off track again. "Mom, as much as I love hearing your voice, please mute it for just a minute so I can answer a few of your questions."

He heard his dad laughing. Jesus, now she had put him on speakerphone.

"Listen, Mom, here are the cliff notes. Autumn and I met while I was in the hospital. She was my physical therapist. After I was discharged, we kept in touch and went out a few times. Her son, Cody, is ten-years-old, and you will love him. His dad, who was married to Autumn, was a Marine. He was stationed at Camp Pendleton in California. He was killed while serving in Iraq a few years ago. And, yes, all of the guys have met her and approve. And, if that doesn't appease you, Alex and Tenley have also both met her and already have 'girls' nights planned for the three of them."

"Well, I'll be damned."

He pulled the phone from his ear and gave it a sideways look, then brought it back up. "Mom, did you just say 'damned'?" His mother was like June Cleaver. She never cussed.

She started laughing. "Oh, Jack! This is great news. You know I was starting to worry that your brother was going to be the only son to give me grandkids."

Fuck me. He loved his mother dearly, but he needed to ask her to tamp down her excitement, or she was going to scare the crap out of Autumn. And that included bringing up future grandkids.

"Mom, please don't bring up grandkids. At least not grandkids produced by her and me. It took a lot to get her to take the chance on us dating. She had a hard time since losing her husband, and with my job, let's just say it's been tough."

His mom was quiet for a few seconds before she spoke in a soft voice. "You really like her, don't you?"

"Yeah, Mom. I do."

"Well, then. I think it's wonderful you're bringing her and her son to dinner. Do you think a ten-year-old will like stuffed cabbage? I plan on making some chicken nuggets and macaroni and cheese for the kids. I can make enough for him too."

He smiled, though she couldn't see him. His mom was a rock star, always thinking of others.

"He might like it. He'll at least try it. I'll ask Autumn and let you know."

"Okay, honey. I'll see you Sunday. I love you."

"I love you too, Mom. Bye."

"Bye, honey."

He hung up and chuckled. Knowing her, by the time dinner was over on Sunday, she would have Autumn and Cody convinced they were already part of the family. His chest tightened at the thought of that. Now he had to hope they wouldn't be getting shipped out.

Frost walked into the secured building on base. He smiled as he made his way to the locker room. His blood was pumping. It was great to be back working with the guys finally.

"Welcome back, man!" Frost was awarded a hard slap on the back from Potter. It was his official first day back on the team. Four fucking weeks was just too long. But he made sure he was one hundred percent good to go before he'd risk the lives of team members.

He smiled to himself, thinking about Autumn and how she was putting him through numerous workouts to be sure for herself that he was ready. He couldn't complain because when they were on the floor, he managed to get another type of workout in with Autumn. She was still talking this morning before he left about the move he pulled on her to get her flat on her back before he stripped her naked and made love to her right there on the living room floor. This was after they had already made love multiple times and were out in the kitchen for the middle of the night snack. He grinned.

"It feels good to be back." He walked over to his locker. He felt some normalcy by being back in action with his team, his brothers. However, it was slightly difficult leaving Autumn in bed naked this morning. Especially when she decided to give him a proper send-off. He was surprised he still wasn't walking around with a hard-on from all their sexual innuendos through the night and into the early morning. He was lucky he wasn't late. After they had made love, she had snaked her way down his body and between his legs, and he felt his cock being sucked into her warm, silky mouth; he thought he had died and gone to heaven. Autumn was a goddess in bed, and he couldn't wait to get back to her. He was addicted.

Ace stepped into the room and thank god for that. It was time to get down to work.

He got a slap on the back from Ace.

"Good to see you back here, man."

Frost grinned. "Good to be back."

182

"Alex wanted to know if you and Autumn would be attending the small gathering at the clinic next month. It's not an opening per se. It's more for the community leaders and government officials to check it out."

"Of course, I wouldn't miss it. She's got to be beside herself right now, knowing the grand opening is scheduled for October."

"She seems to be handling it all in her stride. I just wish she'd delegate more to the others who are there to help her. I'm afraid she's going to overwhelm herself and then get burned out."

Frost knew Ace wouldn't have mentioned anything if he wasn't concerned. If Ace was worried, then he was worried as well, as she was one of his best friends, and he didn't want to see her hurt in any way. Alex was known to push herself beyond her limits sometimes.

"Why don't you let her get through the little shindig next month, and then afterward take her away somewhere for a few days? It would have to be somewhere close by in case we get called in. Maybe during that time, you two can pick out a new wedding date."

Frost knew Ace still felt like shit when the team got called out a few days before his and Alex's wedding was supposed to take place, causing them to have to postpone it. Then with all of the stuff that went down with Tenley and her ex and dad, the thought of their wedding was moved to the bottom of the priority list.

Ace tapped his index finger against his jaw in thought. "You know what...that's a great idea. Maybe I'll see if Stitch will let me use his cabin in the mountains. That way, it's close enough that I can get back in time should we get the call. I just need to find someone to watch Zuma. Tenley and Potter normally watch him if we need to be somewhere, but Tenley's still having some major morning sickness, so I don't want to bother her with the dog."

"We can watch him for you guys if need be."

"Really?"

"Yeah, Cody will love it. Autumn said he keeps trying to talk her into getting a dog."

"Thanks, man. I'll talk to Alex and let you know."

At that moment, Commander Connors walked into the room, and everyone stood at attention. Enough playtime—it was back to the grind. Frost smiled to himself, God, he loved this shit.

CHAPTER NINETEEN

"I'm so jealous of your olive complexion," Autumn said to Alex as they lay in the sun by the pool.

Since the team had gotten called in early this morning, Alex decided to have some of the girls over for a day of relaxing by the pool to try and keep their minds off their men. The girls consisted of Autumn, Alex, Tenley, and Mia, Ace's baby sister. She was in town for a couple of days. She would be taking her board exam to become a veterinarian in a couple of weeks, so she wanted to get in a visit with the gang before she would be shutting the world out to study.

"God, it's hot out, today," Tenley complained, using a paddle fan to try and cool herself. She was just a little over two months pregnant. But looking at her in her itty bitty deep purple bikini, you'd never know.

Alex sat up. "It sure is. I say we get in the pool. I have enough rafts for each of us. That way, we can stay cool while still getting some sun."

Autumn sat up as the other three girls got up and jumped in the pool. Well, Tenley didn't jump; she eased herself in from the side. Autumn glanced at the stunning kidney-shaped pool. The rock formation and waterfall near the deep end was absolutely gorgeous. The green foliage mixed with the pool's exotic features gave you the feeling you were in a jungle. There was even a water slide built into the rocks that dumped the person right into the sparkling blue water. Although the water looked so refreshing, she was still hesitant to get in.

When she was a little girl, she had nearly drowned in the small canal behind her grandmother's house back in New Mexico. Of course, her parents never tried to give her any type of swimming lesson. Ever since, she had a fear of pools and large bodies of water, and basically any water that would be over her head. She made sure that Cody was able to swim at an early age. She knew she should've taken lessons herself, especially since she had a child.

Alex's voice brought her mind back to the present. "Hey, are you getting in? I have a raft for you." Autumn eyed the yellow raft. It seemed small like it wouldn't be able to hold her fully above the water. She saw the way the others submerged in the water when they laid on it.

She pulled her bottom lip, in-between her teeth. "I think I'll just sit on the steps for now and cool off."

Alex scrunched her eyebrows together, and although Autumn may have only known Alex for a couple of weeks, she knew that woman loved to ask questions, and she could tell she was getting ready to fire something off. So, before Alex could even open her mouth, Autumn decided to lay it out for all of them.

"I don't really know how to swim. When I get near water that's deep, I start to freak out. I almost drowned when I was a kid, and ever since, I've been afraid of deep water." She was rambling but now felt embarrassed.

Alex's eyebrows shot upward. "Oh, wow!" The other ladies made similar comments, and they all paddled their rafts to the shallow end near the steps where Autumn was standing.

Tenley hopped off her raft and gestured with her hand for Autumn to get in the pool.

"Get your ass in the pool, and the three of us will teach you. Good lord, woman. You can't be dating a SEAL and not know how to swim. That has to be a cardinal sin in the SEAL hood." They all started laughing. Leave it to Tenley to put a smile on everyone's face.

An hour later, the four women were floating around on the rafts sipping on strawberry margaritas. Tenley's was a virgin, of course. Autumn may have only mastered the doggie paddle, but at least she could say she was able to swim. Tenley told her about the swimming classes at the local community center. She decided that no matter the cost, she was going to go by there on Monday and sign up for their adult swim classes.

She turned her head and looked at the three amazing women floating around her. They looked exhausted but happy, now that they had some alcohol in their veins. They were each so special and selfless. They had spent a portion of their fun afternoon teaching her how to swim, and never

186

once complained. In fact, they had all done a lot of laughing, especially when they were trying to teach her to go under the water, and her ass kept floating to the top.

"I owe you ladies a night out with drinks on me. And, Tenley, since you can't have alcohol, you get to pick where we go."

"Ooo…fun! We love a girl's night out. Don't we, Alex?"

Alex bobbed her head up and down, started giggling, and almost spilled her drink. Obviously, it didn't take much alcohol for Alex to start feeling it. Although if Autumn was honest, she felt a little tipsy herself, and Mia looked like she was feeling pretty good as well. Autumn didn't know too much about Ace's sister except that she lived in New York City. She was a beautiful woman with long jet-black hair and brown eyes. She shared a lot of the same facial features as her brother minus the eye color. She had also just recently broken up with her boyfriend because he had cheated on her. But she was still young—with her good looks, curvy body, and brains, Autumn couldn't see her being single for long.

"Plus, I can be the designated driver and make sure your drunk asses get home safely," Tenley finished saying.

Alex looked at Mia and gave her a wink. "We will have to plan it after Mia takes her Boards, so she can come down for the weekend." All of the ladies cheered and clinked their glasses, making the margaritas slosh into the pool, which just made them laugh even harder. Autumn clung to the raft she was floating on and wondered how much alcohol Alex put in these drinks.

"What you all did for me today is something I will never forget. Thank you." They all stretched out and did a group hug. Autumn felt the tears coming on. These women were what friends were all about. They were the ones you heard about but never got to experience—no judging, and being there for each other no matter what.

Tenley giggled. "With a little more practice, you'll be a pro."

Autumn shook her head and laughed. "I don't think you'll see me on the next Olympic team."

The women all laughed, then Tenley said, "Not unless they create an Olympic event in dog paddling."

Autumn wanted to respond but saw Alex's eyes widen before a big grin appeared on her face. She turned around to see who or what she was looking at.

"Hi, honey! You're back!" Alex said excitedly as she swam with one arm while her other hand held onto her margarita. When she reached the side of the pool, Ace lowered down and gave her a scorching hot kiss. Autumn actually had to look away because she felt her own cheeks heat. Damn!

Ace stood up and scanned the pool, and everyone smiled. He was a good-looking man, just like the rest of the team.

"You ladies having fun?" He asked, grinning. Autumn had a feeling he knew they were all three sheets to the wind, except for Tenley.

Alex spoke for the group. Well, she actually shouted, showing just how much fun they were having and probably how much alcohol they'd consumed.

"Oh yeah. It's been a great time. Hasn't it, ladies?" She asked, looking over her shoulder and winking.

All of the women cheered, including Autumn, who was looking around, wondering if Frost was here too. She had texted him that she was coming over to Alex's to hang out, not that she knew if he received it or not, since all the ladies assumed the guys were being shipped out.

"Where's the rest of the guys? You should've invited them over. We have burgers and hot dogs in the fridge that we can throw on the grill, and I think I have some stuff to put a salad together." Ace grinned, and before he could open his mouth, the rest of the gang pushed through the back door, talking and laughing.

Autumn immediately caught sight of Frost in his black swim trunks and white t-shirt. He was talking with Stitch when his eyes met hers. He smiled, and she could see the sparkle in them.

Frost and the rest of the team were standing in the kitchen when they heard Alex talking to Ace rather loudly. Frost smiled and shook his head, and Stitch started laughing.

"Is Alex drunk?" Skittles asked, looking amused.

Frost shook his head and then laughed when Mia attempted to paddle her way to the shallow end with a drink in her hand and flipped off her raft.

"I'd say all of them are feeling pretty good," Irish said, standing at the glass door watching.

"Yeah, well, my wife better not be consuming any alcohol unless she wants a sore pink ass," Potter exclaimed before heading out the door in search of Tenley. Frost could only shake his head at the man as they all followed him outside. The moment Frost stepped foot onto the patio, his eyes locked onto the yellow raft that was keeping his woman afloat.

"Come on in, guys. The water is perfect," Mia exclaimed.

Everyone kicked off their shoes and divested their shirts before leaping into the water, making the women laugh when the water splashed them.

Frost swam under the water and came up behind Autumn. Her green bikini matched her eyes, and she looked stunning. Even her cheeks looked a little rosy, and he didn't think it was from the sun, knowing she slathered on the sunscreen. If he were to guess right, he would say his woman had a little too much to drink.

He wrapped his hand around her left ankle and pulled her under the water. Suddenly, she started kicking her legs violently and thrashing her arms. When he noticed the panicked look on her face, he knew something wasn't right. He quickly grabbed her around the waist and pushed off the bottom of the pool, bringing them both to the surface.

Once above water, she coughed and clung to him. He could feel her shaking, and he wondered what in the hell went wrong. A minute ago, she was just laughing and seemed to be enjoying herself, and now she was acting like a scared kitten. All he did was pull her under the water.

189

"Whoa, baby. I got you." He spoke in a soft voice, holding her with one hand under her butt while he swam a few feet toward the shallow end where he could stand.

Once he could touch, he wrapped his other arm around her and hugged her. She laid her head on his shoulder. Her face was buried in his neck, and she was still shaking, although not as bad. He kissed her temple. He felt her warm breath against his neck.

Alex swam up next to him. "Is she alright?"

She stirred in his arms, and he loosened his hold slightly. It was just enough for her to move a little, and she looked right at him. Her face was red, and he didn't miss the tears in her eyes either.

"I am so sorry," Autumn whispered.

He kissed her forehead. "That's okay. It's partially my fault. I shouldn't have snuck up like that and pulled you under."

She shook her head. "No, it wasn't your fault. You didn't know." She glanced over at the other women and lowered her eyes, and he knew immediately that something was going on between the four women. After a few seconds of silence, it clicked in his head.

"Oh, fuck! You don't know how to swim, do you? What in the hell were you thinking, drinking and swimming in the deep end?"

The other guys made similar comments as well, and Frost felt Autumn tense up in his arms.

"Frost, she was fine. We were with her. We even taught her how to doggie paddle," Mia said.

"None of you should be in the pool while you're drinking." Stitch then narrowed his eyes at Mia. "Look, you can't even stay on the raft. What happened if you flipped over and hit your head on the side of the pool?" Mia's cheeks turned pink as she narrowed her brown eyes at Stitch.

Frost had to hide his smile because whether Stitch meant to chastise Mia or not, he just confirmed what everyone thought. He had feelings for Mia. Although Ace's expression wasn't giving his thoughts away, Frost knew Ace was aware of the chemistry between his baby sister and Stitch. And, surprisingly, he wasn't against it. All he wanted was for his sister to be happy, loved, and respected by a reputable man, and Ace knew Stitch had those qualities.

"We will talk about this later," Frost told Autumn and hugged her. "And just for the record, I'm teaching you how to swim."

She stood on her tippy toes and smiled as she looped her arms around his neck and placed kisses to the corner of his mouth before landing on his actual lips. "I was planning on signing up on Monday at the rec center down the road, but I think I'd like it better if you were my teacher." She winked at him, and he snorted a laugh, knowing there was no way he'd get much teaching done while holding her in a pool.

CHAPTER TWENTY

Autumn was laughing while listening to Frost's dad tell stories of Frost and his brother, Trey when they were younger. The two seemed like peas in a pod.

Dinner had been delicious. Frost's mom's stuffed cabbage was absolutely mouth-watering. When Autumn found out it was only ground beef, rice, browned butter, and a pinch of cinnamon rolled into a cabbage leaf and cooked in lemon juice and water, she had to get the recipe from his mom before she left.

She felt relaxed as she conversed with his family. She had to admit, she was a nervous Nelly when they first arrived. But Frost had assured her on the drive over that his family would love her. She wasn't so optimistic. As soon as they arrived, Frost's mom came barreling out of the house and, to her surprise, came to her first before her son and wrapped her up in a huge hug. The gesture had almost made her cry.

"Autumn, I have to say your son is a lovely boy. And so well mannered."

Autumn smiled. "Thank you, Mrs. Rhoades. I've always tried to teach and guide him as best as I could. Not to toot my own horn, but he's done really well, considering I uprooted his life and moved us out here."

Jennie smiled warmly. "Yes, Jack explained to us that you lost your husband a couple of years ago. I'm so sorry. The world can be a strange and cruel place sometimes. But I'm glad that you were strong enough to make decisions and move forward."

Lord, if the woman only knew how she had been following Kevin's death. But, she wasn't going even to touch that subject.

As if sensing her unease, Jack's mom shifted the conversation. Jennie took a sip of her after-dinner coffee. "On another note, do you want more children?"

"Mom!" Frost scowled at his mom, and his dad chuckled along with his brother and his wife.

"What? Can't I ask my future daughter-in-law if it's possible I could have more grandchildren?" Jennie was acting all innocent, and it actually made Autumn laugh.

Frost looked up at the ceiling and mumbled. "Jesus, just take me out back and shoot me."

Autumn thought it was funny, and she giggled, then squeezed his thigh, letting him know she was fine with his mother's line of questioning.

Frost's brother's wife, Sammie, spoke up. "Don't take it personally, Autumn, I was asked similar questions before Trey and I got married."

The table got extremely quiet, and Autumn realized they were all looking at her. *Oh shit! Were they seriously wanting me to answer that question? Now?*

The answer was easy, of course, she wanted more kids, but she thought she and Frost would have discussed any future between themselves first. Here she was being asked about adding to the Rhoades' family tree, and not forgetting she was already being called a future daughter-in-law.

She cleared her throat, which seemed to be extremely dry all of a sudden.

"Well, Mrs. Rhoades…"

Jennie waved her hand in the air. "Stop that nonsense. You're family now, you call me Jennie."

Autumn smiled but could feel the heat in her cheeks. "Yes, ma'am. I would love to have more children."

She glanced over to gauge Frost's reaction. For some reason, she was expecting to see a scared or nervous expression, but the look he gave her was far from that. His nostrils flared, and she knew he wanted the same. And from the smoldering look that he was giving her, she thought Frost might drag her to the nearest room and fuck her until he knew for sure he had put a baby in her. That thought made her squeeze her thighs together. *Oh, my god, he has got me so aroused right now; I'm primed and ready to shoot off like a rocket.* Thank God, Frost was able to steer the conversation to sports.

As Autumn and Frost were saying their good-byes to his family, Jennie pulled her in for another hug.

"You are a blessing to this family, Autumn."

Autumn pulled back. "Why is that?"

She took a quick glance at Frost, who was talking with his dad and brother while Cody listened to them. "Because it has been a long time since I have seen my son smile the way he smiles at you. I know it is hard for a woman living with a man like Frost. I went through the same with his dad. Gone at a moment's notice and all of the secrecy and worrying, but I wouldn't trade it for the world. What they represent is a rare breed of men and women fighting to protect our country. In my mind, all military and first responders should be given more respect for what they do and represent. Not everyone has the courage to put their lives on the line every day."

"To be honest with you, Jennie, it took your son a lot to get me to commit to him. However, he made it very hard to say no. After losing my husband, I didn't think I wanted to set myself up for heartbreak if something were to happen."

"And what changed your mind, dear?"

"He did. When he told me about how he was injured saving Tenley's little girl, he reminded me that bad things don't just happen in the war; they can happen at any time. I love your son very much. I just want you to know that."

Jennie took Autumn's hand and squeezed. "I know, honey, and I know for a fact he loves both you and Cody. He would move heaven and earth for the both of you."

Autumn just nodded her head because she knew deep down that is exactly what Frost would do.

On the way home, after they had dropped Cody off at a friend's house for a sleepover, they were both quiet. Frost wasn't sure what she was thinking about, but he, on the other hand, couldn't get past the conversation at his parent's house about his mom wanting grandkids and Autumn still wanting children. He wanted to give her those babies.

He glanced over at Autumn in the passenger seat. She was sitting quietly with her hands clasped on her lap, looking out the window. He reached over and took her hand and brought it up to his lips. She turned and smiled at him. It was hard to keep his eyes on the road she was that beautiful to look at.

"You okay? You seem a little quiet."

She grinned. "Yeah, I'm good. Just thinking about the conversations this evening."

He jerked his head back toward her, and he saw her eyes transform to a brighter green. Was she thinking about making babies, too? Thank God, they were just a minute from the house.

Neither said a word as they got out of the car. Frost met her at the front and placed his hand on her lower back, and guided her to the front door. As soon as they both made it through the door and secured all of the locks, he couldn't take it anymore. All of the talk about babies, grandkids, future daughter-in-law had him so fired up, he was on the verge of exploding.

Autumn kicked her shoes off and went to walk toward the living room when he gripped her waist, turned her around and lifted her, pressing her back up against the door. He could feel the heat from her pussy through his jeans. He took her mouth hard in a deep kiss. She gripped his shirt and ripped it open, sending the buttons scattering all over the floor. It was wild and intense. She quickly moved to his jeans, undoing the button, sliding down the zipper, and using her legs to push them to the floor freeing his erection. All while Frost never let up on the assault to her mouth. He kneeled before her, pausing briefly before running his hands up her thighs, entangling his thick fingers in the sides of her panties and slowly sliding them down her legs. Her pussy throbbed in anticipation. She playfully kicked them to the side, bracing herself for what would come next. Frost began at the inside of her knees, trailing kisses up the sides of her thighs and switching between the two. When his mouth was just about to reach her most sacred parts, he paused again, taking in a slow deep breath.

195

"Frost, I need you."

"I know, baby, but first, let me taste how wet you are."

His words echoed through her, and she had never felt more connected to anyone before, as she did at this moment. Frost took her hot, wet heat in his mouth, and her breath hitched in her chest. Autumn couldn't hold back as she let out a loud moan, and they just kept coming. Her knees were getting weak. She didn't think she could take much more as she burst into ecstasy while cumming in his mouth. Frost stood and wrapped an arm around her before her knees gave out. Letting her bask in the moment before he buried his cock in her, he pressed her back against the door. He kissed along her neck and up to her lips. Then he slid into her, and she let out a moan and then cried out, "harder." She took all of him over and over again. Frost felt her tighten around him again, and he thrust into her two more times when she exploded around him. He only needed one final thrust before he emptied himself into her.

He scooped her up into his arms and carried her to the bedroom. He tossed her onto the bed, and she bounced and started to giggle. Apparently, the talk of babies had everyone feeling horny.

Frost felt her hand glide across his chest and knew his Irish Beauty was awake, although he wasn't sure how she could be. After fucking her senseless, they had made love two more times before she fell into a sex induced coma. He looked over at the alarm clock. It was a little after three in the morning. She was curled up against him. Her head was tucked up under his chin, their legs entwined. He felt her move, and he looked down and met her emerald eyes. They were so bright, it was like they were glowing.

He caressed her back in soft, gentle strokes. "Everything okay?" He asked, looking over at her. She was absolutely beautiful.

She smiled and nodded. "Yeah. How about you?"

He felt like he was on top of the world, but, the whole conversation about kids had kept him awake. He had wondered if Autumn told his mom what she did just to appease her.

He gathered her hair in his hand and slid his fingers through the silky tresses. She had beautiful hair, and he loved the way the strands glided through his fingertips.

"Did you really mean what you said tonight?" He asked.

"About what?"

"About wanting to have kids."

She stilled for a moment as if she was thinking, then sat up and moved on top of him, straddling him. The sheet fell from her body, exposing her ivory skin. She leaned down, the move causing her breasts to press against his chest. Her lips were mere inches from his as she stared intently into his eyes.

"I meant every word. I want more children. I want to have your babies, Jack. I love you and hope one day we get married and start making those babies."

Frost couldn't even swallow because of the emotion clogging his throat. He was hanging on by a thread. He was elated, excited, and my god, so horny.

He flipped her over so quickly it didn't even register to her what was happening until he was hovering above her as he slowly slid his cock into her core.

"Who says we can't get a lot of practice until then."

She laughed, but soon that laughter turned into moans of pleasure. With every stroke, Frost kept reminding himself how fucking lucky he was that this beautiful creature was all his.

CHAPTER TWENTY-ONE

Work for Autumn over the last couple of weeks had been hectic, and she was exhausted. But that was okay because it took her mind off Frost and the danger he could be in.

The guys had gotten called out almost two weeks ago. Frost had mentioned there was a good possibility they would need to leave out on a mission. It was just a matter of time. Although he didn't provide any other information which she expected, and she didn't ask for any. She knew better. She had noticed he seemed a little antsy ever since that day at Ace and Alex's when the guys had gotten called into the base but not shipped out. Now that she thought about it, all of the guys seemed to be a little more on edge since then. Whatever was going on didn't seem good.

As she started her drive home, it was already getting dark. Normally, she'd be home by now, but she'd taken on some extra hours at the hospital since Cody was away at camp.

Today had been an interesting day. That creepy Cecil guy had shown up at the hospital earlier. She had just finished up with a patient when another staff member escorted him to the room she was in. He had shocked her by giving her a bouquet of red and white roses. When she had asked him what he was doing at the hospital, he explained he was there for a meeting regarding a new piece of radiology equipment his company was producing. It was some new state of the art machine.

The flowers were a little creepy, but she became extremely uncomfortable when his eyes roamed over her body as she stood there, especially when she caught him licking his lips while staring at her breasts. Thank God they were booked with back-to-back appointments and had a valid reason to excuse herself. He had invited her to dinner, but she politely declined and told him she was seeing someone. That must have upset him, because his charming demeanor instantly changed to anger, and he acted annoyed.

She turned off the main road and onto the side streets that took her to her housing complex. She still had about twenty minutes to go. She always hated this stretch of road at night because not many people traveled it, and it was dark. She cranked the radio, trying to get the creepy thoughts out of her head. After a few minutes alone on the road, another set of headlights started coming up behind her. At the rate they were approaching, she knew they had to be going well over the posted speed limit. As the headlights got closer, Autumn slowed to the 50mph posted speed and hoped this nut would pass her. But when the vehicle got within a couple of cars' length from the back of her car, they flashed their high beams, and she started to get nervous. She turned the radio down and heard the rev of an engine. It sounded like one of those big diesel trucks. She slowed, even more, when the truck was practically right on her bumper. She couldn't see a damn thing because the reflection of the headlights in the rearview mirror was right in her eyes. It was blinding. She tried moving on the shoulder but knew there wasn't a lot of room before there was a big drop-off into a ditch. All of a sudden, she felt the bump, and the back end of her car swerved to the right.

She screamed out as the person tried to run her off the road. She gripped the steering with both hands and got the car under control and stepped on the gas. She needed to get to help. She still had another seven or eight miles before she would hit any type of gas station or store, and her phone was in her purse on the floor of the passenger side.

She looked up and saw the truck coming at her again. When she glanced down at the speedometer, it read seventy-five. As the truck got closer, she braked and went onto the shoulder. But the truck never slowed down, hitting the left rear of the bumper and sending her headfirst into the deep ditch. She heard the crunch of metal and glass shattering before her head hit the steering wheel, knocking her for a loop.

She heard the rev of the engine again and prayed the person would leave her alone. She tried looking around, but her body hurt, and her vision was blurry. The airbags hadn't deployed, but thank God, her seatbelt worked, although she hit her head. Blood dripped down her forehead.

Knowing she needed help, she unclicked her seatbelt and reached for her purse.

She pulled out her phone and dialed 911. She explained what had happened, and after assuring the operator that she was ok—even though she really wasn't a hundred percent sure—they told her that an emergency crew and police had been dispatched to her location. She tried opening her door, but it was jammed, so she crawled over to the passenger side and was able to get out.

Once outside, she got a look at her car. The front was a heap of twisted metal. Smoke billowed from under the wreckage. Most of the windows had been broken. Her body started to tremble, knowing she could've been killed. She felt so alone right now as she waited on the dark road for the police. The smell of oil and other chemicals infiltrated her nose. She had some cuts along her arms from the broken glass. She was scared. She needed to call someone, so she dialed Alex.

Alex picked up on the third ring, and Autumn explained what had happened and where she was.

"Someone ran you off the road? Did you call the police?"

"Yes. Actually, I can see flashing lights heading this way now." She was trying to stay focused.

"Autumn, are you okay? Are you hurt?" She could hear the concern in Alex's voice and keys jingling.

"I hit my head on the steering wheel. The police just showed up." They were followed by a fire truck and ambulance.

"Okay, good. I'm on my way."

"Okay."

She couldn't believe something like this happened. Thank goodness Cody was at camp and not with her. The police officer asked her if she was okay. She had no intention of going to the hospital, but she did let the paramedic look over her cuts. She would have Alex take her to the hospital once she gave the police her statement and called a tow truck to retrieve her car. She might as well tell them to take it to the scrapyard because it was beyond salvageable. There was no chance in hell her insurance company was going to pay to repair it. Good news, she would get a new car out of this. Bad news, she would now have another monthly expense.

She gave her statement to the officer. She couldn't provide much of a description of the vehicle that hit her since it was dark. Plus, the asshole had their high beams on, so she was blinded. She knew it was a diesel engine truck of some sort, but that was about it.

Alex showed up with Derek. She had managed to keep her emotions at bay until Alex ran over and hugged her. Then she lost it, and the more she cried, the more her head hurt. She just wanted to go home. However, she didn't want to go back to her home. She didn't want to be alone. What she really wanted was Frost here with her to make her feel secure, but she couldn't have that right now and it made her sad.

The guys finished up their debriefing on base and were getting ready to head to Bayside and have a beer before going home. It was a ritual amongst the team. Anytime they were deployed, they always met at Bayside for a beer when they got back stateside to celebrate them all making it home in one piece.

Frost was feeling antsy. He wanted to get to Bayside and guzzle his beer, so he could head home to Autumn. He looked at his watch. It was just a little after six in the evening. She should be getting home just about now.

"It's an awesome feeling, isn't it?" Ace said, coming up and standing next to him.

"What are you talking about?"

"That feeling knowing someone is waiting at home for you."

Frost smiled wide. "Yeah, it is."

"Well, then. Let's get the fuck out of here, so we can get home to our women. I haven't even called Alex yet."

As Frost and Ace were walking out, they heard their names being called. When they both turned, they saw Derek walking toward them, and from the looks of the pained expression on his face, Frost had a feeling this chat wasn't going to be good.

"Everything okay?" Ace asked.

Derek rubbed the back of his neck like he was working out some knots. Frost knew from being around the Commander that when he rubbed the back of his neck like that, it was never a good sign.

Derek looked Frost in the eye. "Hear me out before asking questions." Derek took a deep breath. "Autumn was in a car accident a couple of nights ago."

Frost felt his stomach drop. This news was not what he was expecting at all. A million thoughts started running through his mind.

"Is she okay? Was Cody with her? Why are you just now telling me about this?"

The guys who were on their way out stopped when they heard what Derek said, and they all gathered around listening and looking just as worried as Frost felt. Autumn was a part of their family now, so, of course, they were concerned.

"Calm down, Frost. She was alone, coming home from work when another car ran her off the road. Her car went into that deep ditch on Grand Haven Rd. She has a couple of bruises and a small cut on her forehead, but other than that, she's fine."

Frost felt his temper rise. His fists were clenched at his side. The last thing he wanted to do was calm down. He knew how she hated to travel that road, especially at night. But then he realized what Derek said. "What do you mean she was run off the road? Do they know who it was?"

"No, but the police are investigating. The car hit the back of Autumn's car, so the police are pulling evidence like the paint and the description that Autumn could give, although it wasn't much, considering it was dark out. From her account of what happened, it was intentional."

Frost ran his hand through his hair.

"Where is she now?"

"She's at Alex's. She's been there since the night of the accident. She called Alex when it happened. Alex took her to the hospital, then took her home with her. Her car is totaled, though. She's damn lucky she wasn't hurt worse."

Frost felt the anger build up. He swung and punched the wall, putting a hole in the sheetrock. "Fuck! I swear to God when I get my hands on the sonofabitch who did this, I'm going to kill him."

Derek shot a warning look to Frost. "You let the police handle this, you hear me? No going off on any solo missions." Derek turned to look around at all of the guys. "And that goes for all of you. I want this asshole caught as much as you do, but I will not tolerate any of you jeopardizing your careers. Is that understood?"

A series of mumbles were heard throughout the room.

Alex was fixing dinner when Ace called her to let her know he and Frost were on their way to the house. Ace warned her that Frost was fired up after hearing what happened to Autumn. She understood completely. She also explained to him more of what Autumn went through and how one of her Uncle Tink's employees from his security firm was staying with them as a precaution. She felt little more comfortable, knowing someone else was in the house with her and Autumn. Whoever was after Autumn was intent on doing her harm. Alex could only imagine how Frost was feeling right now.

She pulled the oven open and brought out the pan of garlic bread. A simple dinner was on the menu for tonight; spaghetti and meatballs. As she was pulling down the plates, she heard Byron, the guy on Tink's staff, greet Ace and Frost.

She walked over to the table and started setting it for the five of them. She and Byron had a conversation the first night he was there when he said he didn't want to impose when she offered him to eat with her and Autumn. It took some talking and a threat to call her Uncle Tink to get him to give in and sit down and eat with them.

As she placed the last setting on the table, she felt those familiar arms go around her waist, giving her a good squeeze. She smiled, knowing her fiancé was home and safe. He kissed the side of her neck and nuzzled his nose against her skin. She turned in his arms and was greeted with his gorgeous smile. She lifted up on her tiptoes and gave him a welcome home kiss.

"I love you," she whispered to him as her voice cracked. She got emotional every time he came home from a mission.

He squeezed her even tighter. "I love you, too, sweetheart."

As she pulled back, she saw Frost standing there, looking fierce with his arms folded across his chest. She walked over and hugged him, and he kissed her cheek.

"Autumn's upstairs in the guest room on the right. She was tired and wanted to lay down before dinner. She doesn't know you guys are home."

"How's she doing?"

"She says she's fine, but I can tell she's still shaken up a bit. Most of the muscles in her body are sore from the impact. She has a couple of nasty bruises and a small cut on her forehead. She's been soaking in Epsom salt baths every night."

He took a deep breath. "Thank you for letting her stay here with you."

She gave him an annoyed look. "Seriously, do you think I'd let her stay anywhere else? She even told me she didn't want to go back to her house alone. This really shook her up. Since it's already almost seven and I have dinner made, why don't the two of you stay the night?"

Damn, he loved his best friend. She was always thinking of everyone else before herself. "Thanks, honey. I think that's a good idea." He gave her another hug before handing her off to Ace and going in search of his woman.

Frost opened the bedroom door and saw Autumn curled up in the middle of the queen-size bed. She had a small throw blanket covering most of her body, but her face was in plain view, especially with her long hair pulled back into a ponytail. He frowned as his eyes scanned the bruises and the small band-aide on her forehead. God, he wished he could take it all away from her. But he couldn't. However, he could be with her now and care for her.

He walked over to the bed and toed off his boots, sliding in next to her. He gently ran his fingers over the bandage on her forehead. Then he kissed it, letting his lips linger, hoping it would help make it feel better just the way his mom would do to him when he was younger and would get hurt.

She stirred in his arms and slowly blinked her eyes open. Once it registered who was in bed with her, she smiled wide and snuggled into his arms.

"Hey, sugar," he said, tipping her head up and giving her a light kiss on the lips.

"This isn't some cruel dream, is it? I mean, you're really home, right?" She whispered in a sleepy voice, and she looked so cute with her scrunched up nose.

He chuckled. "Yeah, baby. I'm home."

She looked up into his eyes, and he could see the vulnerability. She was still fearful. Hell, he would be too, if someone had run him off the road on purpose. Her eyes were full of tears, and she seemed like she just needed a good cry.

He pulled her close to his body, and she started sobbing.

"I was so scared. I didn't know what to do. I mean, this truck came out of nowhere and hit me, not once but twice. The scariest part is I have no clue who it was or why. What happens if they try to come after me again? Or worse, they try something with Cody?"

Frost was thinking the same. He had already spoken with Derek, and he was going to call his buddy Tink who owned the security firm. He was paying to have a camera installed on both the front and back door of Autumn's house. That way, if this motherfucker came around the house, they'd have a face to give to the police. He explained all of that to Autumn. She told him she felt a little better knowing that, but she was still fearful. Her boss Nancy told her to take the next week off and not come back to work until she felt ready to.

"Alex said dinner is almost ready. Are you hungry?"

She gave him a little smile. "Alex has been a savior. I owe her for letting me stay here. I didn't want to go back to the house."

He smiled back and ran his fingers through her ponytail. "Yeah, she's a great friend to have." He gave her hip a little squeeze. "You didn't answer me. Are you hungry?"

"A little bit. But can we lay here for just a few more minutes? I missed you and missed being in your arms."

He gave her another kiss. "We can do whatever you want."

She smiled and snuggled up to his side. Her chest was pressed against him, and he could feel the beat of her heart. Having her in his arms and knowing she was indeed okay calmed him to a point. But he couldn't help but think whoever did this would be back and try to harm her again.

CHAPTER TWENTY-TWO

Carlie sat in her hotel room. Two weeks had gone by since she had run Autumn's car off the road. The truck she had used was stolen, and she had ditched it behind an abandoned house a few towns north. She was careful to avoid any places that could have cameras set up.

She couldn't believe Autumn had escaped the car crash with only minor injuries. She had followed the police activity since the accident. They weren't any closer to finding out who had done it. It was still an ongoing investigation. But by the time they found the truck that was used and got any closer to solving the case, Autumn would be dead, and she would be back home in North Dakota.

She picked up the phone and dialed another guy who she hoped would help her out with one last attempt on Autumn's life. Ever since the first guy Skinny bailed on her, she'd been keeping her ears open on the street to land another person to help with the dirty work. It took some time, but it finally paid off.

A gruff voice answered the phone. She explained who she was. Of course, she used an alias. She explained she needed something put inside Autumn's house. Two bags. At first, the guy was hesitant because Carlie wouldn't tell him what was in the bags. She told him it didn't matter to him, just that the bags needed to be placed in the house—Autumn's bedroom specifically. But once she told him that she was offering him one thousand dollars in cash, the guy jumped at the opportunity with no other questions asked. It was set for tomorrow. The guy would pick up the bags from the abandoned house across the street from Autumn's and sneak in while she was at work.

She smiled, knowing that after tomorrow night, she'd never have to worry about Autumn again.

CHAPTER TWENTY-THREE

Frost opened the door and allowed Autumn, Cody, and Alejandra to walk into the house. The four of them had spent the day down at the Boardwalk. Frost took a day of leave, and Autumn used one of her many vacation days to have a little fun with the kids on the rides and in the arcades. It had been two weeks since Autumn's car accident.

They had just stopped at the house to grab their swimsuits before they all headed over to Ace and Alex's for a casual barbeque dinner and swimming. Potter and Tenley were coming over as well.

Cody went to his room, and Alejandra followed him. Autumn used those minutes to look through the day's mail. Frost was sitting at the breakfast bar, reading through his texts. Autumn had been looking over Cody's report card that she had finally gotten in the mail when she heard Alejandra scream and Cody call out frantically for her.

Both her and Frost heard the terror in his voice and took off to his room.

Frost entered the room first, and Autumn followed closely behind. He saw Cody on the floor, holding his ankle. Alejandra was sitting behind him. They were both crying, but the fear Frost saw in the kid's eyes told him something was really bad. That was when the sound he heard registered in his brain. It was the sound of a rattle shaking. He looked toward the bed and saw it. Or should he say them. Two fucking rattlesnakes, and they were pissed off.

"Fuck!" Frost shoved Autumn back into the hallway, so she wouldn't be in danger, then grabbed a blanket that was draped over the back of Cody's desk chair and threw it over the angry snakes. Quickly, he scooped up both kids, one in each arm, and high tailed it out of the room, kicking the door shut on the way out. Autumn took Alejandra from him, and he gently laid Cody on the couch and started looking over Cody's ankle. His ankle was already red and swelling. They needed to get to the hospital.

Instead of calling 911 and waiting for an ambulance, he decided it would be quicker to drive there.

He looked at Autumn, who was wide-eyed and shaking as she kneeled by Cody's head, talking to him. He grabbed her hand. "Autumn. We need to move fast. I'm not going to wait for an ambulance. Grab your purse, and I'll grab Cody. I'll put him in the back seat of my Tahoe with you, and we'll call Tenley on the way to the hospital. Potter mentioned she was working today, and she should still be there. If not, I'll tell her to meet us there."

Frost hoped to hell the hospital had anti-venom on hand.

"Mommy, it hurts," Cody cried, then he threw-up all over himself and on the sofa.

"We need to move, Autumn. Let's go," Frost barked at her.

They moved as a team and got Cody into the back seat. Autumn jumped in next to Cody, and Frost got Alejandra buckled in and already had his phone out and was talking to someone as he got into the car and started it.

As they flew down the road, Frost met Autumn's gaze in the rearview mirror. Her eyes were red and full of tears.

They arrived at the hospital in record time. Tenley was waiting for them at the emergency entrance with a team of medical personnel. They got Cody out of the car and onto a gurney and rushed inside with him. Frost told Autumn to go with Cody, and he would take care of the car and Alejandra. The poor little girl looked so scared. He was scared himself. He knew snakes could get into houses, but what were the odds of two snakes getting in and both confined to one room. And not just any snakes; rattlesnakes. He knew they were around, but it was rare to see one in this area.

"Uncle Frost, is Cody going to be okay?" Alejandra asked, wiping tears from her eyes.

He picked her up and carried her inside the emergency department. "I honestly don't know, sweetheart. But your mommy and her doctor friends here at the hospital are going to do everything they can to help him."

She wrapped her arms around his neck and cried. He walked faster, needing to be there with Autumn and Cody. Cody was already a son to him. If anything happened to him, he didn't think he could survive. He shook that thought from his head. Cody was a strong, healthy boy. He was going to be fine. They got him to the hospital in time. As he entered the hospital, he kept repeating that everything would be fine.

It was mid-morning the next day. They had been at the hospital all night. Thankfully, the emergency room team had the anti-venom on hand and were administering large doses intravenously into Cody, along with antibiotics, fluids, and a mild pain killer. Currently, he was stable. He was admitted in the early hours of the morning and moved to the pediatric unit on the second floor.

Frost sat in one of the two reclining chairs in Cody's room. Autumn was sitting next to Cody's bed. She hadn't slept a wink, and it was showing. She looked exhausted and was also starting to get a little snippy with people, although he wasn't going to say anything, yet.

Cody, on the other hand, had pretty much slept since they brought him to the hospital yesterday evening. It took a while to get the kid some pain killers. A snake had never bitten Frost, but he knew plenty of men who had, and all of them had said it hurt like a bitch. The doctors were pretty optimistic about his recovery. They didn't believe the snake got a "full" bite, therefore, not a lot of venom was released into Cody's leg.

Frost got up and stretched his legs. He needed some coffee. He walked over to Cody's bed, and Autumn looked up at him. He leaned down and kissed her. She grabbed his hand, and he could tell she was hanging on by a thread. He pulled her up and hugged her.

"He's all I have, Jack. I almost lost him."

He rubbed her back. "We didn't, though. Come on, baby, calm down."

In a surprising move that shocked him, she shoved her hands against his chest and pushed him away.

"Don't tell me to calm down, dammit. How can you even ask me to do that when my ten-year-old son is lying in a hospital bed being pumped

210

with anti-venom because some sicko out there with a grudge against me decided to put rattlesnakes in my son's room?" Tears were falling from her eyes. "Terrorizing me is one thing, but going after my son?" She sniffled and walked back over to Frost, pressing her forehead against his shoulder. "Who does something like that, Jack? Who?"

He wrapped his arms tightly around her and buried his face in her hair. "I don't know, but we'll find out. I promise you that."

As he held her, he started thinking about events that had happened to Autumn in the last month or two. Her flat tires, wires that had mysteriously come loose under the hood of her car, the break-in and someone messing with her husband's dog tags, the cigarette butts out by her car several times a week, not to mention being in the car accident, and now this. He popped his eyes open. Son of a bitch! Someone had been watching her and targeting her for a while.

Just then, the door to the room opened, and Ace stood there. Frost looked over Autumn's head and knew right away by the angry and hard expression on Ace's face; he had some information, and it wasn't good. Hopefully, the guys were able to catch something on the surveillance cameras.

Ace came over and gave Autumn a hug and kiss on the cheek. He looked over at Cody, who was sleeping soundlessly. Frost could literally see Ace biting the inside of his cheek. He was pissed along with the rest of the team. They all had a soft heart for women and kids, especially the violent acts towards women and kids they'd seen in not the best places in the world. He looked back at Autumn. "How are you holding up, sweetheart?"

Autumn sniffled again, and it broke Frost's heart, seeing her like this. She didn't deserve this shit. If he could switch places, he would in a heartbeat. He and Autumn hadn't talked about them getting married, but he knew it was just a matter of time until she was officially his.

Autumn explained to Ace what the doctors had told her and how it was a wait-and-see situation to see know if the venom had done any long-term tissue or muscle damage.

211

Ace then asked Frost if he could talk to him out in the hall. After assuring Autumn he'd be right back, he started to walk out. On their way out, he passed his mom and dad as they were coming in. His mom went right to him and hugged him. He saw the tears in her eyes. His mom and dad already considered Autumn and Cody a part of their family. "Oh, Jack, how is Cody?"

He hugged her back. "He's stable right now. We got him here quickly, which was good, but that type of snakebite is bad. He'll be here for a few days."

"Oh, and how is Alejandra? We heard she was in the room when it happened."

"She's fine. She's with Tenley right now. She didn't want to leave Cody's side, though. He saved her from getting bitten. She was closest when they both realized what the sound was. Cody managed to push her behind him. I'm damn proud of what he did."

His dad gave him and Ace a serious look. "I hope to hell you guys find the person responsible for this. There is no way that this was a coincidence."

"Trust me, Dad, when I get my hands on whoever is responsible, they're going to wish they were dead after I get through with them." He then started ticking off all of the incidents that had happened to Autumn over the last two months.

Both his dad and Ace were even more concerned and pissed off.

Ace spoke, "Well, you did the right thing by installing the cameras."

Frost looked surprised. He had hoped they would catch something or someone, but he still had his doubts. "So, Tink's guys got something."

Ace shook his head. "The police already have the kid in custody. They picked him up this morning."

Frost shook his head. "Wait a minute. Did you say a kid?"

"Yep. Seventeen-years-old. Looking for some easy cash. But this kid is only part of the issue. He told the police that a woman paid him to put the two bags in Autumn's room. How they ended up in Cody's remains a

212

mystery. When we told the punk what was in the bags, his face turned white as a fucking ghost. He had no clue."

"Jesus Christ, I hope the police got a description of the woman and any other information that could help."

"Oh, he's singing like a canary, especially when they let Potter in on the interrogation. The kid is detailing every job the woman paid him and another guy to do. You were right. All the tampering with her car. All of those flat tires and engine issues? She was behind it. The other guy was also the one who broke into her house."

"What about her car accident?"

"Potter said the kid was surprised about that, so they don't believe he was involved."

"Where do they meet this woman? How does she get in touch with them? Did they give a description?"

Just then, Frost's phone rang. He looked at the screen and saw it was Nathan. Why was Nathan calling? Unless Autumn called him to tell him about Cody. He swiped the screen and answered.

"Hey, Nathan, I was just about to give you a call."

"Yeah, but what I have to say is more important. Where's Autumn and Cody right now?" Frost didn't like the desperation in the sound of Nathan's voice. Something was wrong.

He quickly explained what happened with Cody and told him that they were all at the hospital. Autumn hadn't called him yet, and Nathan seemed a little upset. Frost could understand why he felt that way, but in Autumn's defense, she probably just overlooked it since she'd been so busy and concerned with Cody and dealing with the doctors and visitors.

"Did you catch who did it with the security cameras?"

"Yeah, it was some low life punk. He said he and another guy were being paid by a woman to terrorize Autumn."

Nathan swore, and Frost got the feeling that Nathan may have some information relevant to all of this crazy shit happening to Autumn.

"Nathan…what's going on? Do you have any information connected to this shit storm here?"

"Yeah, I just arrived at Carlie's house. You know Autumn's sister-in-law."

"Okay, what's that got to do with what's happening here?"

"I've been trying to call her for a couple of weeks to check on her. She never answered, so I decided to catch a flight here. Fuck man. There are pictures of Autumn all over the place. One has a target drawn on her forehead. Some have a knife stuck through them, and that's not the worst of it. There's more, but I got the local Sheriff here now, and they are combing through everything."

"I don't understand. Why would she go after Autumn?"

"According to the notes we found, she blames Autumn for ruining her life and her relationship with her parents and brother. There's more, but I'm going to finish up here with the Sheriff and then catch the first flight down there in the morning. If we can track her down, I believe she'll listen to me."

"Can you give me a description of Carlie or send me a recent picture of her? I can get it to the detectives and the guys on my team."

"Yeah, I'll send it as soon as we hang up. Frost, do not leave Autumn or Cody's side for nothing."

"I won't let anything happen to her, Nathan. She and Cody are everything to me."

"Alright, I'll give you a call when I get in tomorrow."

Frost put his phone away, then ran his hand down his face. His phone beeped with an incoming message. He opened it and looked at the picture that Nathan had sent him, and his gut clenched. Christ, how was he going to tell Autumn that her sister-in-law was the person responsible for everything?

He walked back over to where Ace and his dad were. Irish had joined them. He had been with Tenley and Alejandra and had just come by to see Cody and in any way he could. All of the guys had been coming and going, including some of the guys from the Bravo team.

"That was Nathan. We got a name to go with the face of the woman in question." Ace raised a questioning eyebrow at his statement. "And you

214

are not going to believe it." Frost proceeded to tell them what Nathan shared with him, and he showed them the picture of Carlie.

"We need to get that over to the police right away," Ace said, already taking his phone out and texting Potter since he was at the police station.

"Nathan said the Sheriff in Carlie's town has already contacted the PD here and have briefed them. But I'll send the picture to Potter just in case, and he can pass it along."

"You okay, man?" Ace asked.

"No, I'm not. I need to get out of here for a little bit. I know that I should stay and be with Autumn, but I just need some time to decompress. I've got so much shit running through my head right now. And I don't know how in the hell I'm going to tell Autumn that her fucking sister-in-law is the reason her son is lying in a hospital bed."

Ace clasped Frost on the shoulder. "I understand, man. Come on. Let's tell Autumn we're going to step out for a little while; I'll call the guys and have them meet us somewhere. We'll sit outside, get some fresh air, and make a plan of action."

Knowing it was what he needed, he decided to let the guys take him out for a drink.

Ace had called Derek to fill him on everything, including Nathan's news. He, in turn, called his buddy Tink, and Rocky—both former teammates of Derek—to keep watch over Autumn and Cody at the hospital in his absence. Frost's mom was also there keeping Autumn company.

He walked into the room and told Autumn he was going to run out with the guys and grab some food. The exhaustion could even be heard in her voice. She was running on fumes and needed some sleep and food. She hadn't known he witnessed her breakdown in Cody's room last night. He wanted so badly to wrap his arms around her and console her but knew she needed that time to herself. So instead, he quietly backed out of the room and waited.

Autumn gave him a kiss and hug and told him to take his time, as she was fine. He also explained to her about Tink and Rocky coming by the hospital, and they would wait until he returned. She was a little skeptical

215

about that, but once he told her it was just a precaution, she relented. He knew Autumn could tell he was angry and needed to blow off some steam, but she never questioned it, and he respected her for it. He loved her so much, and soon he was going to ask her to marry him.

CHAPTER TWENTY-FOUR

Frost, Ace, Stitch, Irish, Potter, and Dino all sat around the table. They were all immediately upset once Ace and Frost explained who had been behind all the violent acts against Autumn.

"Is Autumn planning on staying in that house once Cody gets released?" Dino asked as he sipped his cold beer. Paul, the owner of Bayside, heard about what happened to Cody and bought the first round of drinks for them.

"I don't think so, and honestly, I don't want her staying there. But where she is going to move to is going to be a challenge."

"How so?"

"You all know she is very independent. Fuck, if I knew she wouldn't get pissed off, I'd drive over to her house right now, pack her shit up and find another place for her to stay that was safe."

Potter set his beer down on the table. Frost noticed that ever since Potter arrived, he'd been quiet. But that was nothing new, as he was known as the silent one on the team. However, Frost could tell something else was bothering him. He wouldn't question his friend now, though, but when he got him alone, he would.

Suddenly the big broody man broke his silence. "Frost…Tenley and I were talking last night, and we want Autumn and Cody to move into my old condo. The one on the beach. It's a secured complex, which is a hell of a lot more than what that sorry excuse of a house she lives in offers. And the condo itself is equipped with a security system."

Frost looked at Potter. "Are you sure, man? I thought you were talking about trying to rent it out."

Potter shrugged his shoulders and looked Frost in the eye with an intense stare. "We were, but things change." Frost got what he was conveying.

"How much? I'll pay whatever you're asking to rent it. I know Autumn can't afford something like that right now, but I'll pay you whatever."

He shook his head. "They can stay until she feels ready to find another place. There's no time limit on it. It was just sitting there anyway. Plus, I feel like I owe Cody my life. Because of his quick actions, he's the one lying in a hospital bed instead of my little girl."

Ahhh...Frost now understood the mood Potter was in, and he knew better than to try and argue. He would accept both his and Tenley's gratitude with a smile.

"Just for the record, I'm moving in with them. There is no way in hell I'm letting them out of my sight. Not with some lunatic trying to harm either one of them."

Potter's lip twitched. "I never doubted you weren't. Tenley was going to demand that you move in. I think her exact words were, "I'll go over to his apartment and pack his shit up and move it for him."

He looked over at Stitch. "I won't leave you hanging on the rent for the apartment. I'll square up with you for the remainder of the lease."

Stitch waved him off. "Whatever. The lease is up in two months anyway, and we both were talking about looking to find a house of our own here in town."

That was something they had talked about ever since transferring back east. This was where they both grew up and where they both wanted to retire when the time came. Their families and friends were here, and they hoped to grow families and memories of their own. It looked like he and Autumn would be in the market for a house.

Frost took a sip of his beer and swallowed. Then he glanced around the table at a group of men he was damn proud to call his brothers.

"Thank you all for being here and helping with this situation."

"Well, how about we finish up and then head over to Autumn's house and start moving her and Cody's stuff over to the condo," Ace told everyone, then asked the waitress for the check.

218

As they were paying the bill, Frost's phone rang. It was Skittles, and what he had to say just made the day even shittier.

"So, you mean to tell me Carlie's been able to see and hear everything going on in the house."

The team stood around Autumn's living room while Skittles explained about the hidden camera he and Diego found when they were sweeping the house.

Skittles nodded his head sideways. "Somewhat. The camera was located here in the living room. It's not a very complicated system. It only caught video out here. So, she could see the kitchen and living room, but because of how small the house is, the audio portion could pick up anything being said in a normal voice tone in either bedroom. It's a wireless feed that's coming from the house directly across the street." Skittles said, pointing to the dilapidated house.

"It can't be. Autumn said that house was abandoned." Then he remembered the very first time he showed up at Autumn's, the night Cody had hit his head. He had the feeling that he was being watched, and when he turned toward the house and saw the curtain move. "Motherfucker!"

"You're saying she's been living across the fucking street undetected this whole time?" Irish stated. The look on his face said it all. He was visibly upset.

"I doubt she was living there. She seems to be one step ahead. My guess is that she's holed up in some hotel under an alias," Skittles said.

Frost thought of something else. "The day Cody hit his head. He mentioned to Autumn and I that it was a parent who had bumped into him. Though he never saw her face, he did mention she was blonde. I'm wondering now if it was Carlie."

"You think she went to his school with an intent to harm him?" Ace asked, standing there with his arms crossed in front of chest, appearing disgusted.

"I don't know for sure, but with everything else we've uncovered, I'm not ruling it out."

219

Skittles explained the rest. "The police already went over across the street and scoured the place. They let us in to check it out as well. The computer was still up and running with the live feed. And here's the kicker; the electricity isn't even turned on in the place."

"How was she able to plug the computer in? A battery couldn't run it. It would need to be recharged."

"We found an extension cord running to the neighbor's house. She had plugged it into an outside outlet on the side of their house. They didn't have any knowledge of it when the police asked about it."

"They find anything else in the house?"

"No, but it smelled like a fucking garbage dump. There were food containers and trash strewn everywhere. Besides the computer, nothing personal was in there. I honestly don't think she was staying there. I think she was just using it as a base per se."

"Do we have any idea what she may be traveling in or where she could be? I've never seen a car parked over there."

"PD is looking into it, checking with all of the car rental agencies in the area, and also pulling camera footage."

Just as the guys were getting ready to enter the house and start packing, Alex pulled up in her black Escalade with Tenley. Frost and the guys walked over as the ladies got out. Ace hugged Alex, and Potter did the same with Tenley, placing his hand over the little swell of her belly.

"What brings you ladies by?" Frost asked.

"Well, Tenley told me about you guys moving into the condo, so we thought we could come lend a hand."

"You're not lifting anything." Potter scolded his wife.

Tenley rolled her eyes and elbowed him in the ribs. "Oh, knock it off, you big oaf. I know better. I can at least help pack up their clothes. I'm pregnant, not an invalid." Potter snagged her around the waist and hoisted her up close to his body. He said something to her quietly in her ear. Whatever it was had her face turning red. He gave her a quick kiss and set her down.

Alex shook her head, laughing. "We figured you guys would need some boxes for packing, so we stopped by the grocery store, and they had a bunch they were going to throw out. We loaded the back of the car up with what would fit. Oh, and we stopped and got some newspapers to wrap up anything fragile."

"And my mom and Derek are over at the condo, airing it out and giving it a good cleaning," Tenley said.

As the guys went to unload the boxes from Alex's car, Frost walked up to his best friends and gave them each a hug and kiss on the cheek. The two women were dynamos and eager to help any time it was needed. He made a mental note to purchase them each a full spa day with the works as a thank you.

A few hours later, Frost was loading boxes into the back of his Tahoe when a dark grey four-door sedan pulled up in front of the house. The others noticed as well, and Ace, Potter, and Stitch all took protective stances around Alex and Tenley. Nobody was taking any chance with a crazy lady on the loose. They didn't know who was inside the car.

When the driver's side door opened and Nathan stepped out, Frost relaxed. He had forgotten that Nathan said he was coming into town. He noticed Nathan speaking to someone in the car, and he wondered who he'd brought with him. The passenger door opened, and a tall woman with brown hair stepped out. She walked around the car and met Nathan, and they both started walking toward the group. Frost met them midway and shook Nathan's hand. Nathan then introduced the woman as his girlfriend, Valerie. This must be the woman Nathan had told Autumn about. Seeing the woman in person made him feel much better and not so much of a jealous asshole.

Frost explained to Nathan about moving Autumn and Cody into the condo. Nathan wanted to go over to the hospital, and Frost thought that was a good idea. Autumn needed her friends, and Frost knew both Autumn and Cody would be thrilled to see him.

"I sure as hell am glad Autumn met you and your friends. There's no telling what is going through Carlie's head right now. She's unstable."

"I just don't understand why she would blame Autumn," Frost said, crossing his arms.

Nathan leaned against the hood of the car. "I'm sure you know that Autumn doesn't have a family. At least family who supports her. Kevin's parents took Autumn in with open arms, and I guess Carlie was jealous of their relationship." Nathan stared at the house across the street where Carlie had been operating from. "I didn't tell you this over the phone when we spoke yesterday, but the Sheriff believes that Carlie may have been responsible for her parents' car accident. We can't prove it yet, but from evidence gathered from her house, all signs are pointing to it."

Frost rubbed a hand over his unshaven jaw. "Jesus. But why go after Autumn now? Why didn't she do something back then?"

Nathan got a grim look on his face and looked away. "Unfortunately, it's because of me. Letting Autumn and Cody move in with me after Kevin's death led her to believe that I wanted to pursue a relationship with Autumn. Carlie made it known over the years, and I mean years, dating back to when Kevin and I first joined the service, that she had a thing for me. Always had. After Kevin's death, I spent some time with her, but I never once gave her the idea that she and I would be anything more than friends."

"Okay, but Autumn mentioned several times that she and Carlie didn't have the best relationship, so how did Carlie even know Autumn had moved here?"

"Again, because of me. Right after Autumn and Cody moved out here, I went up to Carlie's for a few days to check on her, and I made a comment about planning a trip to come out and visit them."

"Shit."

"Exactly. I feel like all of this has been my fault."

"No, man. Don't go blaming yourself for her issues. Listen, why don't you take Valerie and go over to the hospital. I know Autumn and Cody would love the company. After me and the guys take everything over to the condo and get it unloaded, we're going to stop and get some food and bring it to the hospital."

"That sounds good, but are you sure you guys don't need any help unloading everything?"

"No, we're good. Go spend some time with Autumn and Cody. I'll let the guys keeping watch outside Cody's room know to expect you."

"Thanks, Frost. And I meant what I said; I'm glad they have you in their lives."

"Me too."

A few minutes later, they were all ready to head out. Before they pulled out, Frost went next door to Mrs. Higdon's house to let her know what was going on. She was happy to hear Autumn was moving and that he was moving in with them. He wanted to make sure she was going to be okay, but was shocked to hear that she was moving as well. She was moving in with a friend from her sewing class who lived across town. He made a promise they would call her once they got settled and have her and her friend over for dinner.

CHAPTER TWENTY-FIVE

Frost walked into Cody's hospital room after speaking with the doctor. If Cody's body kept responding to the medications, Cody could possibly be released as early as tomorrow afternoon.

Autumn was curled up on the tiny bed with Cody as they read a book together. The book was a new one that Ace and Alex had brought him this morning. The name of it was *Max*. It was about a Marine dog. Cody had been talking about how he wanted to get it the other week.

He walked over to them. Autumn looked up at him, and the dark circles under her eyes appeared even more visible. Damn, he needed her to get some sleep and eat something. The gang were all out in the hall at the nurse's station. As of right now, Cody was the only patient on the floor, which was a good thing because it meant that no other families were going through what they were right now. At least in this area. On the way to the hospital, they stopped at the Deli to pick up sandwiches and tubs of potato salad and pasta salad. And to thank the hospital staff on the floor for letting them have way more people than they should visiting Cody, they brought them dinner as well, which they were very thankful for.

"Hey, Frost!" Cody said, handing his mom the book to put on the table next to the bed.

"How ya feeling, buddy?" Frost reached out and ruffled Cody's hair. He looked down at his ankle, and it was still the size of a grapefruit and looked really painful.

"Okay, I guess. My leg still hurts."

"It will for a few days, I'm sure. But I got some encouraging news from your doctor just now on my way in here."

Autumn got up and walked over and nestled herself under his arm. He loved having her in his arms. She was a perfect fit. He leaned down and kissed the top of her head. He also noticed that her hair was wet and piled into a messy updo on top of her head, and she had changed clothes. She was wearing her grey sweatpants and one of his sweatshirts that looked huge on her, but he loved it when she wore his clothes.

"How come the doctor didn't come in here?" She asked, looking up at him.

"He was getting ready to, but then he got a call and was needed down on the next floor. But he did tell me that Cody could go home tomorrow."

"Really?!" Cody yelled from his bed.

"Really," Frost told him happily.

Autumn walked away and sat in the chair next to Cody's bed. It was the same damn uncomfortable chair she'd been sleeping in. He squatted down in front of her and took her hands into his.

"Hey…what's with the sad face? I thought you'd be excited that Cody gets to go home."

She looked up at him, and her eyes shone with tears, and she sniffled.

"We don't have a home," she sobbed.

He squeezed her hands. "What are you talking about? Sure, you do."

She was shaking her head. "No, I can't go back to our house, not knowing what happened there. Plus, Nathan explained to me that the person who's been causing all of this is Carlie. I just can't put Cody in harm's way, Jack. God, I don't know what to do."

He pulled her into his arms and lifted her up and took the seat with her on his lap. She immediately curled up against his chest and tucked her head under his chin.

"Mom…we can find another house." Cody looked up at Frost with a sad but worried expression. "Frost, can you help us find another place to live? Please?"

He smiled at Cody. They had no clue what he and the guys had been doing for the past five hours. He had told Nathan to explain the Carlie situation to her, but he wanted to tell her about them moving.

"Well, that is something that I wanted to talk about with the both of you." Autumn looked up at him, and he smiled at her and wiped a few stray tears from her cheeks. "Neither one of you are going back to the house you've been living in."

225

"What?" Autumn asked, looking at him with a confused look on her face.

"The guys and I spent the last few hours packing and moving all of your belongings."

She grabbed ahold of Frost's arm. "Jack...what? Why? I mean, how? I can't afford anything else right now. You know that I was barely making it there as it was."

He gripped her chin between his thumb and pointer finger and tilted her face. He looked right into her Irish green eyes. "I love you, Autumn, and I love Cody as if he was my own son. I would do anything for the two of you, and that includes making sure you are both cared for and living in a safe environment, with me."

She tried covering her quivering lips. "Jack, what are you saying?"

"Potter and Tenley have a condo on the beach. It was Potter's before he met Tenley and moved in with her. They were going to rent it out, but instead, they have offered the condo to you and Cody rent-free until we can find something else more suitable. I'm moving in with you guys. It's a two-bedroom, so Cody; you'll still have your own room. It's also a hell of a lot bigger than the place you were living in. Plus, it's in a better part of town and is equipped with a security system."

"So, you're moving in with us? But what about the apartment you share with Stitch?"

"The apartment with Stitch is not an issue. Our lease is up in two months. And he and I planned to look for our own houses anyway. I'll pay him my share of the last two months, but I'll be living with you and Cody. I don't want to be anywhere else but with the two of you."

Autumn was looking up at him with her mouth agape. He chuckled, then leaned in and kissed her. As he pulled back and he looked at her, an idea popped into his head.

He stood up and placed Autumn on her feet, then glanced over at Cody, who was watching them with wide eyes. "Remember that important question I asked you last week, buddy?" Cody's face lit up with a huge grin, and he nodded his head. "Are you still okay with that?" Again, he nodded.

Frost took Autumn's hand and looked down at her. She had a look of confusion on her face as she looked from her son to him. She was his Irish beauty and his forever. Keeping her hand in his, he got down on one knee. He heard her whisper his name, and he grinned, then gave her hand a gentle squeeze. He took a deep relaxing breath.

"Autumn, sometimes the bad things that happen in our lives happen for a reason. Such as the day I was shot. But I don't regret it because it put me on a direct path to meeting the most loving, caring, smart, and beautiful woman who I hope will make me the happiest man right now and agree to marry me. I love you, Autumn, and I promise to be the best husband to you and the best father to Cody. Will you marry me? Please?" He asked as he withdrew a diamond ring from his pocket and presented it to her.

Autumn couldn't breathe, and she felt her body start to tremble. She tried wiping the tears from her face, but it proved to be useless as they just kept coming. She looked at the simple princess cut ring in a white gold setting. The diamond was stunning, but what she admired even more were the tiny emeralds that surrounded the diamond. It was beautiful and perfect. Hell, he could've given her a ring from a Cracker Jack box, and she'd still say yes to him. She loved and adored this man and wanted to spend the rest of her life with him. She took Frost's face between her hands and leaned down. He watched her with his amber-colored eyes.

"Yes, Jack. I'll marry you."

He smiled wide as he stood and swept her up into his arms and kissed her. Cody was laughing and clapping his hands.

"I love you, sugar," he told her as he set her back down on her feet, kissing her again.

She gave him a big smile. "I love you too."

"And I love you both!" Cody shouted, making Autumn and Frost chuckle. They walked over to Cody's bed and gave him a big hug. Autumn squeezed both of her men knowing her angel in the sky, Kevin was looking down and smiling because she and Cody were happy and living life to the fullest. A few more tears leaked out when she heard the door to the room open.

"We're hearing a lot of laughter coming from in here," Ace said as he and the rest of the gang piled into the room.

Cody had a big smile on his face, and he looked at everyone and shouted with excitement. "Mom and Frost are getting married, and I'm going to have a dad again!"

The cheers went around the room, and Frost set Autumn back on her feet. She was immediately surrounded by Alex and Tenley. They were looking at her ring and welcoming her officially into the family with hugs. Cody even got hugs from the ladies and fist bumps from the team.

CHAPTER TWENTY-SIX

Cecil was sitting outside on the main deck of his yacht. It was a few minutes before noon. His staff had just delivered his lunch to him. As he took a bite of the tender French dip sandwich, he felt the yacht rock gently from the waves on the open ocean. He was anchored about a mile off the beach.

He thought back to a few days ago and how furious he was when Skinny called him and explained what this woman Carlie had done to Autumn and her son. Skinny heard through the neighborhood boys that Carlie had hired a local boy to do her dirty work.

Her mistake was not noticing the tail Cecil had put on her. He knew where she was staying, and every move she made. She had been surprised when Skinny and Roscoe knocked on her door at the extended hotel she was holed up at. She tried pleading with them to spare her life. She offered everything she had, money, cars, even her body for sex. But there was nothing she could do or say for him to have mercy on her. Skinny ended her life with one pull of the trigger.

The focus had been on where Autumn had disappeared to. He had been in luck when a couple of his men came across some information while they were at a local restaurant having dinner one night. They happened to be sitting at the bar when two women were talking to a man named Paul. Paul had asked the woman how Autumn was doing. At the mention of her name, his guys had a feeling they just hit the jackpot. And, indeed, they had. They eavesdropped on the entire conversation. Autumn and her son were staying at a condo on the beach.

He tried being nice, but with the looming contract signing just a few weeks away, his patience had worn off. He didn't give a rat's ass that she was seeing someone. After he whisked her away and showered her in his wealth, she wouldn't look back at her old life. He would give her anything she wanted, as long as she did her part and helped this deal go through. But he needed her now as time was ticking. She had to be groomed to learn how she was expected to act as his wife. He would not allow her to screw up this deal with Vadim. If she showed any sort of defiance, he would hit her where he knew it would hurt her the most; her son. His dilemma had been how and when he could grab her. The SEAL she was living with never left her side unless he was working. The easiest plan was to snatch her while she was on her way to work, but since she had taken a few days off, it hadn't been possible. He thought about just going to the condo and breaking in, but the security around that place was exceptional. However, he and his men put their heads together and came up with a plan.

He relaxed in his seat and lifted his glass of red wine, smiling as he scanned the shoreline. He looked down at his expensive Rolex Submariner watch. Skinny and a few others should be executing the plan right now, and in less than an hour, Autumn would be his forever.

CHAPTER TWENTY-SEVEN

Cody sat on the floor in his room with Alejandra. The two were playing Call of Duty on his new XBOX that Potter and Tenley gave him as a thank you gift for saving Alejandra from getting bitten by the snake. His ankle was still sore and swollen around the bite, and he was still taking some medications, but he was glad he was able to come home.

Alejandra was over because Potter was at the base with the team for work, and Tenley got called into the hospital. His mom was going to be taking them out for ice cream in a little while. She just needed to finish up some chores she was doing around the condo.

As he and Alejandra battled each other, he heard a knock at the front door and wondered who it was. He tried tuning out the sound coming from the game as he heard his mom talking to someone. Then he heard a man's voice and his mom raised her voice. He knew right away that something was wrong. He turned the sound to the TV down and held his finger up to his lips in a silent move, telling Alejandra to be quiet. She nodded her head in understanding.

When the guy raised his voice and asked where her son was, Cody knew his mom was in trouble. He wondered if his Aunt had sent this guy to get them.

He thought back to a few days ago when his mom and Frost explained to him that if he ever came in contact with his Aunt, he needed to get away from her as quickly as possible and call for help. He had everyone's phone number programmed into his phone.

His bedroom was the first door on the right in the hallway. He peeked his head around just as his mom told the stranger that she was alone, and Cody was at a friend's house. What made his body fill with fear was seeing a gun pointed at his mom. She looked scared, but he knew she would do anything to keep him and Alejandra safe.

While the guy and his mom shouted at each other, he quietly ducked back into his room and closed the door until it was almost latched. He didn't want to make a sound. He walked over to the TV and turned it off. He grabbed hold of Alejandra's hand and whispered to her what was going on. He pulled her into the closet and shut the door. She wanted to say something, but he held his finger to his lips in an attempt to quiet her. Again, she gave him a nod of her head in understanding. He listened carefully as the shouting grew louder. The man was yelling at his mom, telling her that she needed to go with him and that the boss was waiting for them. He mentioned another man was down on the beach, waiting in a boat to take them out to a yacht. He never heard his mom talk about anyone with a yacht. But right now, he didn't have time to wonder; he needed to help his mom.

He pulled his phone from his pocket and dialed 911. He explained everything to the dispatcher. The dispatcher wanted him to stay on the line until the officers arrived, but he knew that if he didn't help his mom, it might be too late. After he disconnected the call, he handed the phone to Alejandra. "Call your dad and tell him that a guy came here and took my mom. You heard what I told the 911 operator. If you can't get hold of him, just start going down the list until you get hold of one of them. Okay?"

"Okay, Cody. Where are you going?" She whispered, and Cody could hear the fear in her voice.

"I have to help my mom," Cody said, moving towards the door.

Alejandra grabbed his arm. "No, stay here with me. I'm scared, Cody."

He hugged her tight.

"It'll be okay. Just start calling. Tell them where you are and that you're safe."

She looked at him as tears spilled from her big brown eyes. "Okay...be safe, Cody."

Autumn didn't know what to do as she faced down the barrel of a gun. She didn't know what kind it was, and she really didn't care. A gun was a gun, and she knew her life depended on her keeping calm, though she felt she could be sick. She didn't know who the guy was that forced himself into the condo. All he kept saying was that they had to go because his boss was expecting them. He was tall with dark blonde hair that was slicked back. He was wearing a set of coveralls that the maintenance workers at the condo complex wore. That was the only reason she had opened the door when he knocked on it. She thought there was a problem. Whoever he was, he knew she had a son because he had asked where he was. Thankfully, she was able to think before answering him and lied, telling the guy that Cody wasn't there, that he was at a friend's house. She had to do whatever she needed to do to get this gun-wielding guy out of the condo and away from the kids while finding a way to alert the police. Her phone was on the table in the kitchen. She tried moving that way, but he cut her off and threatened to shoot her if she tried anything stupid. There was absolutely no way she'd be able to get to it. For a second, she thought about throwing something at him, hitting the panic button on the alarm, and bolting out the door. She dismissed the idea as quickly as it had come to her. One, she wasn't the fastest runner, and two; if he started shooting, he could hit her or possibly someone else. Her heart sank as she knew her only option was to go with him.

He grabbed her arm and led her out the door. Once they got down the stairs, he led her onto the beach, and she wondered where he was taking her. Then she spotted the little rubber boat sitting at the shoreline. There was another tall guy standing by it, watching them as they walked toward him. He was on the phone. When they got closer, she heard him say that Skinny had her, and then he placed the phone in his pants pocket. She looked around, hoping that the few people enjoying the day at the beach would notice something was wrong.

The guy pressing the gun to her back, who she now assumed was Skinny, shoved her into the boat, and she fell face-first, scraping her legs and arms on the rough seams of the rubber boat. The other guy reached for her, lifted her up, placed her on one of the little seats and told her not to move. Like she had a choice with a gun being pointed at her.

Once the three of them were seated, the tall guy started the motor, and they pulled away from the shoreline. The motor wasn't very big, so they weren't able to go fast, but the further away from the land they got, the more nervous she became. She glanced around the boat, hoping to see a life jacket, but there were none. They hit a large wave, and the little boat went airborne. When it came back down and smacked the water, she lost her balance, but Skinny grabbed her arm before she fell.

He grinned at her. "We don't want you to get banged up. The boss would be pretty upset if you got injured."

She gave him a dirty look, and he laughed. She glanced at the other guy, and he was in a dead stare with her. His evil eyes roamed over her body, and he licked his lower lip, sending a shiver down her spine. These guys were bad news. She thought about jumping into the ocean, but they were already too far out, and with the rough waves, she wouldn't be able to tread the waters. Since the day Frost found out she couldn't swim, he'd been taking her to the community center pool and teaching her. In a short time, she had learned several new strokes; however, she knew she wasn't that strong of a swimmer to tackle the open ocean, especially in rough waters.

She turned and glanced over her shoulder and saw the giant yacht in the distance.

She looked at Skinny. "Is that where we're going?"

The way he grinned at her, she wanted to cringe. What did they want with her? She closed her eyes and tried not to think about the worst. She opened her eyes when she heard him speak.

"That beautiful boat is your new home."

She jerked back like he had slapped her. "What?" He just nodded his head, and the other guy started laughing. She looked back toward the shoreline in the distance, and her thoughts went to the kids. She wondered if Cody heard what was taking place and called for help. Her eyes started to fill with tears. Would she ever see her son again? And Frost? Oh, god, what was happening here?

A few minutes later, they pulled alongside the yacht. It was massive. She'd seen some like these when she'd passed the marina and always wondered what one looked like on the inside. But now she had no desire to. They circled around to the backside, and a door opened, then a ramp lowered. The guy steered them up the ramp and into a little boat garage of some sort. Jesus, this thing had all of the bells and whistles. She was looking around not paying attention when Skinny grabbed her arm again. She was going to have bruises from him yanking her around. He pulled her out of the boat and walked her through another door, then up two flights of stairs. When they entered a living room, he told her to wait here. She gave him a look like where else would she go.

She scanned the room. It was designed in a modern art deco theme and fit for a king. Pristine white leather sofas that looked as if they'd never been sat on before. Black and gold pillows were scattered around. The coffee table and matching side tables were stainless steel. Black and gold artwork adorned the walls.

She was so enthralled, she hadn't heard "him" enter the room.

"It's beautiful, isn't it?"

She jumped and turned with her hand against her chest in shock. She could feel how fast her heart was beating. But what was more of a shock was that the guy staring at her was Cecil. The creep who kept showing up places. He stood there, holding two glasses of what looked like champagne. He was dressed casually in khaki shorts and a white polo shirt.

He walked toward her. "Before we set sail for our future, I thought we could make a toast. Come here, Autumn," he demanded, but she took a few steps backward, and he tsked at her, then set down the glasses on the coffee table. He took another step toward her. "Rule number one, when I ask you to do something, you do it. No questions asked. You will obey me; you will show me respect. You belong to me now."

Her head was swimming with thoughts. What was he talking about obeying and belonging to him? It had pissed her off, and she should have considered the consequences before she opened her mouth. "Obey you, belong to you? Are you crazy? I will never belong to you. You can't do this to me!" She shouted at him. All that did was earn her a swift backhand across the face that she never saw coming. Pain exploded along her cheek, and she fell to the carpeted floor.

Cecil took advantage of the situation and jumped on top of her and straddled her body. She moved to strike him with her fist, but he caught her hand before she landed her punch. He gripped both of her wrists with one hand and held them over her head. She tried fighting him and bucking her hips to get free, but he was too heavy.

His face was red and angry. "You will learn that when I want something, I always get it. I thought maybe we could enjoy each other's company before moving into the bedroom to get more acquainted with one another. But I see we need to get right to the discipline aspect of this relationship.

She gave him a look of astonishment, and he grinned. "Oh yeah, darling, discipline. You disobey, and you suffer consequences." She shook with fear. This man was off his rocker. She needed to get away from him. If she could get outside, maybe she could find some sort of floatation device and jump overboard. She'd rather take her chances in the open sea than hang around here and be his wife. She wasn't going to leave behind her son, Frost, and all of her new friends. No way in hell was she going to give up now.

She should have seen this coming. All of the coincidental run-ins she had with him over the last couple of weeks, she should have seen the signs. But why? This guy obviously had a lot of money and was attractive. He could land a woman with no problem. Why her? What could she give him that any other woman couldn't?

He eased his body lower on top of her, using his weight to keep her in place. He used his free hand and tugged on her blouse, causing it to rip and expose her breasts. He lowered his head and licked her cleavage. She screamed for him to stop, and he just laughed at her.

"You can scream all you want; nobody is going to hear you. In fact, I want to hear you scream." He licked her again.

"You are one sick bastard," she said through clenched teeth.

He gripped her jaw and squeezed. "You will shut this pretty little mouth of yours if you know what is good for you." Then he sneered at her.

"Or maybe since you like to use your mouth so much, I'll fill it with something."

He reached down and started to undo his belt. *Oh, hell, no!*

She jerked her knee upward and nailed him in the groin. He screamed and released her hands as he gripped his crotch. She didn't hesitate. She got to her feet and ran toward the set of stairs. As she climbed higher, she heard him swearing at her, saying she was going to regret doing that.

She made it to the upper deck and looked around for anyone who could be waiting for her. When she saw the coast was clear, she ran toward the starboard side, then made her way toward the bow. On the way, she spotted a flotation ring hanging on the wall. She felt a little relief and grabbed it, knowing this could be her only option to escape. She was going to have to jump. She put the ring over her one shoulder and climbed over the railing. She closed her eyes and said a prayer. When she finally got the nerve to release her hand, Cecil appeared, and he wasn't alone.

"Don't you, do it?" He shouted. "Think about it, Autumn. If you jump in that water, I'll leave you there. You are too far out to swim to shore. Nobody will find you." He reached for her. "Come with me now, and I'll forgive your lack of obedience."

Autumn was crying and shaking. There was no way in hell she would go with him. She gathered all the courage she could and looked him in the eye.

"Go to hell, you son of a bitch!" Suddenly, the boat lurched, and her foot slipped. She lost her grip on the railing, and her head hit the metal, instantly knocking her out, and she fell into the water below.

Derek was in his office at the base and was getting ready to head out to meet the team at one of the training facilities when his phone rang. He picked it up from the desk and saw it was Cody calling. He smiled. He loved that kid and was happy for Frost and Autumn.

"Hey, Cody…"

But it wasn't Cody on the other end of the line, it was his granddaughter, and the fear he heard in her voice put him on edge, and his protective instincts kicked in. "Pop, it's me, Alejandra," she whispered.

"Honey, what's wrong? You sound frightened. Is everything okay?"

He heard her sniffle and knew she was crying. "Some guy just came here and took Aunt Autumn." She started sobbing.

Fuck! Knowing his guys were out on the obstacle course, he took off out of his office in a sprint while talking to Alejandra and trying to get information from her. His feet pounded on the asphalt as he ran across the parking lot.

"Alejandra, listen to me, sweetheart. Tell me everything you saw or heard."

"I could only hear them shouting. Cody said he heard the man say something about needing to get to a boat out on the beach and then going to some yacht. Oh, Cody said the man had a gun and was pointing it at Aunt Autumn."

Oh, dear Jesus. He had to stay calm for Alejandra's sake. He put everything his body had into his sprint, thanking God he still kept in tip-top shape, even though he commanded his teams from behind a desk.

"I'm scared, Pop." Hearing her quivering voice broke his heart. There wasn't a damn thing he could do for her at the moment except to keep talking to her.

He was breathing hard. "I know you are, honey. Where's Cody? Is he there with you?" He made it to the building in record time, and Ace saw him, and he signaled to him to get everyone.

"He went to follow them. He said he had to help Aunt Autumn."

"Where are you, sweetie?"

"I'm in Cody's closet. He told me to stay in here and to call you, and if you didn't answer to keep calling all of daddy's teammates until someone answered."

Damn, that boy was a natural protector.

"He did well, and you stay in that closet until either your dad or a police officer comes to get you, okay?" As the team gathered, Derek looked at Frost. "Alejandra, don't hang up, but I need to talk to your daddy and the guys, okay? You may not hear me, but I'm still on the line, okay, honey?"

"Okay." She sniffled again, and it broke his heart, knowing she was scared.

"Good girl. Just hang on for a few minutes."

He muted the phone so Alejandra couldn't hear their conversation. Potter was looking at him with a concerned look.

"Why is Alejandra calling you?"

"There's been a situation at the condo. According to Alejandra, some guy showed up at the condo and forced Autumn to go with him. Something about taking her to a boat."

Frost's face instantly took on a hard, pained expression. "Took her? How? Did he threaten her?"

"Alejandra said he had a gun." Derek looked at Potter. "She's safe in Cody's closet where Cody put her."

"Where's Cody?" Frost asked with his phone to his ear. He was trying to get in touch with Nathan since he was still in town.

"He went to follow Autumn."

"Fuck! Do we know where they were heading?"

"No, but Alejandra said Cody mentioned taking Autumn to a yacht."

"A yacht?"

"Considering they took her in a small boat, the yacht is probably anchored somewhere offshore."

"What do we need to do, commander?" Stitch asked.

"Alejandra said Cody called the police, but she's scared. Let's call them again and make sure they are in route to the condo. Have them dispatch their water patrol unit to look for a yacht offshore near the condo." Skittles pulled his phone out and contacted the local PD. Most of the guys had friends on the force.

"I'll contact the guys over at SWCC and tell them that we need two Mark Vs ready to go pronto. With those, we should get out on the water quickly. Potter, you and Skittles' head to the condo and meet with the

239

police there. Ace, you take Dino, and Stitch in one boat. Frost, Irish, Diego, you guys are with me. Grab some gear before you board. These fuckers aren't getting away." He put his phone back up to his ear. "Alejandra…you still there, sweetie?"

"Yes," her angelic voice floated through the line.

"Your daddy is on his way to get you, okay? Now I am going to hang up, and your daddy is going to call you."

"Okay, Pop."

"You are so brave, sweetie, Love you."

"Love you, too, Pop."

His heart melted every time she called him Pop. He watched as Potter put his phone to his ear and began speaking with her while he and Skittles sprinted to his truck.

He looked at Frost. "Let's go get your woman."

Frost was full of rage. These assholes came into his home and not only threatened Autumn but took her at gunpoint. Carlie was the only one who came to mind who wanted to hurt Autumn. With all the money she had taken over the years, she could afford to rent a yacht and hire some muscle.

Right before they boarded the boats, they had gotten a call from PD, saying they found Carlie's body at a hotel in Hampton Roads. They said she had been murdered. There went the Carlie scenario, Frost thought to himself.

Once the teams were loaded up in the two boats, they were on their way, and the boats sped over the water in haste to get to Autumn before the yacht could get any further out to sea.

Skittles called and said PD had a sighting of a small craft east of the condo about a mile offshore, so they were heading in that direction. Shortly after, another call came in about a large yacht in the same vicinity. As a precaution, they called in the Coast Guard in case this guy managed to get into international waters.

"What the hell is that?" Irish asked, pointing toward an object in the water. He was looking through a set of binoculars. "Is that someone on a surfboard?"

Frost picked up the other binoculars next to him and put them up to his eyes. He focused in on the object in question, then his breathing stopped when he realized it was Cody. He was paddling his surfboard, heading towards the direction of a yacht they finally caught a glimpse of. His first thought was, what in the hell was the kid thinking? His second thought was the fear for his safety, as he could see that Cody was struggling to get through the rough water. At least he had been smart enough to put his life vest on, but he was heading towards a very hostile situation.

As the two Mark Vs followed by a police boat flew over the choppy waters gaining ground on the yacht, Frost saw two people emerge onto the starboard deck. He didn't need any other visual to know that the woman with the red hair was Autumn. She had something over her shoulder and started climbing over the railing. Holy shit, she was going to jump.

Frost watched as a man went to reach for her, but at that exact moment, the police boat that was following had moved ahead and cut off the yacht, causing it to make an abrupt maneuver to avoid colliding with it. The sudden movement caused Autumn to lose her grip on the railing, and he watched in horror as her head made contact with the metal bar, and she tumbled into the ocean with the life ring coming loose, and she disappeared under the water.

Frost saw Cody approach on the surfboard, where his mom went into the water and saw him removing his life vest before disappearing under the water. As their boat came to rest at the same spot, Frost dove into the water along with a couple of the other guys. He spotted Cody's foot as he was going under. Ace saw it as well, and both he and Ace dove under the water after him.

They spotted Cody about four feet under, as he was trying to bring Autumn up. Her body was limp, and Cody was struggling. Frost grabbed Autumn while Ace took hold of Cody, and they both surfaced with the pair. Cody was coughing as Ace helped him to the boat. Autumn, on the other hand, wasn't breathing. He yelled to Stitch and Irish, and they hoisted her out of the water. By the time Frost was out of the water and in the boat, Stitch and Irish had already begun CPR. Frost estimated she had been under the water two to three minutes.

He knelt down in the boat next to her and took her cold hand into his.

"Come on, baby, breathe," he pleaded with her as he squeezed her hand, trying to infuse strength into her. He couldn't lose her. Not now. Not when he finally had his future in front of him. Cody couldn't lose her either. She had to make it through this.

After a few rounds of breaths and chest compressions, she finally made a gurgling sound, then coughed up a mouthful of water. Her eyes shot wide open, and the coughing became uncontrollable. They rolled her onto her side, so she wouldn't choke. Frost pulled her into his arms and sat back against the side of the boat and buried his face in her hair. The emotions racking his body right now had him on the verge of totally breaking down. He could have lost both her and Cody today. He honestly couldn't say if the wetness on his face was from the water or tears.

Autumn felt like she was stuck in a nightmare. She was wet, cold, and confused. Her head and face hurt. She knew she was on a boat in the arms of her fiancé. What she couldn't remember, though, was how she got there.

The last thing she remembered was some guy named Skinny, forcing her at gunpoint into a boat and them going to a yacht that the creepy guy Cecil owned. She put her hand to her head, feeling a rather large bump. Did someone hit her there? And why was she soaking wet?

She felt Frost's arms tighten around her, and she tilted her face up toward him as she lay against his chest. He, too, wassoaking wet.

"What happened?" She asked in a very hoarse voice. It was even painful to speak.

She saw how Frost was biting the inside of his cheek. His normal amber eyes had turned a dark brown, and his gaze was intense and fierce.

She shivered as she kept her eyes focused on his. Someone had put a blanket over both of them.

"What do you remember?" He finally asked her. His voice was low and deep.

She explained what she could remember. He lifted his hand and pushed some loose strands of hair out of her face and cupped her cheek.

"You hit your head pretty hard on the railing." She gasped and covered her mouth. He continued to tell her how Cody had paddled on his surfboard to help her and how all of the guys had jumped in and found Cody pulling her up. He recounted she wasn't breathing when they pulled her onto the boat, and Stitch and Irish had to do CPR.

Tears fall rolled down her face, and she shook. No wonder he seemed so angry. She almost died today. Cody could have died. He risked his life to save hers.

She grabbed Frost's shirt. "Where's Cody, now?" She asked, fearful that something bad happened to him.

"He's in the other boat. He's safe with Ace and Dino. They'll meet us at the beach."

"What about Cecil and those men who kidnapped me? What happened to them?"

"They're all in police custody. They'll be going away for a long time." He stroked her hair, and she laid her head back against Frost's chest and burrowed under the blanket to stay warm. She closed her eyes as the boat rocked over the waves and they made their way back to shore.

Potter came walking back down the beach, holding Alejandra in his arms, and Frost smiled. She was wrapped around him like a little monkey clinging to a tree. He couldn't blame the poor thing. What she heard and had to guess was happening had to traumatize her a bit. Diego and Skittles were with him. As soon as Potter set her down on the sand, she took off running towards Cody, who was standing with the rest of the team. Frost smiled when she gave Cody a big hug.

"She, okay?" He asked Potter, who was watching the interaction between the two kids.

"Yeah, just shaken up a bit. She was right where she told me she'd be. She was worried about Cody and Autumn. How are they? Diego said Autumn hit her head pretty hard, then was underwater for some time."

"Cody seems fine. He just has a couple of scrapes, and, of course, he is exhausted. Autumn's being checked out right now. Stitch is with her in the ambulance. They wouldn't let me in. They only allowed Stitch because he's a medic. She's alert, so that's good." He paused for a minute, trying to gather his thoughts and emotions. The adrenalin rush was starting to flee his body. He had dealt with this feeling numerous times, but knowing what he could've lost today scared the ever-living shit out of him. "I could've lost both of them today," he said in a flat voice, biting his lip.

Potter clasped his shoulder and gave a hard squeeze. "But you didn't. Your boy did good. I can't believe he paddled out there on a fucking surfboard."

"Yeah, he did."

"Because of his quick thinking, he also prevented my little girl from getting caught up in the middle of all of this. He is a natural protector. Reminds me of us."

Frost thought about Potter's statement. He wondered how Potter was so calm and collected right now, knowing what Alejandra had been through the last few weeks. Jesus, that poor girl wasn't going to be allowed out of his sight from now on. He couldn't blame him either. He didn't want Autumn or Cody out of his sight, either.

They both stood there silently as the police pulled up along the beach. They watched as the officers escorted Cecil and his men in handcuffs off the boat and into a waiting police car. The team had found out a little while ago, that one of the guys who worked for Cecil had already confessed to murdering Carlie. It was a sad situation when you really thought about it. If Carlie had just accepted Autumn into the family instead of getting caught up in jealousy, she could've been part of a great thing. Instead, she lost her life. Even after all of the terrible things she'd done, he prayed she

244

was now at peace with her brother and parents, and hopefully, they'd forgive her.

Stitch caught his eye as he jumped out of the back of the ambulance. "They're going to take her to the hospital just as a precaution. She swallowed a lot of water, plus I'd feel better if she got a CT on her head."

"Thanks, man." He gave a Stitch a man hug, and Stitch gave his back a good slap.

"No worries, man. She's safe, and those assholes are going to jail for a very long time. The FBI's been after Cecil for quite some time."

That was a surprise to Frost. "Really?"

"Yep. From what they say, he's been behind a ring of multi-state vehicle thefts. Anyway, come on, let's get you to the hospital.

CHAPTER TWENTY-EIGHT

Autumn stood on the parade grounds on base. It was hot out, but this was an important day. While she waited for the ceremony to start, she thought back to all of the events in the last few weeks leading up to now.

It had been almost a month since the incident with Cecil. They avoided the subject as much as possible. She and Frost accompanied Carlie's body to North Dakota, where she was buried next to her parents and brother. She hoped she would find peace when she met her parents again. Since then, a lot had happened. As a matter of fact, they were life-changing.

For starters, she and Frost were married two weeks ago in a small but quaint ceremony at Ace and Alex's house. The guest list only consisted of Frost's teammates, his commander, and Juliet, and, of course, his family that included his mom, dad, brother, sister-in-law, and their two little kids. She had invited Mrs. Higdon, but she couldn't make it because she and her new roommate were on a Caribbean cruise.

Alex and Tenley were her saviors and apparently had a little experience in throwing together a quick wedding.

Both she and Frost told everyone not to buy any gifts and explained that sharing in their day was the best gift they could have. So, when Frost's commander presented them with an envelope at the end of the evening, it had surprised them. The contents of the envelope had brought tears to her eyes. It was a cashier's check payable to her in the amount of 1.2 million dollars. It was from her sister in-law's estate. The amount included the money owed to her from her husband's life insurance policy, along with the money owed to her and Kevin when Kevin's parents passed away. The additional money was what was leftover since she and Cody were her only remaining family. She had questioned how this all came about, and the commander explained how each team member, along with Alex, Tenley and Juliet, played a strategic role in getting everything completed and legally binding before the ceremony.

The second life-changing event was when she and Frost purchased a new home. It was a model home in a fairly new neighborhood next to where Alex and Tenley lived. Since it was a model home, it came with all the upgrades, including the Jacuzzi tub she'd always wanted in the master bathroom. They moved in a few days ago. It was four bedrooms and three and a half baths and had a huge backyard for the kids to play in. She and Frost were planning to start trying for a baby.

She also resigned from her job at the Naval Hospital and started working part-time three-days a week at an orthopedics office just down the road from their new home. Of course, she wanted to work full-time, but Frost explained she didn't have to. Since she was married to him now, she and Cody were covered under his insurance, plus working part-time meant she'd be able to help pick the kids up from school. When school started in a couple of weeks, Cody would be attending the public middle school just down the road. And in her free time, she told Alex she'd volunteer at her clinic once it opened.

She took a deep breath and smiled, looking with the rest of their friends as they all watched Cody stand tall and proud in his Sea Cadet's dress white uniform as he was awarded the Honor Ribbon, which was awarded to a cadet directly responsible for saving a human life at the risk of his or her own life.

He was receiving the award for his bravery and courage for putting his life on the line when he not only saved Alejandra from being bitten by the rattlesnake, but also for saving the life of his mom.

Frost and his team were involved in the ceremony. With permission, they were all dressed in their dress whites as they all stood at attention and saluted Cody when the Secretary of the Navy presented Cody his ribbon. Yes, she couldn't believe the freaking Secretary of the Navy was here, presenting her son with an award. Apparently, Commander Derek Connors and his daughter Alex possessed some good connections.

She smiled as Cody saluted the SECNAV, then shook his hand as he accepted the award. She was so proud of him, watching him grow into the wonderful young man he had become. And although at times she wished he would never grow up so she could always have the little boy she'd loved these past ten years; she couldn't wait to see what the future held for him. If her gut was right, she had a feeling that one day, her little boy would be standing where his dad was currently standing. She thought back on their wedding day when Cody asked Frost what he should call him now that he was married to his mom. Frost told him it was up to him. When Cody told him, he wanted to call him dad, she swore she saw a tear slip out of her man's fierce eyes, though she'd never call him out on it.

"Daddy...can I go see Cody now?" Alejandra asked Potter in a cute, whispered voice. Potter looked down at his little girl, who was tugging on his sleeve, and Autumn could see the love shining in the big bad SEAL's eyes. She had been bouncing up and down for the last thirty or so minutes, waiting to see Cody. Tenley was having a hard time keeping her still during the ceremony. She wanted to stand with him while Cody got his award, and Tenley had to explain to her that sometimes being family, they'd have to stand back and just watch.

The two kids had definitely grown very fond of each other over the last two months and held a special connection.

"Yeah, sweetie. You're allowed to go see him now," he told her as he released her hand, and she took off in a sprint.

They all watched as she ran over and gave Cody a big hug, and he, in return, gave her a hug and a kiss on the cheek. The two of them were so cute together as they walked back toward the group holding hands and smiling at each other and talking. Cody, in his dress whites and Alejandra in her pretty red, white, and blue dress and her black curly hair blowing in the breeze; they made the perfect little kid couple. She took a picture with her phone to remember this moment. It kind of reminded her of an image you'd see on a postcard.

Autumn had to wonder if she didn't just have a little Alpha male on her hands. Not that she minded because his dad was a big Alpha-male and the perfect role model. He would teach him the ropes with respect to women and how they should be protected, loved, and cared for. Everyone knew it was hard for Potter to watch, and all the guys ribbed him about it every chance they got.

"Jesus Christ, shoot me now," she heard Potter mumble as he gripped the nape of Tenley's neck and pulled her into him. His large hand caressed her baby bump. "I will love that baby in your belly no matter what sex it is, but Christ, I hope it's a boy. I can't go through this again."

Tenley's smile reached clear to her eyes as she looked up at her husband, then batted her thick eyelashes at him.

"Well, then I guess this isn't the best time to tell you that we're having twins."

Autumn never thought she would see the day when a man so intimidating like Potter looked scared out of his mind. Who knew it would take his wife telling him she was pregnant with twins to conquer that feat?

Right at that moment, Alejandra tugged her dad's hand and looked up at him with her huge brown eyes. "Daddy, Cody and I are getting married like you and mommy and want babies like mommy too."

Potter's naturally tanned face took on a tint of green, almost as if he was going to be sick. He looked at Frost with a stern expression.

"Frost, I think tonight is the perfect night to sit down and have 'the' talk with your son." Everyone laughed.

Frost caught Autumn around her waist and pulled her against him. She turned and gazed into his beautiful amber-colored eyes. He smiled at her, showing off his dimple that she adored.

"I love you."

"I love you, too," she smiled, hugging him tighter. Ever since he wore his dress uniform during their wedding, she loved seeing him in it. However, tonight she was looking forward to peeling it off him. Cody was staying over at Potter and Tenley's, and this would be the first night they'd be alone in their new home, and she couldn't wait. Tonight, they would start working for that baby.

She snuggled closer against his chest despite how hot it was out, and she turned her head and glanced around at everyone. They were a special group of individuals and ones she was proud to call her family.

EPILOGUE

Irish sat by Ace and Alex's pool, his feet dangling in the cool refreshing water. It was hot and humid, although not as hot as where he and the team had just come from. They had been living in a South American jungle for the past two and a half weeks. The ladies planned a welcome home barbecue for them. Another few weeks and the season would start to change, bringing the cooler fall temperatures. He was looking forward to it. He could adapt in any type of weather, but there was just something about the fall temperatures that he loved.

He was deep in thought, thinking about the conversation he had with the guys a few weeks ago at Stitch's cabin. He caved and told them about "Blue," the blue-eyed goddess he met in the parking lot at Bayside. At first, they teased him, and it was expected, but when they all realized he was serious, they told him that if he truly felt something, he shouldn't ignore the feeling because, in a blink of an eye, it could all be gone. And that couldn't be a more accurate statement after seeing Ace, Potter, and Frost all fall in love, and then almost lose their women because of assholes in this world.

But, unfortunately, "Blue" was going to have to stay on the back burner for just a little while longer. He needed to make a quick trip home to Michigan to see his mom and dad.

During this last deployment, his dad Ollie had a heart attack. Derek had informed him when he had arrived home. Even though doctors said it was a mild heart attack, it would make Irish feel better if he saw that his dad was indeed doing okay with his own eyes. The doctor said his dad should be just fine with a proper diet and exercise. Irish's other concern was the farm his family lived on. Over the years, his mom and dad sold off a lot of the livestock. He had a feeling it was getting to be too much for the two of them now that they were getting older. They only kept a few goats around, and that was for the benefit of his little niece Sienna who lived with them.

His thoughts went to Sienna and how she might be dealing with everything going on with his dad. As she was only five-years-old, she probably didn't really understand. His parents were her legal guardians after his drug addict sister gave her up at birth to continue her life with her drug dealer boyfriend. Neither Irish nor his parents had seen or spoken to Maggie, his sister, since that day.

Damn, he hated being so far away from his parents and niece. He hadn't seen them since Sienna's birthday last October. That little girl was a spit-fire but so adorable, and she knew it too. She had him wrapped around her little finger and was one of the few females who held a place in his heart.

He had plenty of leave accrued, so his Commander told him to take a couple of days to go and spend some time with them. He was actually looking forward to it.

He felt the cool pool water hit his face and then heard a giggle. Alex. He wiped the water from his face and grinned as she swam over and held onto the ledge next to him.

"You looked so deep in thought; I thought you needed a distraction. Want to talk about what has you acting like a hermit and ignoring your friends? This is supposed to be a fun party, you know." She gave his leg a nudge with her elbow and smiled up at him.

He was silent for a moment as he sat there staring at her. Alex was a beautiful woman and smart as hell. Ace was a lucky son of a bitch to land her. Irish wanted someone like her—someone beautiful on the inside and out. Someone who could like him for him and not just the SEAL. His mind went back to "Blue," and he wondered if she could be that someone.

Alex's voice broke his train of thought. "Are you thinking about your mystery girl, "Blue?"

Christ, he regretted telling Alex about "Blue." He didn't know the woman's name who had consumed his thoughts for the last couple of weeks. But every time he thought about her, all he saw were those glacier blue eyes that sparkled like diamonds. So, until he found her, he and apparently everyone else referred to her as "Blue."

His lips twitched, and he took a slug of his beer. "Maybe," he replied, and she smiled.

"Well, now that you're back, you can look for her. You said she mentioned she just moved here, right?"

"Yeah, but I'm going home to Michigan for a few days. I don't know if your dad or Ace told you, but my dad had a heart attack while we were deployed. I just want to go home and make sure everything is good with them."

She covered his hand and squeezed it. "No, he didn't say anything. I'm so sorry. Do let us know if there's anything we can do." He smiled at her. She was like a mother hen to all of the guys, and they all loved her.

"I will. Thanks."

He smiled to himself as she swam off. His thoughts immediately went back to "Blue," and he chuckled. He should never have mentioned the woman to the guys. They named her blue because he was so fascinated with her eye color. They were majestic like an ice glacier in the Arctic. He took a swig of his beer. He had to find her. It would be his next mission.

Bailey Anderson sat on her balcony overlooking the Atlantic Ocean. It was a beautiful evening as the sun was starting to set and the moon began to show its face. She closed her eyes as she felt the slight warm breeze pass over her face. She'd been living in Virginia Beach for a few weeks now and had already fallen in love with the town she now called her home.

She looked down at the large sweatshirt she was using to cover her legs. She smiled, thinking about the gorgeous man who had helped her with her flat tire the first night she arrived in town. It was his sweatshirt. He had lent it to her since it was raining out that night, and she was soaked and cold. She didn't have much of her belongings at the time since they were in the moving truck that wasn't scheduled to arrive until the next day.

She remembered his intense steel blue eyes and that faint scar that ran from his bottom lip to just under his chin. He was a perfect gentleman, but the way he looked at her before he got in his car and drove away was a look that she would never forget.

She shouldn't be sitting here thinking about a man right now. She moved away from her home to get away from a man, a man who was in cohorts with her greedy and selfish parents. He wanted to marry her and make her a trophy wife. He wanted to control every aspect of her life.

So then why was it that she couldn't get her mind off Irish, the stranger who came to her aid the very first night in her new town? Was fate trying to tell her something? Only time would tell, but she was determined to meet him again. After all, she had his property to return to him.

Irish and Bailey's story available now!

BOOK LIST

The Trident Series
ACE
POTTER
FROST
IRISH
STITCH
DINO
SKITTLES
DIEGO
A TRIDENT WEDDING

The Trident Series II – BRAVO Team
JOKER (2021)
BEAR (2022
DUKE (2022)
PLAYBOY (2022)
AUSSIE (2022)
NAILS (2022)
SNOW (2022)
JAY BIRD (2022)

ABOUT THE AUTHOR

Jaime Lewis, a *USA TODAY* bestselling author, entered the indie author world in June 2020 with ACE, the first book in the Trident Series.

Coming from a military family, she describes as very patriotic; it's no surprise that her books are known for their accurate portrayal of life in the service.

Passionate in her support of the military, veterans, and first responders, Jaime volunteers with the Daytona Division of the US Naval Sea Cadet Corps, a non-profit youth leadership development program sponsored by the U.S. Navy. Together with her son, she also manages a charity organization that supports military personnel and their families, along with veterans and first responders.

Born and raised in Edgewater, Maryland, Jaime now resides in Ormond Beach, Florida with her husband and two very active boys.

Between her day job, her two boys, and writing, she doesn't have a heap of spare time, but if she does, you'll find her somewhere in the outdoors. Jaime is also an avid sports fan.

Follow Jaime:
Facebook Author Page: https://www.facebook.com/jaime.lewis.58152
Jaime's Convoy: https://www.facebook.com/groups/jaimesconvoy
Goodreads: https://www.goodreads.com/author/show/17048191.Jaime_Lewis

Made in the USA
Coppell, TX
17 February 2022

73676502R10148